'So very funny, Spencer is terrific'

Jenny Colgan (*The Bookshop on the Corner*)

'Spencer Brown is endlessly inventive and delightfully, dependably silly'

Richard Ayoade (*The IT Crowd, Submarine*)

PRAISE FOR THE REBUILDING OF TOM COOPER

'A gloriously self-aware satirical romp through the terrors of relationships, family life and survival. Philip Roth meets Cold Feet'

Helen Lederer (*Absolutely Fabulous, Losing It*)

'Hilarious and heart-warming'

Andi Osho (*Live at the Apollo, Curfew*)

'A joy-seeking missile'

Richard Ayoade (*Ayoade on Top, The Grip of Film*)

'Very funny. Peep Show combined with Outnumbered. But you know. In a book'

Josh Howie (*Josh Howie's Losing It, BBC Radio 4*)

'An aspirational figure for the men of today'

Omid Djalili (*The Infidel, Live at the Apollo*)

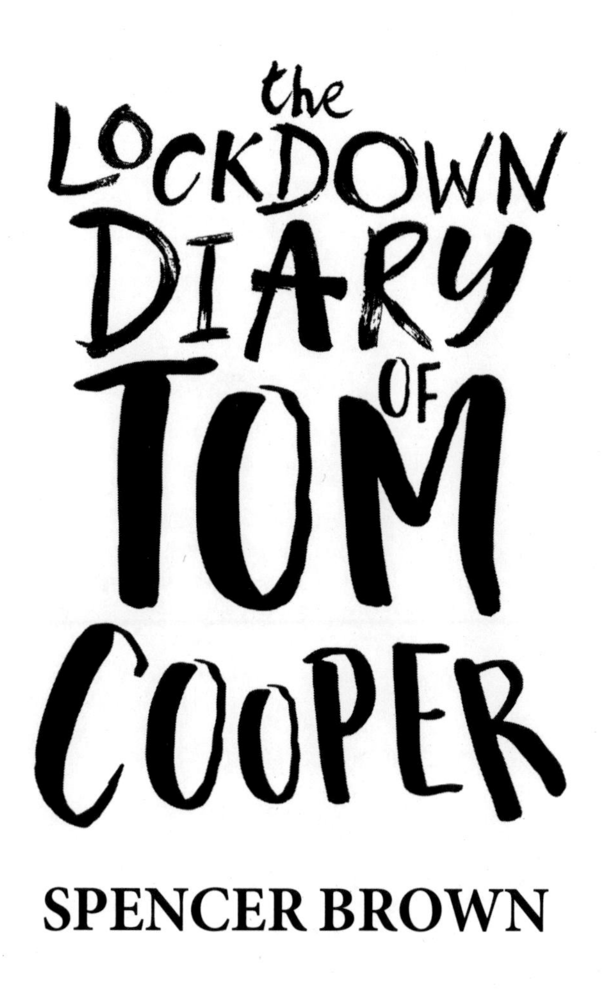

SPENCER BROWN

Marotte

www.marottebooks.com

First published in 2020
by Marotte Books Ltd
51 York Avenue, London SW14 7LQ

www.marottebooks.com

A CIP catalogue record of this book is available from the British Library.

ISBN 978-1-9161526-5-6

Typeset by Elaine Sharples
Printed and bound by PULSIO SARL
Cover design by Liam Relph

For Noa

Tuesday 17th March

'Are you going to die, Daddy?'

They're the first words I hear when Carrie comes into my room this morning.

'What do you mean, Carrie?'

'Someone at nursery said there's a bad disease and everyone's going to die.'

I think for a second, not sure how to approach this. And then she starts to cry.

'Oh, my love,' I say, pulling her close to me, her tears wetting my cheek.

'If you died, how would we… how would we… how would we…'

She can't get her words out. I draw her in even closer.

'How would we… how would we…'

'It's all right, my love, Daddy's not going to die.' It calms her just enough to let her finish her sentence.

'How would we… reach the cereal?'

That wasn't quite the ending I was expecting.

'What? What do you mean, love?'

'The cereal,' she explains. 'How would we *reach* it?'

'Um, you're talking about Daddy *dying*. The cereal isn't what you're really worried about.'

'Yes it is. It's on a really high shelf.'

Jesus. Why not just step on my corpse? Maybe she's thinking she's already eaten that.

'I'm not going to die, love – the coronavirus doesn't really kill people of my age.' (I looked it up – it's a 0.4% chance.) 'So Daddy can just get the cereal for you.'

She seems relieved for a second. But then a new thought strikes her. 'What about children? Does it kill children?'

Thank God. The one question I can answer without making things worse. 'No – it doesn't really hurt children. That's the one good thing about it. It's more dangerous for old people – like Granny and Gramps. That's why we're not going to see them for a while.'

'But we haven't seen them for ages.'

'No,' I reply, 'that was different. That was because they're not very helpful. This is to protect them.'

'OK,' she says, wandering off surprisingly reassured, despite the fact the Coco Pops are still six feet above ground.

But the statistics are still echoing round my mind. 0.4%. God. I mean, it's ridiculously low, but it's still roughly one in two hundred. If that was the chance I'd be hit by a car when I walked them to school, I'd never leave the house. And if I *did* die – what would happen to *them*? Their mum (Sally, my now ex-wife) is currently thousands of miles away, stuck in Canada with her new partner and a slightly raised temperature. Not only is that shitty for them, it also means there's no one to pick up the slack if something happened to me. It's not like they could go and stay with my parents – they're pensioners. It'd be as good as signing their death warrants. I don't want my kids losing their father and grandparents in the same bloody week. Would they have to go into care until Sally could make it back?

I'm overreacting. It's more likely I'd just get ill. But how would we cope then? Who would make the meals? How would we get the shopping? Come on – you can deal with that if it comes up. Hopefully it won't. Until then, all I need to do is make sure that they know I love them. Just in case.

And I should probably move the cereal to a lower shelf.

***

'Mark – I need you to look after the kids if I die.'

'People normally start with a "hi".'

I'm sitting at my computer, sharing a beer online with my best friend over Skype. It's rubbish, but thanks to social distancing (which Mark and I are observing properly because we're responsible human beings), it's the closest we're going to get for a while to going to the pub. That said, it's nice to just be chatting to another human being. Amanda, my girlfriend, is currently self-isolating, feeling really shitty with (what's hopefully) flu, so we're only communicating via WhatsApp. Worse for her, she came down with it when she was visiting her parents, so she's stuck at their house. Within the same four walls as the people that birthed her. The thought sends a shiver down my spine. I try to take my mind off the thought by refocusing on the conversation at hand.

'Sorry – stressful day. How's Karen doing by the way? Maybe I can have a quick chat with her after we've finished?'

'Oh no, you can't talk to her,' he says, stopping me with the fervour of a lollipop lady who has taken it upon herself to also build a wall.

'What?'

'Sorry – you're just my friend now.'

I feel a little taken aback. 'I don't understand.'

'Well – we had a chat about it and we realised if we're stuck inside together for months, we're really going to wind each other up, so we're each going to need someone to complain to.'

'Why does that mean I can't talk to her?'

'I can't have it that I'm slagging her off to you, then she comes on and does the same thing about me. You'd know too much. So we've decided to divvy up our joint friends.'

'And you've got me?'

'Yeah. She's got loads of other friends. I've mainly just got you.'

'Well, what if I want Karen?'

'You can't want Karen – she's my wife. It's fine if we're both equal friends with you – but if your relationship becomes the main one, that's basically an affair.'

'Yeah, we'd probably start having Skype sex,' I reply, sarcastically.

'Can be done. I've done it. With her. When I was away. She was really good at it.' *Didn't need that shared.* 'Just be thankful, Tom. You're lucky – being single. This is going to be a fucking nightmare for couples.'

'Yeah – it's going to be great for us lot. Loneliness, isolation, no breaks from childcare for the foreseeable future…'

Perhaps whatever situation you're in, it's going to be awful. The whole thing reminds me of a joke I once heard – can't remember who it was. It was about the question you have to ask yourself when you're thinking of getting married: which would I rather be – lonely or irritated? Coronavirus is just going to get people to that point a hell of a lot faster.

But even if Mark's being ridiculous, it's nice to be talking to another adult human being for a change. I'll let the whole no-Karen thing be for a few days, before I start insisting that I talk to her as well.

But maybe *I'm* the one being ridiculous? Is this whole not-seeing-friends-thing a complete overreaction? The pubs are still open, other people are still having play-dates, me and Mark aren't seeing each other, but the kids are still all over each other at school…

'Oh no – Amelie isn't,' Mark replies when I mention it. 'We took her out.'

I can't quite understand the words. 'What do you mean you took her out?'

'It's as it sounds.' He pauses. 'Don't tell me yours are still there?'

'Yeah – the schools are open. Don't we have to send them?'

'Technically, I guess, but everywhere else in the world has closed up – letting the kids go to school seems like a really bad idea.'

'I know, but… how… how did you do that?' I am still genuinely uncomprehending.

'We just said she has a cough,' he shrugs.

'You're *pretending* she's got coronavirus?'

'Yeah – but to stop her *catching* coronavirus. Karen and me sat down and decided it was for the best.'

And there it is: the real reason it's shit being a single father. How the hell can you make a decision like that if it's just you? I can imagine the two of them egging each other on, comment after comment, until eventually they're sure, they're confident, definite that they're doing the right thing. But when you have to go against what the government is saying, what society is saying, *alone*, you just feel like a crazy person. God, I really hope it works out with Amanda and me. It'd be great to have someone to make those decisions with. Someone to share the burden. Oh, and because she's awesome. That's the main reason. Not just because I want the occasional break from responsibility and childcare. Maybe won't mention that when I message her later…

Wednesday 18th March
8:15 am

'Right, kids – handwashing. You need to learn to do it properly. If you're going to keep going to school, you're going to have to improve your personal hygiene.'

The kids look unimpressed, standing in the bathroom like they're about to experience the most boring lesson of their lives. But this is necessary – if I'm going to continue following the government guidelines (which I'm beginning to agree are massively stupid), I at least need to get them to wash their hands properly.

Arthur has an alternative suggestion: 'Maybe we just shouldn't go…'

'It's school. You have to go.'

'Amelie's not going,' Arthur counters.

'That's different. Amelie's got a cough. You have to either have a cough or a temperature to be off school at the moment. Those are the rules.'

'But she hasn't got a cough,' Arthur replies. 'I heard you talking to Amelie's dad last night. He said they were just pretending.'

'She's got a pretend cough?' asks Carrie.

'Um… Maybe *slightly* pretend,' I reply, 'but…'

'I think *I've* got a pretend cough,' says Arthur. 'Can I be off school too? I think I've got one now.'

'I have as well!' Carrie echoes.

They both start coughing, and I've got to admit it does sound convincing. Then I remember the upstairs neighbours and feel massively self-conscious. They're going to think this is a hotbed of infection.

'Stop!' I shout. 'Please stop coughing. PRETEND coughing,' I add – loud enough so the people in the attic flat can hear. 'You can't PRETEND to cough anymore.'

'Can I have a pretend temperature?' asks Carrie.

'That would be better,' I reply. 'But no. You can't have a pretend anything. You're going to school and that's that.'

'*Why*?' insists Arthur. Justifiably so.

I sigh, and let the truth flood out.

'Because Daddy's weak and doesn't have the courage of his convictions.'

That seems to satisfy them. I just needed something they could believe in.

'Right – handwashing,' I say, trying to get this whole farce back on track. 'Now, you have to wash your hands for twenty seconds. That's counting up to twenty, all right Carrie?'

'I can count to twenty!'

'I know – that's why I'm telling you like this.'

She counts to twenty in about four seconds.

'It has to be slower than that.'

Second try – six seconds.

'OK – this is the problem. And the government knows that so what they've said is that you have to sing "Happy Birthday" *twice* while you're doing it.'

'Who to?' Carrie asks. It's not a question I was expecting.

'Um… I don't know. It doesn't matter. It doesn't have to be *to* anyone.'

'Then how do we do the "Happy birthday dear…" bit?' Arthur queries.

'Just leave it out.'

'But won't the song be shorter then?' he asks.

'OK. Just, um… to me then: Happy birthday dear Daddy.'

'But it's not your birthday,' Carrie protests.

'I know it's not my birthday, but it doesn't matter.'

'Then I'm not singing it to you.'

'Why not? It doesn't matter.'

'Because when it is your birthday you won't feel special,' Carrie explains.

'It's like when you tell us not to wear a coat in the house,' Arthur adds. That is a very astute observation.

'OK – then not to me.'

'Then who to?'

'I don't know – the coronavirus,' I respond flippantly. It is not taken like that.

'How old is the coronavirus?' asks Carrie. Speech to kids really needs a forward slash s at the end.

'It's not old, it's new,' Arthur points out.

'Well, this one is, but there've been other ones. Covid-*18*. No one ever talks about that one. It probably feels very lonely, whereas in reality I'm sure it was nice and didn't really hurt anyone.'

'I'm not singing "Happy Birthday" to a silly virus,' Carrie snaps. She seems adamant. Why do things always have to be so difficult? 'We need to find out whose birthday it is.'

All my resolve is gradually crumbling. 'Fine.'

I go onto Facebook, and scroll through my notifications. Kate Belfiore has a birthday today. I have no idea who that is. But who cares? It's a birthday.

'Good news guys – it's Kate's birthday today!'

'Who?'

'Kate. Kate Belfiore. You remember?'

'No.'

'Doesn't matter – it's her birthday! And that's true! Now, let's get to some handwashing. Twenty seconds! Sing it twice, remember? She's a bit deaf.'

The kids start washing their hands and singing. Kate Belfiore has literally no idea how much goodwill she's getting right now from the under-tens. The annoying thing is that, like Cinderella's godmother's, Kate's Belfiore's magic will wear off at midnight. That means I'm going to have to find someone else first thing tomorrow morning. As if getting them dressed and reaching up for the cereal wasn't enough.

'OK – let's get you to your infected schools!'

'Daddy – I need to go to the toilet first.'

'A number one or a number two?'

'Two.'

I eye one of our remaining two toilet rolls and think of Carrie's technique of rolling it round her hand like she's trying to mummify it. The supermarket's still completely out, so I'm starting to think about alternatives (kitchen roll/baby wipes/£2.99 Dan Brown novel), but how long till other people get the same idea? Better to try to conserve it.

'Call me when you've finished. I'll wipe for you.'

'Thanks, Daddy.'

The joys of parenting a four-year-old… I wander out to let her get started, reminding myself to set a good example washing my hands afterwards. I won't go overboard though. Ten seconds should do it. It's only a poo.

***

After dropping them off, I settle in for my third day of homeworking. By the time I pick the kids up, I feel pretty proud of what I've achieved: I've got through a hell of a lot of biscuits and the flat has never looked so tidy.

When we get back, we FaceTime Granny Jan. She's finally agreed to self-isolate after a week of me trying to persuade her. A typical conversation:

'Mum – you have to stay in the house.'

'Of course, I'm not stupid. I'm only going to go out if I need to do the shopping. And for Zumba.'

'No, no – not for Zumba. You can't go out for that.'

'I've got to keep fit, Tom.'

'Go for a walk – just stay away from other people.'

'I don't like walking – it's boring.'

'Well you can't go to Zumba.'

'Fine. I'll just do tai chi this week then.'

'You can't do tai chi either.'

'No one's near each other. It's very slow. A lot of people do it in China.'

'Really not doing anything to help your case. Even if it's the number one leisure activity in Wuhan.'

'Fine. I won't do that. I'll stay in the house.'

'Good.' Another thought hits me. 'And you'll cancel your hair appointment?'

'No. There's no need. That's not going out. She comes to the house.'

'For God's sake.'

'You said not to go out, not not to have people come in.'

'You've got to be sensible, Mum, you're old.'

'I am not old – I'm middle-aged.'

'You're not middle-aged. There's no chance you're living to a hundred and forty. I'm sorry, Mum – but you're nowhere near the middle. I'd just like to see you reach 75.'

Eventually she agrees to cancel her hair appointment. When she hangs up I can tell she's unhappy.

That was six days ago. We haven't talked since. At 6:30 pm, I assemble the kids around my phone (propped up on the first can of tinned vegetables I have ever bought) and dial her up.

What appears on the screen is not pretty.

It looks like Granny Jan, but also… not like Granny Jan. Her face is the same, but her usually voluminous hair is now plastered down in two strange feather-light curtains either side of her head.

'Aggh!' screams Carrie as she appears.

'Hi Carrie! Hi Arthur!' Granny Jan waves on the screen.

'Who's that?' asks Arthur.

'It's Granny Jan, of course,' I tell them, smiling, desperately trying to pretend that it does not look like Granny Jan's corpse.

'That is NOT Granny Jan,' Arthur replies.

''Course it is – sorry, Mum, they're just not used to seeing you on the screen.'

'I'm scared,' says Carrie. 'Make it go away.'

'No, no – it's just Granny. You're just not used to FaceTiming.'

'Yes we are,' says Arthur. 'We FaceTime Mummy every night.'

'What's happening?' asks Granny Jan, confused. 'Is something wrong with your screen? I can see you perfectly.'

'Yeah,' I reply, knowing that this is all my fault. It's fair enough that I made her cancel all these things, but I really had no idea of the consequences. Maybe the hair appointment was a step too far. 'I think something's wrong with the screen. Maybe we should call you back.'

'I think you dialled the wrong person,' says Arthur.

'Maybe you called Kate Belfiore?' suggests Carrie.

'Mum – we'll call you back in a sec.'

I hang up, the words, 'Is Granny Jan dead?' trailing from Carrie's mouth just before my finger reaches the button.

Fuck.

Hopefully she didn't hear.

I sit the kids down, and explain to them that Granny might be looking a little different to normal, but that they shouldn't say anything. We need to be understanding in this strange and unusual time.

When we call back, my mother is wearing a sunhat.

I feel terrible… Maybe I should have just bought her hairdresser a hazmat suit.

After the call, I sit there thinking. Is this a taste of things to come? Are we all going to be emerging in three or four months' time looking like Robinson Crusoe? Obviously there're bigger issues at stake, but is this the moment we suddenly find out what everyone looks like sans expensive haircuts and hair dye? Without regular…

Shit.

Hair dye.

I suddenly realise I might have an issue here as well.

I started dying my hair a few months ago – just before I started seeing Amanda. Something that's now starting to look like a terrible decision. Shit. One kid says you look like Santa, and suddenly you're three months into a relationship and *living a lie*. My hair appointment was meant to be next week. That means *my* dye's due to start coming out. Christ – what's Amanda going to think?!? We're still only messaging, but she says she's getting better, so it can't be long until we're seeing each other's faces on a screen, or in actual life. I'm going to look like an idiot – like I've gone grey over two bloody weeks. I know this is a stressful situation but that's ridiculous. I'm going to be fat as it is (in the three days I've been working at home, I literally haven't stopped eating), the least I can do is be fat with flowing chestnut locks.

Maybe I should I just tell her the truth. Honesty is always the best policy. No – I've got to maintain the façade. As much as I condemn all these hoarders, we must be going into lockdown soon (every other country in Europe seems to be!), so I need to stock up. I need to stock up on hair dye.

When I check the news later, it turns out that things *are* going the same way as the rest of Europe. The schools are closing. Nurseries too. It's going to be disastrous, but I think I agree it's for the best.

And I know lockdown's coming. They haven't announced it, but I can feel it.

So I need to get to a chemist.

Thursday 19th March

I arrive at Boots just before nine. There's a bit of a queue, but it's not too bad. My plan is to get in and out quickly then go to the supermarket before starting my 'home-working'. I still need to get some toilet roll as my whole Dan Brown plan doesn't look like it's going to bear fruit. Turns out he hasn't written anything in a while. Jeffery Archer has, but rumour is they're already out. Guess I wasn't the only person who'd had the idea...

As soon as the doors open, I dart straight to the men's section. I vowed never to dye my hair myself in case I messed it up, but here I am – buying six packs of *Just For Men* and hoping that no one sees me. I try to be big about it – flattening the curve will require everyone to make sacrifices.

OK – what colour am I – light brown? Dark brown? *Mid-*brown? I could ask someone but they'd probably give the answer 'slightly grey' and I don't think they do that one as an option.

I head to the till as quickly as possible with an eye to being at the front of the queue, and getting out with my dignity intact.

But it is not to be.

Somehow, within the three minutes it has taken me to scoop up an armful of embarrassment, the queue is now twenty people long. I look to the front doors, and there's more of them coming in, flooding through the entrances like zombies into a shopping mall. And they're going straight to the back of the queue... without even getting anything. What the hell is happening?!?

In a rare moment of decisiveness, I realise I don't have time to think. I have to act now. The quicker I get in the queue, the smaller the damage will be. And any hesitation might also mean the supermarket is out of loo roll/the Jeffery Archer restock.

I join the queue and an old lady takes her place behind me. I can't see anyone around that I know. This might be all right.

Then I hear a coughing from behind. A 'can I get your attention?' one rather than a 'highly infectious and you probably shouldn't be in the same room as me' one. Still, not currently the most appropriate way to get someone to look at you. It's the old lady.

'My husband used to use that,' she whispers. Not that quietly.

'Oh, right,' I say, smiling, trying not to look mortified. I attempt to change the subject before anyone can overhear. 'Why's everybody queuing?'

'They've got paracetamol and hand sanitiser!' she says, triumphant.

'Really? I mean – I knew that.' I didn't. It's a complete result – I stocked up on ibuprofen a few weeks ago only to read it makes Covid worse. Paracetamol's gold-dust at the moment. 'I totally knew that.'

'Of course you did,' she comments. 'No, one would be in here at 9:00 am just to buy six packets of *Just For Men*.'

She's not keeping her voice down.

'We probably shouldn't talk,' I explain. 'You know – in case I have a mild form of the virus – I don't want to risk giving it to you.'

'Oh, yes,' she replies, stepping back. I'm really hoping this means an end to our conversation, rather than just that she continues it louder.

The queue moves forward, and my Machiavellian machinations seem to have worked. But then I see who's in front of me in the queue. Martin.

He's one of the dads from school. Massive, stupid, and completely unsophisticated. I kind of got in a fight with him in the playground a few months ago. And then I started seeing his ex. Used some of his left-over extra-large condoms. They're back together now. Him seeing me like this means she is *definitely* finding out.

I look around, desperately searching for something to hide my stash under. There's a big bag of panty liners on the shelf next to where we're queuing. They're the only thing I can see that's big enough to hide multiple packets of hair dye, so I grab them. And just in time.

Martin turns around, almost as if he has sensed me.

'Oh, it's you?' he scoffs. 'Aren't you meant to be staying in your house?'

'What do you mean?' I ask, confused.

'Vulnerable groups,' he says. 'I think weaklings count.'

Every time he talks to me, it feels like I'm back at school being bullied. I turn to the mouthy pensioner behind me to roll my eyes, but she's having none of it, looking away like she doesn't know me. What – suddenly I'm a stranger now? What happened to me and your dead husband bonding over being the unacceptable face of male vanity?

'That's very funny, Martin. Good to have a laugh when things are so difficult.'

'Not a joke. And what are you buying?' he says with a grin. I look down with a grimace before replying to check what he can see.

'…Panty liners,' I reply.

'Ha, ha! I always knew you were a woman!'

'They're not for me. They're for my girlfriend. Who's on her period.'

He shakes his head. Probably more information than was needed. I doubt my imaginary girlfriend uses them as pan scourers. And why did I feel the need to call her 'imaginary'? I actually do have a girlfriend.

But Martin has spotted something, and there's a glint in his eye.

'Panty liners, you said?'

'Yeah.'

'Except, they're not panty liners, are they? They're incontinence pads.'

I look down. Fuck, he's right. They look almost exactly the same, but no, these are definitely 100% adult incontinence pads.

'My husband used to use those as well,' the old lady pipes up from behind. For fuck's sake – where were you when I needed some support on the eye rolling?

'Been pissing yourself, have you?' he says. 'I know this Covid thing is scary, but I thought even you could have held it in?'

I want to say I got the wrong ones, but that would involve me putting them back and swapping them, revealing the eight months' supply of hair dye underneath. Then I'm incontinent *and* embarrassed about going grey. Doesn't exactly make things better.

'How old is your girlfriend?' he laughs, intoxicated by his own hilariousness. 'Eighty?' I feel the woman from behind perk up – maybe she can get herself a toyboy.

Martin gives one final snort, then turns away from me, confident in the utterness of the devastation in his wake. He's right. His victory is absolute.

A few minutes later I reach the front of the queue, utterly ashamed, plonking my haul down in front of the cashier.

'I'll get some hand sanitiser and paracetamol as well please?' I ask, thinking I may as well try my luck.

'No problem,' she replies. 'Just one packet though, ooh, and that's the last hand sanitiser!'

Silver linings. Paracetamol! That means I can now survive this disease for more than two days if it hits me.

As I leave the shop, I pass my elderly queue-mate arguing with the cashier. She's looking unhappy.

'But that's all I came in for. I'm old – you should save the hand sanitiser for us.'

'I'm sorry, madam, but when it's gone, it's gone,' the cashier replies.

As much as I'm annoyed with her, I realise I don't have a choice. I step over to the till (maintaining as much social distance as the action of giving her mine will allow).

'Here you go.'

I walk away with a bag full of hair dye, some incontinence pads (can't work out why I went through with paying for those) and some unexpected paracetamol, my head still held low. Then the old woman calls after me.

I turn around, worried I've dropped something.

'You *are* like my husband…' she says.

Great, more mockery coming from the OAP roast squad.

'He was kind too.'

Silver linings…

***

The supermarket shop goes more smoothly, apart from a brief set-to with a man in his thirties who I accuse of being a hoarder ('I need a lot of pasta!' 'So does everyone else.' 'But I don't like eating many things!'), and I manage to get pretty much everything I want. The only strange thing is that I'm suddenly having to buy all the expensive stuff that I wouldn't normally touch – Lurpak butter, organic milk, Charlie Bingham's ready meals… Gone are the economy free range eggs – in their place I now have to shell out £2.40 for some Burford Browns. It makes me feel like I'm a rich person. A rich person getting one last luxury shop in before he declares bankruptcy.

By the end of it I have about thirty quid's worth of shopping that costs me over sixty. On the upside, I did manage to score a nine-pack of toilet roll, so that puts us up to eleven. I've got to work out how many we use a day – see how long we can survive until we need to restock. I'm also quite excited about trying the high class eggs. This is how things must have been for people during the war.

***

Back at the flat, work is starting to worry me. I haven't come up with anything decent since I've been at home. I really didn't think the office (with its free coffee, ping pong tables and bean bags) was particularly helpful, but it turns out that being able to play Space Invaders on a 1980s arcade machine *does* make you more creative. Who would have thunk it?

But I'm *trying*. I'm trying really hard. This could be a really difficult few months. There's a good chance the business could go under or they start laying people off. If I lose my job, I'm fucked. How am I going to support the kids? How am I going to pay our rent? So I really need to come up with some ideas for this bloody campaign.

After two hours I've generated about a page of ideas. They're not particularly good, but at least it's something. Maybe I need some coffee? Coffee definitely seems like the most accessible of the creativity hacks that I'm used to. I think about going down to Starbucks and getting a takeaway but that seems like a bad idea. What if the person serving is all coughy? Ha ha coffee. No? Nothing? I decide against it. I go online to see how much a home coffee maker is, only to discover they're bloody expensive. Finally I find a Nespresso thing with a milk foamer for just over a hundred. Ouch. But maybe it'll make a difference. It's the only option I've got to make the place more 'office-like'. And it's definitely cheaper than a ping pong table. Plus I doubt one would fit in our living room.

At lunchtime, I get a call from Larousse. He's filling in for Amanda while she's self-isolating. He likes to pretend he's down to earth because he's got a Welsh accent, but apparently his dad left him about 20 million and he has a seven bedroom house in Notting Hill, so there's only so down to earth you can actually be. That said, I've heard he added a basement recently, so technically that's more down to earth than ground level. I'm also pretty sure his actual name is Larry.

'All right, Tommy? How's it going?' asks Larousse.

'Not too bad – just getting used to this whole home-working thing.'

'You'll be all right. I got the document you sent. There's some good stuff there. Not much of it, but good stuff.'

'Thanks. I'll do more this afternoon. And I've ordered a coffee maker, which comes tomorrow, so hopefully that should give me a bit of a boost to get more done in the mornings.'

'A coffee maker? Are you serious? Everyone else is stocking up on pasta and rice, and you're ordering bloody coffee makers?!?' he says, barely able to contain his own amusement.

'I just wanted to be productive.'

'God, Tommy – how middle class are you? Quick! The world's ending – get me a cappuccino! Down the supermarket worried they're going to run out of avocados and hummus, are you?'

'I…' He's really starting to wind me up. Particularly as they had run out of avocados. It was really annoying. I try to change the subject. 'So do you not have one?'

'Yeah – of course I've got one – a Sage Oracle, it's excellent – but I didn't go out and get it just because the bloody coronavirus kicked off!' I look it up online, it's over a thousand pounds. Jesus. And yet somehow he has still succeeded in making me feel ridiculous.

'Yeah – maybe it was stupid,' I reply. 'Anyway – I'll get some more ideas to you this afternoon.'

'Don't worry about that. We need you to work on some copy for a radio ad we're recording Monday – I'll send you over what we've got. You can sit in on the voiceover.'

'Great.' That does actually sound a bit exciting.

I suddenly realise I can hear something in the background down the phone line. It sounds like children.

'Is that your kids?' I ask.

'Yeah – we've had them off since Monday.' Christ! How is everybody doing this? Does no one obey the rules?!? 'Wife and I just chatted about it and sending them in didn't seem like a good idea. Bit of a hassle with both of us trying to work from home, but the nanny's managing to keep them occupied most of the time.'

'Nanny?'

'Yeah…' He pauses before continuing, suddenly realising he's been caught out. 'Probably shouldn't have said that. Don't tell anyone. She's agreed to self-isolate with us till things calm down a little.'

I literally can't speak. This man was taking the piss out of me for spending a hundred quid on a coffee machine, and he has *staff*?

'Probably be better for her as well,' he continues, clutching at a straw from the stable she's probably sleeping in.

I come off the call feeling utterly deflated. The media keeps telling us everybody's in this together. Rich and poor. What a load of bullshit. Turns out it's everyone except for those who can afford to pay servants to go into bloody quarantine with them…

That evening, someone sends me through a link of Gal Gadot's *Imagine* video. It's sickening. All these damn rich people, pretending they're experiencing the same things we are in their massive bloody houses and park-like estates. I wonder if *they* have staff? I'll bet some of them do. It's not like they'd put them in the video – their housekeeper suddenly appearing and coming in to harmonise on the middle eight…

Meanwhile I'm lying in my bed, trying to think of whose birthday I should pretend it is tomorrow, wondering how the fuck I'm going to get through this. Tomorrow will be my last day of home working without the kids around. I've got to keep my job. So I need to make it count.

Friday 20th March

The coffee maker arrives and my new found caffeine high allows me to get some serious amounts of work done. This was the best investment I could have made! Come Monday, when the kids are at home, I'll realise it probably wasn't as good as a live-in nanny, but for a single father on a budget it was definitely the way to go. Well, until the supermarket runs out of Nespresso pods.

By lunchtime, I've got a draft of all the scripts sent off and I'm cooking an organic bacon sandwich, when I get a phone call from Mark.

'They're doing my fucking head in.'

'Who?' I ask, not even bothering to comment on the lack of greeting. It's becoming pretty standard for us at the moment.

'Karen. The kids. All of them.'

'You love Karen – you two are the best couple I know.'

'I know, I just… I need to get out. Can you meet me in the park?'

'We're not meant to be meeting people.'

'I know the rules – we'll walk eight metres away from each other and talk on our phones.'

'Won't that be awkward?'

'We can put headphones in and talk through them.'

'Can't we just Skype on treadmills or something?' I say, really wanting to enjoy my overpriced bacon sandwich in peace.

'Do either of us own a treadmill?'

'OK. I'll see you in the park.'

Twenty minutes later, we're in the park, and what follows is the weirdest conversation ever. Me and my best friend walking what is probably ten metres away from each other, with our headphones in so we can actually hear what the other one's saying.

'I can't take this,' Mark rants.

'It's only been a week.'

Mark looks genuinely surprised. 'Has it really? My God, I'm fucked. I'm absolutely fucked.'

'Calm down – a lot of people have got it worse than you. Like, look at this guy's dog,' I say, pointing out a dachshund being dragged along by a jogger. 'Did you see the expression on its face?'

'Not a person,' he replies. 'But no, I didn't see the expression on its face. The dog is ten metres away from you so it's twenty metres away from me.' Maybe now's the time to point out that this ridiculous charade was 100% his idea. It's almost like he's forgotten the point of being in public together is to point at things and mock them.

'OK – just get it off your chest – tell me what's happening.'

He sighs. 'It's impossible. I'm trying to work – but I've got the kids screaming downstairs. Then I'll talk to Karen and she's in a terrible mood, and has a massive go at me 'cos she's been dealing with them close up. So I take over while *she* works, and after about two minutes of thinking "isn't this nice?" I want to kill them. Then I have to suppress that feeling for the next ninety minutes and of course – *not* actually kill them, and then she comes into the kitchen having finally calmed down, and I have a massive go at her. It's fucking shit.'

'Doesn't sound great.'

'You know, Tom, I didn't realise how much I liked working. Work is amazing. I always thought I went just to make money, but it's like this brilliant opportunity to not be around your family.' He starts to slow down. 'To actually *miss* people.'

'Yeah, well… I don't want to be a dick or anything, but it is kind of what you signed up for. Wife. Family. Being with them for the rest of your lives, that kind of thing…'

'Yeah, I know. And I *do* want to be with Karen forever,' he replies. 'Just not this much.'

'Well, at least you like her. Normally. Think of all the people who are shacked up with someone they don't love anymore, someone who hits them…'

It knocks him out of his indulgence for a while. 'Yeah, you're right. It could be a lot worse. First world problems, I know. But it's still difficult.'

'Hey – at least you've got someone,' I say, taking my turn for self-indulgence.

'You've got the kids,' he replies, in the weakest counter argument ever.

'Isn't that just worse?'

He pauses for moment. 'Yeah, you're right – that's worse,' Mark replies. I laugh. 'Not a joke,' he continues. 'You'll see on Monday. It's a fucking nightmare…'

We don't talk for the rest of the time, but I think just getting out has made him feel better. But when I get home, the words are still just hanging there… *It's a fucking nightmare…*

And I can't help but be worried he might be right.

Afternoon

Thinking about other people puts me in a giving mood, and, after

I finish the rewrites for the voiceover, I decide to text Sue, my elderly neighbour, to see if she wants anything from the supermarket.

She calls me the instant I press send.

'Tom! That's so nice you got in touch. That would be so kind. Can I give you a list?'

After five minutes of her reciting items that I didn't know were still being produced/sold to the public (frozen cauliflower, Baxter's consomme, corned beef, pudding rice, canned fruit cocktail and 300g of fresh liver), she asks me if I'd be willing to get a few things for her friend Pamela as well? I tell her 'no problem', but then Pamela refers me to Rosamund, who refers me to Cath, and by the time I'm done I have the shopping lists for four pensioners splayed out in front of me.

As much as I feel like a good person, I can't help worrying I might not get it done before I have to pick up the kids from school.

Turns out, the best thing about pensioner food is that no one else wants it. Although they're still out of eggs (I doubt they'll be willing to pay up for the Burford Browns), everything else is a breeze. The corned beef actually has a *deal on*. It's crazy. If I could convince the kids to start eating tinned sardines, I could probably get enough stuff to last us until winter.

The bad news is that I've currently filled up a full-size trolley as well as a basket. They've also *all* requested toilet roll, which seems impossible, but when I tell the shelf stacker guy that it's for elderly neighbours he goes out back and gives me some from a secret stash. Still, it doesn't look good. I'm walking around with a quantity (and quality) of food that makes me look like a black market dealer during World War II rationing.

And that's when I hear someone calling me from behind.

'Excuse me!'

I turn round to come face to face with the pasta hoarder from a few days ago.

'Oh... how the tables have turned...' he says, smugness running through his veins like a glucose spike. 'The other day you accused me of hoarding pasta – and look what's happening now. *You're* hoarding. You're hoarding...' he picks up a packet from my trolley, 'blancmange mix!'

Even more than his accusations, the fact that he's handling the food sends me into panic mode. 'You shouldn't be touching that. You're not following the proper social distancing rules.'

'You should have thought about that when you accused me of hoarding pasta!'

'You were!'

'All I had was three bags.'

'You had *seven*.'

'I DON'T LIKE RICE! ... I'm naming and shaming!' he says. 'I'm NAMING AND SHAMING.'

'No – don't do that,' I panic. 'It's not for me. It's for my neighbour.'

'A likely story – just 'cos you eat...' He picks up another item, 'tinned prunes rather than pasta, it doesn't make you any better.'

'Please don't touch my stuff.'

He pulls out his phone, and I manage to hide behind my coat before he starts filming. Eventually someone from the supermarket asks him to stop.

'No problem, I've already got the footage... posting... now!'

I go to the tills, my head held low, having to explain once more to the cashier why I've got so much loo roll.

I drop the various bags off at the pensioners' addresses, making sure I stand back after ringing the doorbell. Everybody is very appreciative, but still...

'How much did it cost you?' Sue asks as I drop off my final delivery.

'Just my reputation,' I reply.

She looks confused. I feel bad. Old people don't like to be confused. 'I'll work it out and text you. Oh, and disinfect the blancmange and prune packets before you touch them – they might be infected.'

It's when I'm walking the kids home from school that I see I'm mentioned in a couple of tweets. One is Sue (who I'm surprised is on Twitter) thanking me for being a good neighbour. The other is trending at number three with the hashtag 'named and shamed'. There's no face on it though. Turns out I did manage to get my coat up in time.

That said, I should probably change into a different jacket.

Saturday 21st March

After a family breakfast of the most delicious golden-yolked eggs I have ever tasted (note to self: if I get rich I am never buying the economy ones again), I head out to the park with the kids.

The whole thing is so weird. There are people everywhere – the sun's out, it's warm – it seems more like a spring bank holiday than the middle of a pandemic. I let the kids run ahead of me as it's going to be the nearest I get to alone time for a while – they're under strict instructions not to get too close to people (or lick anything), so hopefully it should be fine.

But what's worrying is that people everywhere seem to be letting their guard down. Walking too close, going over to friends to have a chat. Not that I blame them 100%. When the weather's like this, it just doesn't seem *real*. The joggers are the worst – they never seem to give you any space – as if coughing is contagious, but spraying you with out-of-breath pant spittle is fine. At one point, I actually shout, 'Two metres!' as one skims my shoulder. Carrie overhears and finds it hilarious and starts shouting, 'Two metres!' at everyone who walks past. God, I'm raising my kids well.

But beneath it all, I can't help feeling generally unsettled. I suppose we all do at the moment. We're living through the weirdest time in human history. Surely there can't have ever been anything like this before? A time when everyone had to just stay in their house, only leaving for essential tasks? Well, winter maybe – you know, in the old days, before they invented decent clothes. But not *recently*.

Or maybe it isn't weird at all. Maybe this is just what it is to be human – knowing something's coming – something that could kill you, hurt you, take away your loved ones. All the time. This is how existence has been for our species for millions of years. Since we were conscious. We've just forgotten what it feels like.

I'm distracted from my thoughts by a group of cyclists all sitting down close to each other on the grass and chatting, as if there's nothing wrong. It really pisses me off. How the hell are we going to make it through this if this is what people are doing as social distancing? Surely lockdown can't be that far off?

But still, the sun gives me hope.

Maybe this whole thing is going to be all right.

As long as the sun keeps shining…

Sunday 22nd March

Sunday begins with the daily chore of working out whose birthday it is for the handwashing ritual. I can't find anyone – but there's something better. Mother's Day. 'Happy Mother's Day to you!' It fits perfectly. They just need to sing it twice every time they wash their hands. I'll tell them to imagine they're being parented by a lesbian couple.

It's about ten minutes later when I come to a realisation.

I too have a mother.

And I haven't sent her a card.

Shit.

Shit, shit, shit, shit, shit.

I sit the kids down. 'You know we're FaceTiming Mummy today to say happy Mother's Day?'

'Yeah.'

'Well you know who *else's* Mother's Day it is today?'

'Amelie's mum's?' Carrie says.

'No. Well, yes, but also…'

'Mrs Harrison's from Science?' Arthur asks. 'I don't like Mrs Harrison.'

'I don't think she has children,' I reply.

'She does – two…' he explains.

'Really?!? Can't believe anyone would… any stork would… Anyway, that's not the point. The point is it's also *Granny Jan's* Mother's Day. She's a mother. A *grand*mother. So – what I need you two to do now is draw her a card.'

'Shouldn't *you* draw her a card?' Carrie asks. 'She's your mother.'

'No – Daddy needs to learn how to bake bread, otherwise the family will starve, so today: this is on you.'

An hour later, I have some bread dough 'proving' in the cupboard and over most of the work surface, and the kids announce that the card is done.

Just in time. My phone starts ringing almost to cue. My mother's FaceTiming. I wanted to beat her to it. At least the card's finished.

I answer, and Mum appears on the screen.

She's wearing a woolly hat and an expression of disappointment.

'I didn't get a card through today.' Wow. Straight in with the accusations. She must have been talking to Mark about how to open a phone call.

'Happy Mother's Day!' I reply, 'And of *course* you didn't get a card. We're trying to be safe. I did think it through – it's not just like I *forgot*!'

Mum looks sceptical.

'Look – what if I sent a card through to you, and we had an asymptomatic version of the virus? Now you'd have it too. Doesn't really seem worth the risk.'

She hesitates. '... I suppose not, no.'

'So... really – not sending a card is the nicest thing I could have done.'

'Well, I got one from your sister.'

'Then it seems like she wasn't being as thoughtful as I was. Think about who loves you more.' Dick move. I feel guilty almost immediately. 'Actually, I doubt the virus could last the trip from Australia, so she was probably thinking about that. Looks like we actually both love you *equally*.' Saved it. 'The good news is – we've drawn you a card. Kids.'

The kids lift up the card, which shows Granny Jan doing Tai Chi.

'It's you doing your old person karate!' says Arthur. 'We drew a really weak person coming to take your money who you might be able to beat.'

'Oh right,' says Granny Jan.

'I drew your hair,' says Carrie. 'Do you like it?'

'It's really nice, darling.'

'I did it so your hair looked like it did before the virus came, so you don't look scary.'

I hold my head in my hands.

Strangely, Mum actually seems OK about it.

'Thanks, my love. That's what I really look like, isn't it? It's good you drew it like that. I won't be posing for any photos while it's like this.' I decide not to tell her that Arthur has just reached over and taken a screen shot to use as a reference for his next masterpiece.

'So – you got to see it on the day, and I'll put it in the post tomorrow.'

'But…'

'That was a test. Just checking you were being cautious too…'

Monday 23rd March

The first day of home-schooling begins.

I have to say I'm pretty impressed with what Arthur's school has sent through. They emailed to say they've set up all this online work – various tasks and worksheets to download. I really can't believe they're going to so much effort. I just think the whole package is amazing.

That is, until I open it.

There's almost nothing. One page of easy maths questions, some colouring and the task 'make a rainbow.' I can feel my son's mind expanding already.

Apparently, the rainbow thing is what people in Italy have been doing – putting drawings of them in windows to show solidarity. It's meant to give the kids hope; take them out of the doldrums they're in and make them know that the world is going to be OK.

Although, considering the first words I heard as Arthur burst into my room today at 6:00 am were 'No, schooooooooolllll!' while he performed a malcoordinated version of the Running Man, I'm thinking he'd probably be OK without the rainbow.

I decide it's best to keep them to their regular schedules and start them off with work at nine. Which actually means ten. It's only fair. After all, they're technically 'working from home'. I start to explain what they have to do at 9:50, as I need to be on the phone with work for ten.

'All right. Carrie, you've got some colouring and some letter writing that your nursery has sent through. And Arthur, you've got colouring, worksheets, and then you need to "make a rainbow". What's "making a rainbow"? Aha! I'm glad you asked. Look at this picture.'

I show them the example photograph the teacher has sent through.

'See, your teacher has arranged all these different objects in different colours together, so they form a *rainbow*. There's a red book on the left, then an orange… which is orange… then something green… actually she's missed out yellow… But do you understand, Arthur? Yeah? Good – so that's what you have to do, and then you take a picture of it and upload it on the school website.'

'What can we use?' Arthur asks.

'Anything you can find,' I reply. 'Richard Of York Gave Battle In Vain. Red, orange, yellow, green… you know that one yeah?'

Arthur nods.

'Can I help?' Carrie asks.

''Course. Arthur – you explain it to Carrie. I'll log in for you on the website so you can upload your photo when it's done. Now Daddy's going to go into the other room to do his work, all right? Try not to disturb me.'

I hand them my tablet and leave them to it. There's not much work, but it should buy me a couple of hours to get this recording done. I reach the bedroom, just as my phone rings.

'Hi, Tom? It's the engineer, Derek – I'm just dialling you in with Larrouse, and Seb, our voiceover artist. Everyone – Tom's on the line.'

'Morning, Mr *Coffee*,' Larousse laughs, getting in his dig before

I even have time to speak. A response comes to mind. Saying it may involve getting fired.

'Hi T…' Seb's voice cuts off, just as he starts to talk.

Damn it – I look down at my phone. I'm on Wi-Fi – must have just been a glitch.

'Are you there, Tom?' asks the engineer.

'Yeah, I'm here. Sorry – just cut out for a second.'

'No problem. Right, Tom,' Larousse interrupts, 'I was thinking that Seb approached your script with a k… o… t… and kind of… h… and b… but not too s… don't you think?'

What the?!? I look down at my phone again – still says I'm on the Wi-Fi. Shit. I guess the Wi-Fi's not so reliable when half the country's watching Netflix.

'Well, if that's what you think, L,' I reply, 'I'm happy to go with it.'

'Cool, let's do a take.'

Seb starts his voiceover and cuts out immediately. Arse. I need to get some normal 4G reception so I can actually hear him. I head to the bathroom, the only place that has a decent signal. It kicks in just as Seb finishes.

'What do you think? A little warmer maybe?' Seb asks, ironically the only thing I've heard in his last minute of constant speaking.

'Maybe. But I liked it – that was a great start,' Larousse replies. 'Tom?'

'I… I'd like to hear a second one,' I hesitate. Or a first one. For all I know he was doing it in a Scooby Doo voice. A Scooby Doo voice that wasn't quite warm enough.

He starts and I can hear it! Excellent. Annoyingly, I find the best place for reception is actually sitting on the loo itself. Lid down of course – I'm not an animal.

He finishes and it's actually pretty good. Kind of how I'd envisioned it, and not a request for a Scooby Snack in sight.

'That was great, Seb, I think the warmth worked well,' I reply. 'Maybe if we could do another one, but a bit faster at the top as I'm worried it's not going to fit in the slot.'

'Cool, no probs,' he replies. Just as Arthur comes in. And starts pointing at the loo.

Fuck. I mime the words 'wee or poo?' at him, and he replies 'wee.' Thank God. I rise from my throne, and Arthur relieves himself while I continue the conversation.

'What was that?' asks Larousse, 'I'm getting something on the line. That's not Seb, is it Derek?'

'Sorry that's me,' I reply, wishing Arthur would finish his wee quickly. 'The tap's dripping. Can't get the plumber out 'cos of the virus.'

'Oh right.'

Seb finishes another take. At the exact moment Arthur decides to flush the toilet. I try to ignore it.

'That was great,' I tell him. 'I think we should move to the second script, then come back to this one again at the end…'

'Tom?' Larousse asks.

'Yeah?'

'Are you on the toilet?'

'Umm…'

Carrie takes this as her cue to come in.

'I've finished!' she exclaims. Unnecessarily loud. It's only been ten minutes. That was meant to be a day's work for her. WTF?

'Tom?' Larousse continues. 'Are you… are you… in the toilet wiping your kid's arse?'

'No, I'm…'

'I've finished too!' says Arthur.

'Two of them?' Larousse questions. He sounds genuinely shocked. 'Derek – can you just put Seb on hold for a second?'

'Sure thing.'

'Tom – we're all doing this from home, but you've got to maintain a little professionalism.'

'I'm in the bathroom – the kids needed to come in to use the loo – they haven't "finished" finished…'

'They're still pooing? For God's sake, Tom.'

'Give me a break, L. There's nothing I can do. Not all of us are self-isolating with a bloody nanny.'

'Sorry guys,' interrupts Derek. 'Seb and I are still on the line – I haven't worked out how to put you on hold yet. New software.'

'You're self-isolating with a nanny?' Seb asks.

I have to admit considering how shocked he seems, he does manage to make his words sound reassuringly warm.

I'm losing my fucking job.

***

I manage to explain the whole thing to Amanda at lunchtime – we're speaking now, even if she doesn't feel up for FaceTime. But it's reassuring. Even though L's filling in for her, she's still technically my boss, so he can't fire me without her permission. I start to worry that she might be torn between her loyalties to me and the job. Turns out she's not. She mainly seems to find the whole thing funny.

But it hasn't been a great first experience of how this whole home-schooling thing is going to go. I managed to shoo the kids away until the voiceover was finished, only to go to the kitchen afterwards and find Carrie's craft medium of choice is now crayons and toilet paper. Seeing her stick-figure's hair consisting of glued-on strips of Andrex sent shivers down my spine. How many times have I told her it's currently a precious commodity? This is how onlookers must feel when an R&B star starts spraying five-hundred-pound bottles of Dom Perignon around a nightclub. If the Dom Perignon was a basic necessity. And actually theirs.

They've also posted Arthur's rainbow picture online via the school website and ask me to look at it, but I get distracted with work, and have to put my fatherly approval on hold for a few hours. It's four o'clock when I finally get round to viewing their masterpiece.

A red book, an orange (as suggested), a rubber duck, some broccoli… and three packets of *Just for Men*. In various shades of brown. Well, at least they got the light/mid/dark in the right order.

I feel part of me die inside. They've put it on the school notice board. Which means it's basically been viewed by every parent in Arthur's year group.

'Arthur, you do realise the B is for blue not brown yeah?' I say. I've lost all hope of growing older with dignity; I may as well try to educate them so they can look after me in my twilight years.

'Sorry,' says Arthur. 'I got mixed up.'

I almost don't feel anything when I scan along to see the indigo slot is filled by the packet of incontinence pads. At least they got the colour right this time.

It's a few hours later when I have an idea of how to minimise the fallout. I pull up the picture and comment, 'Ha! Ha! This is why, when you do a shop for an elderly neighbour, you don't leave it in your house!' I think about linking in Sue's tweet thanking me, but it doesn't seem right. Also, her hair is completely white, so maybe it wouldn't help my argument. I notice Arthur's picture has had ten times as many views as anyone else's. I check my phone – yeah, it's gone round on the year group's WhatsApp chat. There's also a comment from Martin (the first time he's ever posted), saying, 'Heard his current girlfriend's 70!' OK, it's official. I'm screwed.

It's such a relief when I finally put the kids to bed. How long are the schools going to be shut for? This is impossible. And it's day *one*. At least if I had someone else to help, I could go for a walk on my own, get some space, but instead I'm going to be with them non-stop for all their waking hours for God knows how many months. I don't think things could get any worse.

It's 8:30 when Boris announces we're going into full on lockdown.

It's 9:45 when I realise I have to pay for the third season of *The Bureau* on Amazon Prime.

Life really doesn't let up.

Tuesday 24th March

I'm getting the kids ready for our once daily allowed exercise when Mark Skypes me.

'I'm going fucking crazy. I need to get out. Can we do another one of our distance walks in the park?' He calls to Karen without even waiting for an answer. 'Babe – I'm going out with Tom.'

'You're only allowed to go out for exercise once a day now,' Karen calls back. 'If you go out with Tom you won't be able to come out on the family walk later.'

'This is the gift that just keeps on giving,' he mutters under his breath.

'Sorry mate – I can't do it,' I reply. 'I've got the kids.'

He sounds genuinely annoyed, before realising that my situation is probably even worse than his. 'Course you have. Yeah, sorry man. I'm being really self-involved. That must be really hard.'

It's nice to hear someone say it. My mum hasn't. My dad hasn't even joined a call on FaceTime. So it's really nice to have someone acknowledge what you're going through. I think everyone's having such a tough time at the moment that we forget there're plenty of people who have it far worse than us. I need to remember that too. I tell him I'll call him later, and then head off towards the park.

***

It's even stranger being outside now we're in lockdown. It doesn't seem like anything's different (I guess physically it isn't), and yet there's this weird sensation hanging over me. Like I'm not free anymore. Is this what it would be like to be living in a dictatorship? Heading down to Gorky Park for an afternoon stroll, just knowing that if you take a step out of line… Even the park itself seems different. People seem better at keeping their social distance now, but that's not it – it's just this cloying feeling of foreboding – like a pre-revolution French aristocrat walking around his sumptuous grounds knowing that beyond the walls of his estate everyone wants to kill him.

The kids seem fine though. Carrie's definitely getting better at not licking things, and has stopped shouting, 'Two Metres!' at people. I keep seeing these newspaper articles about 'how to talk to your kids about coronavirus' – seems like the best thing is not to talk about it at all. They seem to think everything's fine.

The issue comes on the walk home. The kids are running ahead of me while I message Amanda to see how she's doing. In the near distance, I can see an old man walking towards us.

'Kids! Make sure you give the man some space. Walk by the wall – two metres remember!'

Issue dealt with. Except it isn't. I press send and look up again. The old man has started swinging his stick.

And not just a little bit. We're not talking a jaunty little wiggle so he looks like he's about to launch into a *Singing in the Rain* style number. No, he's swinging it from side to side at arm's length in an arc of retribution as an attempt to enforce the two metre rule. What the…?

'Carrie, be careful, the man's…'

And then he whacks her full on around the head.

I can't quite believe it – I run towards her as fast as I can – the old man is still walking, his cane whirring around him.

'What the hell are you doing?' I ask as I run past. 'You just hit my daughter.'

'Then she can't have been far enough away,' he says.

'She was next to the wall – she couldn't have got any farther.'

He stops for a moment, as I reach Carrie. She's finding it difficult to open her eye and the skin is all red around it. Luckily, she's not bleeding.

'She needs to learn to give old people space,' he spits. 'We're a vulnerable group.'

'She knows that! It doesn't mean you can go round hitting kids with a stick.'

I get Carrie to open her eye, and she seems fine – she can answer my questions normally and doesn't seem to be seeing double, so it's not dangerous. I think.

I turn back to the man to see he's carried on, still swinging his stick from side to side, a whirling dervish of self-importance and -righteousness. What a horrible old git. I can't believe he just walked off after basically committing assault. She's all right – but what if she hadn't been? If he'd fractured her skull or given her a concussion? Taking a kid into A & E doesn't seem like the best idea right now…

It makes me realise how completely mind-warping this whole pandemic thing is becoming, making it seem like it's the only thing that can hurt us right now. Like you can no longer trip over and break your wrist, you can eat any old shit as long as the supermarket has it – *it's not an issue while the pandemic's on!* – you can't have a heart attack, you can't end up with diabetes. The other day I washed my hands after handling raw chicken and I didn't give it half the time I do after I've touched the post – as if salmonella is on a break, coronavirus having taken up the slack.

And it's not just diseases – what about the kids' education? I've been letting them watch TV and play around on the iPad today so I can get my work done. That's not going to work out if they're off school till the autumn. I can't have my kids being six months behind where they should be by the end of the year. I need to pull my finger out.

'Come on guys – let's go home.'

We walk off, and I look back to get one last glimpse of the person who just hit my daughter and got away with it. I'm filled with resentment and anger. To think we're doing all of this for him. But then, abruptly he stops swinging his stick. It's weird. It feels as if the daggers I'm sending him have actually got through.

Then suddenly, I see why, watching as a policeman crosses the road and has a word. After a quick telling off, the old man walks onwards, his head no longer held as high, his stick tapping a path on the ground by his side as it should be.

And it makes me feel a lot better than it should. As if a little bit of order has been restored once more…

***

'So, are you moving in with Amanda?'

I get the text from Mark at about six. As much as anything, I think it's mainly a reminder to call him, but it throws me for a loop. I've been so overwhelmed with getting my head round 24/7 childcare that I haven't thought about how things were going to work with me and Amanda in lockdown. Maybe that's not true. I think it's been there in the back of my mind. I just didn't want to confront it.

I look online, and it's been announced that, in terms of seeing people, there's no exception for the person you're dating. That means I won't see Amanda for ages. I can't believe it – it just feels like such a kick in the gut. Unless, of course, we move in together…

Is that something we should be talking about? We've only been together for a few months, but these aren't normal times. It seems too serious for this early on, but what's the alternative? And we wouldn't just be moving in. We'd be moving *in* in. Trapped in a flat with nowhere to go – hers is nicer, but it wouldn't have room for the kids – I'm pretty sure she wouldn't want to come to mine. God! Why is this even going through my head? This is madness.

But what if this lockdown goes on for half the year? That's longer than we've been together. We'd be out of the honeymoon period. That's rubbish – you can't have a relationship without a honeymoon period. We'd see each other again and it would just be super weird. But no, I can't ask her. It's too much. Not with the kids.

We chat on the phone a few hours later. I can sense she's been thinking about where our relationship is going as well, but neither of us wants to mention it. Instead, we just talk about random terrible things that are happening in other countries. It's easier; easier than talking about the terrible thing that's happening between us.

Wednesday 25th March

After printing out the single hour of tasks the school has set for today, I manage to find some extra colouring for Carrie and some maths questions for Arthur. I've decided to teach him his three times table as well. If I can get him up to seven, he'll be able to work out how many days of horror our family is going to endure collectively every week. That's useful stuff.

But we're also out of food. I go online, as going to the supermarket with the kids would be a nightmare. Annoyingly, most stores don't seem to be allowing new customers – that's ridiculous. Tesco has a more subtle approach, allowing me to do a full shop before showing me that there's not a single delivery slot available, ever. But then I remember something. I did an Ocado shop once. I must have a login. I go through my old emails and find the details – system, you have just been beaten.

I log in and the shop page appears. For about half a second. Then suddenly, I'm in an online queue. What just happened? Why did the website tease me I was in, and then put me behind one hundred and eighty thousand other people? That's just not nice.

Right, I look at the numbers: 186,742. Oh no – 186,74*1*! RESULT. Some people have no patience. I need to work out how long it's going to take me to get to the front of the queue.

Underneath is the helpful information: 'Waiting time: more than an hour.' No shit Sherlock. Difficult to believe you can't deal with nearly two hundred thousand customers within sixty minutes…

But after a quarter of an hour, I'm already in the one hundred and seventy thousands. Maybe this *can* work out. If I keep it open on my phone, I can do my work and teach the kids at the same time. I should be at the front by the end of the day, and then, boom! Delivery Slot!

By 11:00 am, Arthur knows his three times table, Carrie has drawn a frog and I have written two pages of copy. More importantly, I've broken the top one hundred thousand.

By 2:00 pm, the kids have taken their first steps to learn programming, the whole family knows how to book a table in French and the top 50k is within my sight.

By 4:00 pm, school is over, the kids are watching TV, I'm on a conference call and I'm in the top five *thousand.* People seem to lose faith as they get nearer, but surely the secret is to stick this out. I can do it. I just have to believe.

By 6:00 pm, I have baked bread once again, made the kids dinner, got some positive feedback from Larousse, and now I'm into triple figures.

It's at seven when I watch the last few numbers tick down. The kids are getting ready for bed, and I know today has been worth it. I'm going to do this. We're going to *eat.*

It's as I hit the top twenty, that a message appears on my phone: '10% battery remaining'. I didn't even take in that the 20% one had appeared – I must have dismissed it without registering when I was being basically Superdad. Shit. My phone seems to drain exponentially at this point, and has a habit of dying randomly thanks to its crappy Apple battery – I start running round the flat looking for my charger. Kitchen: no. I haven't charged it today – it must still be by the bed. I run to the bedroom, but it's not there. What the hell?!?

'I've finished!' shouts Carrie from the bathroom.

'Wipe it yourself!' I shout back. If I can pull this off, any day now we're going to be awash with toilet paper.

But I can't find it. *Anywhere.* I run into the living room. Queue space: nine. Battery: 5%.

'Arthur! Do you know where my phone charger is?'

'Yeah – I used it to charge the iPad – it's in our bedroom.'

Awesome. I dash into their bedroom. The iPad's there, but the charger's not. I check every plug socket. Empty. Queue space: five. Battery: 4%. Back into the living room.

'Arthur! It's not there.'

'I don't know then.'

'You can't not know – you *have* to know!'

'I'm sorry. I don't. No wait – Carrie was using it with her Lego.'

What?!? I look down at the phone. Queue space: three. Battery still on 4%. I just have to hold on for a couple more minutes.

I run into the bathroom. Carrie's already used half a roll. Doesn't matter – eye on the prize. 'Carrie – where's my charger?'

'Behind the sofa – it was a monster and the Lego men hid, but it chased them.'

'Doesn't matter right now.' I see the queue: I'm next. I'm next! And I'm still on 3%!

I run to the sofa, and it's there! It's bloody there!

Five seconds later, I've got it plugged into the wall, and as the lead goes into the phone, I see the list of groceries appear on screen. I did it! I bloody did it!

And then the phone dies.

Without rhyme or reason it just dies.

'No!' I scream. 'I was on 3% – that's not fair! It's not fair! I was on 3%!'

I boot up the phone again, and log on. They've closed orders till tomorrow morning.

For the first time since my divorce, I start crying. I actually start crying.

Carrie comes in.

'Are you OK, Daddy?'

'Yes love,' I say, trying to shake it off. 'I'm fine. Daddy's just a bit stressed, that's all.'

'It will be all right, Daddy – we'll look after you.' And I know she can't – that the duty of care is completely the other way round – but somehow, strangely, it makes me feel better. She comes over, and wraps her arms round me, and we just sit there for a second as she hugs me and strokes my hair.

'Thanks, love – I feel a lot better now.'

'That's OK, Daddy. Oh, and you need to tell me whose

birthday it is so I can wash my hands,' she says smiling and giving my hair one final stroke.

I make up a name, and she wanders off back into the bathroom. I tell her to be quick. It looks like I'm going to have to take a shower.

Thursday 26th March

Yesterday having gone tits up, I realise I'm going to have to brave the supermarket again. This time, with the kids.

I go online and get in the Ocado queue before I leave (this time with a plugged-in laptop) to set something up for the future. Amanda was saying last night that the slots you get are in like two weeks' time, so I need to try to tee one up for then.

When we reach the shop, there's a queue stretching round the block. On the upside, there's less than a hundred and eighty thousand people in it, so comparatively it doesn't seem too bad. Turns out it's actually not that many people – everyone's now giving each other the requisite social distance, so it's basically a short queue stretched out like pizza dough – same amount of substance, but with lots of air.

In about half an hour, we're at the front. Things are really different post-lockdown. We get given a trolley at the door – they've got a limited number inside the shop so they can use them to monitor how many people are inside. It makes shopping almost quite pleasant – lots of space around you, which means none of the old people are threatening to hit you with sticks either.

They've got eggs and toilet roll back too, so that's a relief. Although it seems sad to be returning to white-shelled economy ones, I've got to think about the budget. In fact, the main new shortage seems to be on beer. Plenty of lager left over, but not a single can of IPA. God, this area really *is* middle class.

'Back again, hoarder?' comes a voice from behind.

I turn to see the pasta guy. Not a-fucking-gain. And he's got six bags. They're all different shapes. Like he's trying to get around the system that limits how much you're allowed of each product.

'I told you,' I reply, 'that wasn't for me – it was for my elderly neighbours.'

'What's elderly, Daddy?' asks Carrie.

'Old, lovely.'

Carrie looks confused. 'We don't have eld-ar-lee neighbours. They're all young.'

'Yes we do – Sue... Sue's friends.'

'Who's Sue?' Carrie asks. 'I don't know a Sue.'

'Yeah you do,' says Arthur. 'Sue's Harry's mum.'

'Oh, yeah – Harry's mum. She's not eld-ar-lee though. She's young. Well, not young. Like Daddy.'

'Thanks, love. You just don't know them.' The pasta hoarder puts on a smirk of satisfaction when I turn to address him. 'They're just local old people.'

'But we don't like old people,' Carrie says. *Shut up, shut up.*

'Yes we do,' I reply, pasting on a smile. 'Just not ones that hit us with sticks.'

'No,' says Arthur, definitively. 'You said we didn't.'

'No – that was just *that* old person.'

'Was that Sue?' asks Carrie.

'No, Sue is a girl's name – that was a man.'

'This doesn't sound true, Daddy,' she continues.

'It's completely true.'

Carrie looks at me confused, then smiles, comprehending, as if she has finally understood. 'Is this like when we had to pretend all the shopping was for the old people in Arthur's rainbow photo?'

'No, that was different. We're not pretending here.'

'Do we need to pretend this shopping is for them too?'

I look over to the hoarder. He's already got his phone out and seems to be filming me. I didn't even notice this time, so I haven't covered my face or anything. Damn. People are going to finally discover the identity of the star of one of last Friday's top three trending tweets in the UK. Maybe the follow up will make it to number one.

Suddenly, his face drops. 'Bugger. It's died.' He walks off, cursing.

'Crappy Apple battery…'

Evening

I let the kids talk to Granny again in the afternoon so I can focus on my work, and they come out raving about the idea of clapping for the NHS at eight o'clock tonight. I haven't even heard about it – I've been too busy trying to work – but it's for the NHS, so despite the fact that over the last 48 hours I've developed a hatred for absolutely everybody, I decide to let the kids stay up and do it.

At 7:58, we head to the front window to clap. There's not a soul in sight, and it seems like it'll just be us cheering into the void, but we stand there, waiting for eight o'clock regardless.

Staring out into the night, I suddenly realise how quiet the world has become recently. There are no planes, no road noise in the distance, the pub beer garden a few streets away is absent of people chatting under its heaters. Instead there's just silence. It's almost magical. As if, for the first time in years, the world has finally been allowed to breathe.

'Is it time, Daddy?' Arthur asks.

'Yeah,' I reply. 'I think it might just be us, but we should still do it.'

They nod, and I lift Carrie up so she can look out as she claps. And that's when we hear something.

At first it's just a quiet pitter-pattering from a few streets away. People locked up in their houses, letting the world know that they're still there, that they care, that they're *thankful*. Then we hear a few claps from our street, and gradually people turn on their outside lights – those who own whole houses stepping out onto their porches and bringing their hands together in appreciation.

'Come on kids,' I say, a smile beginning to appear on my face, 'are you going to clap or what?' I bring my hands together with Carrie nestled into my elbow, my feelings a mixture of the warmth of community and a hideous English embarrassment at the vaguest expression of emotion. It's ridiculous. Why can't we be more like the Italians? I'm sure they don't feel self-conscious when they're singing out of their windows. But, as the kids add their voices to the fray, the discomfort begins to recede into the background. And soon all there is, is the cheer of the neighbourhood around us. Of the country. And we're part of it.

And, strangely, it actually makes me feel good. Like maybe there is hope after all.

Like maybe we can get through this together.

Friday 27th March

Still no online shop. I'm beginning to think that I may have to keep going to the real-life supermarket. It's not exactly the front line, but I'd rather not be doing it, particularly with the kids. Not that I can think about that now: there's copy for a sofa ad that needs to be written and there's only one man that can do it! Actually, there are probably lots of men (plus an equal amount of women) that can do it, but only one who has been assigned the task and will get fired if he fails to. Go, wholly dispensable team member, go!

I've only just got started when Larousse calls up at ten.

'Right, Tommy, change of plan.' That doesn't bode well. 'The sofa peeps have now realised that no one's going to be hitting their showrooms for another couple of months.' *Um… just now?* 'So they're thinking that they should be selling sofas to… people who can't actually try them.'

'Oh… OK,' I reply, trying to pretend that 90% of last week's work hasn't gone up like an item of furniture that doesn't comply with the 1988 Fire Safety Regulations (hey – I do my research). 'So a sort of "they look nice" angle?'

'No,' he says in a tone that implies I'm an idiot. 'We want people to know they're really *comfy*.'

'OK,' I say, again trying to compute. 'So we… *tell* them they're really comfy?'

'Tom, Tom, Tom – you're thinking small. They need to experience it for themselves.'

'You mean like… sit on them?'

'Exactly.'

'But didn't you just say…?'

'I know what I said. I just said it.'

'OK, so what? You're saying they need to find… comparative things they have in their house?'

'Yeah.'

'Like… another sofa?'

'Don't be a dick.' *Really didn't mean to be. I'm very confused.*

'I'm just trying to follow. So… "soft as a sponge cake", is that the kind of thing you mean?'

There's silence down the phone line for a few seconds.

'That's the first sensible thing you've said all day.'

'Is it?' I reply, mildly dubious.

'Yeah – we just need to work out which sofas match which cakes. The NYC loft couch might be a sponge cake, soft, bouncy. The Chesterfield one would need to be harder.'

'Maybe they could just let it go a bit stale.'

'I like that – less cooking involved.'

I'm getting more confused. 'Sorry – "cooking"? I thought we were talking Mr Kipling's or something?'

'No – they're branded, we can't use those. You're being ridiculous – they're gonna have to make the cakes themselves.'

'What – so we give them the recipes...?'

'Exactly – that's great.'

'Well, what if they're not very good at cooking?'

'Trade-descriptions-wise it can't touch us. "This sofa's softer than I was led to believe." "Judge – please sample this woman's banana bread and tell me she's not 100% responsible."'

I pause for a second. 'I'm just not sure people want to be baking cakes to test the softness of sofas...'

'People are bored – they've got nothing to do.'

'Maybe when they've got a nanny,' I mutter.

'What?'

'Nothing,' I say, regretting the words as soon as they've left my mouth. 'Maybe they're working – like us. I just don't think everyone has time to bake at the moment. You might not be able to get the ingredients. And, if you can, maybe you won't want to use them for a cake that you're then going to sit on.'

'They're not going to be sitting on them.'

'It was a joke.'

But I've started something. 'Maybe it shouldn't have been, Tommy. We could ship out free cake moulds in the shape of cushions.'

'...Right...' I reply. 'Do you think they'd be open to other approaches?'

'I guess so, but… I kinda think we've nailed it.'

'Cool. Well, why don't you pitch the cake/cushion-shaped mould option, and I'll work up some alternatives.'

'OK, Nespresso.'

'Please don't call me that.'

'Ha, ha, ha!' He hangs up.

I call Amanda immediately.

'Oh God, he's going to lose us the contract,' she sighs, the moment I finish explaining what's happening.

'I know – why do you think I called you?'

'OK – you come up with some other ideas and I'll deal with this.'

'Thanks. And by the way, can you tell him not to call me "Nespresso"?'

'You'd have to make an official complaint. And then it's going to come out that you're the guy who spends big on coffee pods.'

'OK, OK… And there's no chance of you firing him?' I ask, hopeful.

'You know April Salinger – the woman who kind of owns the company?'

'Yeah.'

'His aunt.'

'OK. I will receive his abuse in good spirits.'

'By the way, I'm starting to feel myself again… Do you want to do a Zoom call at the weekend?'

'I would like that very much,' I say, trying not to seem quite as excited as I am.

'Great. Talk to you later, "Nespresso".'

***

In the evening, it comes out that Boris has now got coronavirus. It's weird, and actually affects me a bit. I've always liked Boris. Oh, Boris is a school friend's cat. His owner posted it on Facebook, so it must be true. I didn't even know animals could get it. Well, bats obviously, but I'm pretty sure I haven't mis-specied his pet for the last ten years.

Even more weirdly, I find out later that the cat's namesake (who happens to run the country) has it too. Not a good day for Borises. Part of me wonders if it's a PR stunt, but I don't think so. This thing just seems to be everywhere. I don't particularly like him, but I can't not hope he's OK. And that he doesn't pass it on to his… five or six children… Really? That unspecific? Hm. Some might say the number of offspring of the leader of a civilised country should be a little more definite than that…

Saturday 28th March

I'm sat on the sofa, reading the news on my phone, when Arthur comes in with a massive grin on his face. Well, slightly less massive than it was yesterday.

'Daddy! Daddy! My tooth's fallen out!'

It's his first one – it's kind of exciting.

'I'm going to get some money from the tooth fairy!' he shouts. 'I'm going to be rich.'

'You are!' I reply. He won't be. I'm stingy. And he's also unaware of the current value of the pound.

'I'm going to write her a letter.'

'Um… OK,' I reply. 'Why would you do that?'

'So she'll write back.'

Hm. Unless there really are tooth fairies and I haven't got the memo, I'm pretty sure that sounds like extra work for me. Why have I never heard of this? It doesn't matter. Point is – I need to nip it in the bud. 'I don't know where you've heard that, Artie, but I'm not sure they do.'

'Of course they do! Amelie's writes to her the whole time. I've seen the letters.'

'I think that's just for girls.'

'Don't be silly – it's for everyone. If it was just for girls it would be secksual… secksual…'

'I don't know what that is.'

'Secksual discrimination. It's when you treat people differently because they're a boy or a girl. Joel's dad got fired because of it.'

'Oh. I heard they were just doing layoffs…'

'I think I'm going to ask her why they take teeth. I wonder what mine will be called. Amelie's is Petal Shimmer…'

And then he wanders off to put his tooth under the pillow and write a note to a non-existent creature, fantasising about what he's going to do with his two pounds…

Christ. This is really taking the buzz off finding out about Joel's dad.

***

I call Mark the moment they're unconscious.

'OK – this whole tooth fairy thing: money, letters – talk me through it.'

'Oh, has Carrie lost a tooth?'

'No – *Arthur*. Carrie's four. If she's losing teeth, I have severely failed as a parent.'

'Oh, OK – it's just the money. Boys don't do the note stuff, do they?'

'I don't know – that's why I'm asking. Unfortunately, he's off school, and not seeing any of his friends, so he doesn't have a proper male role model.' *Damn, I was quick to disqualify myself from that.* 'So, as Amelie's the only other kid he's communicating with at the moment, she's his best reference.'

'Right – OK, so… we normally give her two pounds. I think.'

'What do you mean – "I think"? Get Karen.'

'You can't talk to Karen.'

'Is that still going on?'

'Until I get some new friends, yes.'

'OK – well, tell me about the notes.'

'Karen writes those too.'

'GET KAREN.'

'No, I'll do it. I'll go and ask her.' He leaves the screen before I can protest. Two minutes later, he's back. 'Right – yeah – you have to write notes back.'

'I realised that, but he wants to ask questions – like "what do they do with the teeth?" – what if I give a completely different answer to everyone else?'

'Er – yeah, that's another one for Karen. One sec.' Two minutes later. 'Right – apparently it's all on the Internet. Just type it into Google.'

'OK – what about a name? I don't want to call his tooth fairy Petal Shimmer – do you know any others?'

'Karen—' he calls, wandering off again.

'Mark?' He's gone.

Another two minutes later: 'On the Internet as well. There's a fairy name generator.'

'Really? Awesome.'

'Oh, man – you'll never guess what bloody Karen did today…'

'Sorry, no time – us fairies have shit to do.'

I hang up and go to the kids' room, trying to reach under Arthur's pillow without waking him, retrieving the letter with the finesse of a cat burglar with a dental fetish.

I go into my room, and sit with my back to the door so he can't come in, then boot up the laptop. Right: fairy names. The good news is they have a box that lets you choose the sex, so I can skip all the Rosebud/Petal crap. I tick 'male' and press 'generate'.

The first name it gives me: Raven Demonbound. Jesus – they're meant to be giving the kids money for their teeth, not possessing them. Why not just go the whole hog and call him Damian Soulstealer?

I press 'generate' again and get some more names. This time they sound like they're from a *Lord of the Rings* porno. Which I'm pretty sure exists… Lord of the Cock Ring, or something… I review the options. Number one: Lichen Elfensplatter (*Oh, Lichen, you've covered me in your elfensplatter*), two: Bold Goblinwand (*Now it's time to deal with that bold goblinwand you've just shown me)* Sparrow Gnomefluff (*The wand has lost its power! Luckily, Gnomefluff will prepare you to perform once more)*. They're not quite what I hoped.

Eventually, I settle on Pip Goldember (after realising 'Goldmember' was a misreading – thanks, Mike Myers, for lodging that in my subconscious), then I look up why they take teeth. Apparently: to grind up and make into fairy dust. They use it to fly. Obvs.

I write down Pip's response in my very best writing and feel pretty pleased with myself. Thank you, Google. Thank you, weirdo who came up with a fairy name generating website.

But, just as I'm slipping it under the pillow, I remember something: two quid. Shit. I need some money.

After twenty minutes of searching it becomes clear that there aren't any pound coins in the house. I start searching through pockets, the bottom of bags, underneath the cushions of the sofa, but there's *nothing*, not even coppers. Fuck.

I call Mark again. 'Do you have any pounds? Could you drop them off at my house?'

'I'll ask Karen.' Jesus.

Five minutes later, he's back. 'Sorry mate – don't have any.'

'Thanks for trying…'

Damn it. I hang up feeling like a terrible, terrible father. How the hell can I get some pounds? We're in lockdown. He said his tooth was wobbly the other day – I should have planned ahead. I do have a tenner – I could try and get some change from Tesco. But taking the kids seems like too much ('I know you were asleep and there's a deadly disease going round, but Daddy really needs to get himself a snack.' What snack? 'I'm not sure but it's not going to cost between £3.01 and £5.' Maths joke. Because then I might not get two pound coins in my change. You'd never guess I used to be an accountant.). Actually, I just remembered – they stopped taking cash – damn it.

Maybe I should redo the note. Tell Arthur that Pip Goldember is self-isolating after someone coughed in the hollow oak tree by the Burbling Brook. No – that's going to raise all kinds of issues. Arthur will be paranoid he'll catch it from the paper. This is *rubbish.*

I look at the ten pounds in my hand. Could I rip a bit off? Give it to him in pieces until eventually he loses enough teeth to sellotape together a whole one? What about I get Pip to tell him that he's transferred the money straight into my bank account and he can spend it from there? Yeah – that's good. Definitely nails the magic of childhood. Maybe next Christmas I could tell him his presents are still in the shop as well?

Gradually, the only option I have begins to dawn on me.

I have to give him the tenner.

I fight the idea, but there's nothing else to do. It's going to set a dangerous precedent. Twenty teeth per kid, multiplied by two – I'll be dropping four hundred pounds on bloody milk fangs over the next few years. That's three and a half years of

Netflix. No – I can't do it. It's too much. I'm going to have to write a PS.

I sneak back in and get the note from under the pillow, and add in a postscript:

'PS. I have given you ten pounds, but that is for the next five teeth. This will help teach you to save!'

I slip it back under, completely unsatisfied with the whole business.

Tooth fairies really aren't what they used to be.

Sunday 29th March

'I got something! I got something!' Arthur screams as he bursts into my room at half six in the morning, Carrie in his wake. He's beside himself.

'What do you mean you got something?' I reply, deeply surprised. Part of being an excellent father: feigning ignorance when you're moonlighting as the fair folk.

'Some money! From my tooth fairy. His name is Pip Goldmember!'

'"Ember"... it says. Probably... So what did he say about the teeth?'

'That they grind them up to make fairy dust. They can use it to fly and to find the answer to any question in the world!'

'Wow! Isn't that cool?'

'I'm going to write to him again tonight!'

'No!' I blurt out, a little too quickly. 'I'm just saying I don't know whether that's a good idea. I'm sure he's very busy with teeth from other children.'

'No. Amelie said everyone has their *own* tooth fairy. They're just for you.'

'Really? She's said that? That's… great. So glad to hear that.' Thanks Karen – looks like I'm now involved in a penpal relationship with a seven-year-old boy where I'm pretending to be a magical elf. God. Put like that it sounds like I'm a predator in an online chat room.

'I can't believe he gave me ten pounds! Amelie only gets two!'

'Er…' I say, my enthusiasm waning even further. 'I'm sure that's not just for one tooth.'

'It is!' he replies. 'It is!'

'Can I… Can I see the note?'

He hands it over, and my heart sinks as I touch it. It's soaking.

'Why's this wet?' I ask.

'Carrie knocked my water over it.'

I look at the paper. The whole bottom part of is sodden. Erasing everything below Pip Goldmember(I mean 'ember')'s name. Christ.

'He doesn't have very nice writing, does he?' Arthur says, completely misinterpreting my expression of horror. 'Amelie's fairy's is far nicer… Probably because he's a boy.' Less of that, Arthur. It's technically secksual discrimination…

But I have bigger fish to fry – I'm about to lose a few years' worth of Netflix budget, and right now decent TV is all I have. I pretend to look at it very deeply, studying it like a monk with an ancient manuscript. 'Actually, I think I can read something here…' *a hidden message from our Lord?* '…something the fairy wrote.' *The all-hallowed Pip Goldember?*

Arthur takes it off me, and stares at it deeply too. 'I can't see anything.'

'It must be a secret message he's written that only adults can see,' I explain.

'No, there's nothing here. What do you think, Carrie?' She looks too.

'I can't see anything… but maybe it's because I don't know how to read.' *You could still see the letters, you moron.* I really shouldn't be paying for her Montessori.

'There's nothing there, Dad,' Arthur states definitively.

'Like I said: must be only adults that can see it.'

'But how are your eyes different? How would that work with "Science"?' *For God's sake, kid, you're prepared to believe a small magical creature has flown in to steal your teeth to make magical powder, and now you're bringing in 'Science'?!?*

'Fine,' I reply, unable to suppress a sigh. 'There's nothing there.'

'Were you joking?' asks Carrie, unsure.

'Yeah,' I nod. 'I was just making a joke.'

'It wasn't very funny,' says Carrie.

'It was a "Dad joke",' says Arthur. 'They're not funny.' I really wish they'd never heard that term.

'Yeah, definitely a "Dad joke",' replies Carrie as they leave the room, laughing conspiratorially.

Shit. Ten quid a tooth. At least I can get it straight from the cashpoint. Do those still work? Well if so, maybe this can work out. I'll be saving time after all. Just have to get my hourly rate a little further away from minimum wage…

***

At 2:00 pm I sit down at the computer to talk to Amanda face-to-face for the first time in three weeks. It's exciting. I've downloaded Zoom (note to self: if I ever learn to go back in time, buy Zoom stock early 2020), I've showered, put on my best shirt, and I'm feeling ready.

Until the moment I press 'Join'. And see myself appear on the monitor.

There're a few seconds before it connects to Amanda's feed, and I have time to examine myself in detail. What the hell has happened?!? Maybe Granny Jan had a virus on her laptop that's now affected mine. I look *awful.* The bits on the side of my head that had begun to go slightly grey, are now somehow stark white, like I've been drained by a White Walker – the bags under my eyes are deep, my skin looks sallow. I've either been infected by Covid-19, or something worse… webcam.

A second later, Amanda appears and I shoot across the room, dragging the laptop with me, skulking away into a dark corner like Golem from *The Lord of the Rings*, contorted into the walls, trying to hide from the light. I look at the screen – it's better. I don't look so bad in the shadows. I mean you can barely see me at all, but honestly, that's an improvement.

But then I look at Amanda. Her face has an expression of sheer horror. Like she's seen me and discovered the truth about the man she's dating. Except she can't *still* be seeing me – the screen is basically black.

Then I notice something – she's scanning *her* screen in panic, almost as if… she's thinking the same thing about herself. It can't be. She looks amazing. I look more closely – I mean, she's got a miniature bit of brown at her roots. But that's nothing – it can't be that – she looks incredible. I decide I have to reassure her.

'Hey – wow, you look stunning! It's so nice to actually see you.'

'I'll call you back—'

She hangs up.

What just happened? Was that her or me? Did she just see how horrendous I looked? Or was she just being ridiculously self-conscious about nothing? It's got to be me. Surely?

I check the kids are still watching TV in the living room then run to the loo. Opening up the bathroom cabinet, I catch myself in the bathroom mirror. I look fine – damn you webcam. But this is something that needs to be dealt with. The open door reveals six packets of *Just for Men* lined up on its shelf. I look at the happy faces of the men on the packets. I want to be happy like them – they weren't caught buying this stuff in Boots. They didn't have their girlfriend hang up on them during a Zoom reunion. I'd hoped not to have to crack them out this early, but it doesn't look like I've got a choice.

I decide to start with the 'light' one. *Is* my hair light brown? Probably not, but better to err on the side of caution. I mix it up as per the instructions and apply it, setting the countdown on my phone, then sit on the side of the bath looking up '*Just for Men* results' images on Google. I watch a few videos, which make me a little bit hopeful, then wash it out.

It looks exactly the same.

Shit. I look at the mid-brown. Maybe that's the answer. No – I need more than one step up. I need the dark. It's got to be better for your hair just to do it twice anyway rather than three times. I have to commit.

I reapply, and set the timer again, going back onto Google, this time discovering *Just for Men*'s one star review on Consumeraffairs.com. Oh no – itching… *yellow pus*? That can't be right. Surely?

'Agggghhh!'

I hear the scream. Strangely, it's not from me.

I run into the other room and Carrie has fallen off the sofa. She's holding her shoulder. She looks fine and the timer's got my back, so I perform my fatherly duties free of worry.

'What happened?'

'I fell off.'

'Were you sitting on the arm?'

'Yeah.'

'Haven't I told you not to sit on the arm?'

'Sorry, Daddy.' I kiss her on her shoulder, and she looks up at me, her injury seemingly healed. 'Why is your hair wet?' she asks.

'Oh,' I reply, 'I'm washing it.'

'It looks darker.'

'That's just 'cos it's wet,' I tell her, casually pulling out my phone to see how long I have left. 'It'll look the same when it's…' I look at the phone. It's died. AGAIN.

DAMN. APPLE. BATTERY.

'Is your ear wet?' she asks. 'It's darker too.'

I barely even hear it. By the time she's finished the sentence, my head is bent over the bath and I'm rinsing like I've got coronavirus dandruff. The shampoo is in and I scrub for long enough to sing individual Happy Birthdays to an illegally large public gathering.

After it's done, I stand up and look in the mirror. It's all steamed up from the washing. I won't be able to tell while its wet anyway, so I pick the hairdryer up from the floor and start to dry it. I really wish I'd never listened to Sally when she'd said not to get one of those bathroom cabinets that heats the mirror. That would be really useful right now. Then I have a brainwave. I point the hairdryer at the mirror and it unsteams in about 20 seconds. Oh my God. Well, even if this has gone wrong, I've just discovered a major life hack.

The mirror clears, and suddenly I'm face to face with the results. My hair is almost black. Not just my hair – the top part of my ear too. Damn it. I should have three-beared it. Too light, too dark; mid brown would have been just right. But no, I had to go with full-on dark, the extreme option. So now I'm Daddy Bear: sleeping in a hard bed, my lips dotted with porridge burns, with hair that looks absolutely ridiculous.

I dry it off, and walk back to the computer, my head bowed. Maybe it'll look better on the monitor. I open up the camera and see myself. It's awful. I look like a vampire with anaemia, like Phil Dunphy off *Modern Family* series 3-9 before he got his dye job sorted. Every bit of colour has been drained from my skin.

I go to the bathroom again – I think there's still some of Sally's old make-up there – maybe if I put on some foundation, it'll look better on screen.

I stand there, unable to comprehend what I'm currently doing, brushing my ex-wife's make-up over my face to try to take the edge of what I just did to my hair. Every stroke just makes it look worse, but I try to remember: it's all about the monitor. I'm not leaving the house anymore – if it looks OK on screen, I'm golden.

I switch on the laptop camera again. Awful. Like an ageing Las Vegas entertainer whose show just closed and has had to let his stylist go.

But, it's better. It's terrible; but it's better.

I close the camera, revealing the Zoom window. It's still open. And Amanda's 'in the meeting'. God, why does Zoom make everything so formal?!? Still, I can't just leave her hanging there. I have no choice but to tell her. I need to face up to what I've done.

I enter the meeting, and there she is.

In full on make-up; her hair a dazzling platinum blonde.

She sees me and laughs. We both laugh.

'There's something wrong with the colours on my camera,' I say.

'Mine too,' she replies.

And then we never mention it again. And have the most lovely conversation for the next hour and a half; a beautiful woman who looks like a movie star from the 40s and a vampire who's trying to 'pass'.

I've got a feeling she's a keeper.

Monday 30th March

I spend the morning trying to come up with some non-sponge cake related ways of selling sofas. It's hard. Harder than a three day old sachertorte. I start off some slogans: 'So comfy you can take our word for it'…'What would you rather be self-isolating on?'… I'm sighing as I think of them. What about just a woman looking really happy lounging on a corner sofa, reading a magazine saying, 'Yeah – lockdown is hell,' then the slogan: 'Sofas you want to be trapped inside with'? Yes, you too could be one of the smug, pampered rich… I don't know – what if they lift the lockdown before the ad even gets released? This might just be another waste of time. The Covid figures are still going up exponentially, so I doubt it, but…

I stop myself immediately, trying to get everything into perspective. It's just a stupid advert. But, then again, it's my job. I mean, adverts are superficial and unimportant at the best of times, but I've still got to feed my family, to keep a roof over our heads. But thinking about all these people out there risking their lives while I'm trying to flog furniture, worrying about the lockdown ending too early for the ads to get out, makes me feel like a bad person… For fuck's sake.

I shake myself out of it, and write down some more ideas while I put in a call to the people I booked our package holiday with. We were due to go a week today, and although there was actually no chance of it happening, they said on the website that they were too busy to communicate with anyone till a week before departure. Of course, nobody answers. It's annoying being in another queue. But, on the upside, I do get to work while listening to some really uplifting hold music. For the next two and a half hours.

I'd really been looking forward to the holiday as well. It would have been the first time we'd been abroad for a year and half – the first time ever without Sally. And when I think about it – just me and the kids getting cooked for and waited on for a week – I feel really down. Even with the substandard food, sunburnt tourists, and general tackiness that would no doubt be everywhere, it sounds like bloody heaven.

It's in the afternoon that I read about Carluccio's going under. It puts me into even more of a funk. I don't know why, considering everything that's happening, but it does. All the people dying – it's difficult to believe it's real – it's just too much to take in, but *Carluccio's*.

Sally and I used to go there after Arthur was born – having a Carluccio's croissant and coffee was our little treat after a night of not sleeping. It's not like the food was the greatest thing I'd ever eaten. But those moments – they seem like a freeze frame of when Sally and I were actually happy. And now, somehow, they're gone forever. It makes me wonder how much else is going to change when this is over. I'd just assumed this was going to be a three (four, five… seven) month break in our lives. A hiatus and after that, everything would return to normal. But maybe it won't. Maybe things will never be the same again.

Will we hug our friends? Shake hands when we go to the pub? Will there even *be* pubs? How many things that were part of our lives are going to disappear into the ether – bars, restaurants, shops, … people? I feel a bit shaken thinking about it. I haven't lost anyone… but will I? How many people are going to be traumatised from losing their mothers, their fathers? And even the people who don't lose anyone – how many people's lives will be different from the way they could have been? There must be people who will have never met the love of their life because of this? Guys who will lose the last bit of hair that could have got them the first date with that girl who afterwards would see past it?

I don't want to think about it. I need to try and have faith, to hope for the best. Life *sort of* how it was; with a few more cases of mild OCD and some better-stocked larders. But sort of how it was…

***

I check on the kids just before I go to sleep, noticing there's another note under Arthur's pillow. I feel a bit annoyed that the correspondence seems to be continuing, but try to suck it up. But when I open up the envelope, I get a shock. Inside is a tooth. Weird. I feel a bit freaked out that he lost another one and didn't tell me.

Except, seconds later, I realise it's *not* a tooth – it's a broken off bit of paracetamol. I can't quite believe it. My son is trying to pull a fast one on the tooth fairy, *and* wasting the most in-demand painkiller currently on the market. I go in and look at him again. He's sleeping with a cherubic expression on his face – not a hint of guilt. For all he knows he's about to leave a fairy stranded with no way of flying home because their fairy dust has been cut with headache pills and he's sleeping like a baby. And that's assuming Pip's using the fairy dust himself. What if he deals? Passing that kind of crap off as 'dust' might lead to full on fairy-gang warfare.

I also feel a little guilty that Arthur got hold of the paracetamol in the first place. It's my job to keep it out of reach. That's why I always put the pills tin on one of the top shelves next to the… cereal. Hmmm… Perhaps they were working on contingency plans for surviving my upcoming demise. Fair enough: a kid's got to eat breakfast.

Still, Pip doesn't have to be quite so tolerant. Arthur hasn't heard the last of this. I unfold the note and start to read.

Question one: *how do you grind the teeth to make fairy dust?*

Easy: 'pestle and mortar'. Next. *Do you know the answer to every question?* 'Of course, I do – I'm a fairy.' *Are you a scientist?* Hmm – that just sounds sarcastic, but I'm going to pretend it doesn't. 'No, I know the answers because of magic!' Done.

I put the reply back under the pillow – no cash, no explanation. I'll let him fill in the blanks himself. Evil little fraudster.

Tuesday 31st March

At breakfast, I realise we once again have nothing to eat for the rest of the day, so we're going to have to go back to the supermarket. Annoyingly, I've still had no luck with the online shop. I literally don't know how anyone is getting one if they're working. It's basically a full-time job.

I have to work all morning and the kids need to do their school stuff, so we head down at twelve and the queue is four blocks long. It's really difficult knowing how to approach the supermarket now – do you buy just enough to keep you going, or stock up? I thought it was the first, but then I saw this video with all these Italian mayors telling people 'buy enough for ten days' (in an Italian accent)(… and also in Italian), and it sort of makes sense. The less we're in the supermarket, the better. Surely, if the whole country moves to an every-ten-days shop, stock should work out fine?

Not that that argument will cut it with some of the angry pensioners I find inside. One of them tells me I'm selfish because I've got two big milks – (he's got one and I imagine he lives alone), another starts having a go because I've failed to give him his 'two metre space', while he blocks a whole aisle trying to work out if he wants Baxters French Onion or Highland Broth. In all fairness to him it's a difficult decision – if only they'd start making a Cream of Tripe, he'd be done with it in a second.

When we get home, I decide I've got to take the shop-to-cupboard transition more seriously. I watched a video last night of some doctor doing a full-on disinfection of his shopping. Is this how far we need to take it? I mean I'm doing all the other stuff – maybe it's important not to cut any corners?

Luckily, I've got some Dettol in. It's one of the upsides of Carrie having had a bad tummy a month ago and missing the toilet in the middle of the night. I bet that stuff's impossible to get hold of in shops now. Maybe I should take out half and dilute it with floor cleaner then sell it on? Arthur could probably give me some tips on cutting the good stuff. Forward slash 's'.

I define my areas: clean and unclean. The guy on the video suggests putting a line of tape halfway down the middle of your work area. I'm doing it on a table – tape would probably take the surface off. Plus I don't have tape. It'd be another trip to the shops, which I'm pretty confident is more dangerous than a slightly ill-defined boundary.

I add some Dettol to water and it does it's usual brown to white thing, and then I start to wash it over everything. It just looks really disgusting. Like I'm rubbing my vegetables with really dilute semen. Yum. I think about using the Dettol spray that I bought after the accident instead. It's quicker, doesn't look like ejaculate, and even *smells* nice, but I can't bring myself to do it. It seems like something I should be saving for a special occasion. Maybe I'll treat myself to a quick spritz on Easter Sunday. Only a few weeks to go!

As I disinfect and move the food onto the clean side (Probably. Without tape on the table it's the Wild West down there), I can't help but think – is this overkill? I know it's worse than flu and is killing lot of people, but this: it's just so extreme. Like we're dealing with Ebola or something. Like we've just returned from a scavenging mission in a radioactive wasteland, and a lack of proper decontamination will lead to certain death or at very least an unattractive mutation.

Then again, three hundred and eighty people died yesterday, and for all we know that's just the beginning. Sure, it might be unnecessary to go this far, but what are a few red peppers that taste like disinfectant compared to a single life? If one person lives because of it, I'd hope everyone in the country would eat a pine-scented apple to save them. It's enough to send me back to the sink and start scrubbing my bag of Royal Gala. On the upside, the strange taste might mean the bag lasts a bit longer. Should save on supermarket trips...

By bedtime, I'm starting to feel a little bit down. I go into the kids' bedroom to have a look at them. It seems to help me centre myself; to get everything into perspective so I remember why it's all worth it. But then I see something under Arthur's pillow. ANOTHER note.

I can't believe it. I thought he was done after last night's paracetamol incident, but no – it appears he's decided to double down. And his tone is starting to become a little less polite.

Dear Pip.

Where's my ten pounds? I gave you a tooth. You didn't give me any money. Also, as you know everything – what is the cure for koronervirus?

Arthur.

Wow. My son's getting an attitude. Also, I'm beginning to wish that I hadn't claimed fairies knew everything through magic. Not that answering the 'koronervirus' question is impossible. Just that I've got until morning to beat the world's leading scientists into developing a working vaccine.

Right, I need to make this reply count: definite, solid, final, otherwise this correspondence thing is going to go on for the rest of his childhood. I don't mind writing the occasional letter – but right now it's like I'm in a dead drop relationship with a spy who can't help oversharing.

It takes me about half an hour to come up with something. But I think I nail it.

Dear Arthur,

I'm so sorry there was no money under your pillow. I left another ten pound note for you yesterday. Perhaps someone took it? It might be that it's just too much money and tempts burglars and thieves. Perhaps in future I'll just leave you two pounds like the other tooth fairies. That <u>*never*</u> *seems to get stolen.*

Of course, if it turned out that the tooth wasn't actually a tooth (ha ha!), the money would just disappear (it's a magic thing), but obviously that's not what's happened in this case! I know you wouldn't do that, Arthur Cooper, my good friend.

Also, I'm afraid I find myself unable to answer your question about koronervirus (actually spelt coronavirus). For some strange reason, my fairy dust doesn't seem to be working properly. It's almost like it wasn't made from real tooth. So that's that then. Unfortunately, you can't ask the same question more than once, which means we'll never find the answer. Oh well.

Your friend and fairy,

Pip Goldmember.

PS. I know where you live.

In the end I delete the PS. But having dealt with the problem makes me feel more positive. I think I'll treat myself to season three of *The Bureau* tomorrow…

Wednesday 1st April

When Arthur comes into my room, he looks upset, confiding in me that he might have just lost an opportunity to end the current pandemic after doing something a 'bit naughty'. Whoops. May have slightly overdone the level of consequence there. Probably not the best thing to drop on a seven-year-old.

We talk about it a bit, and eventually he admits what he did. I tell him not to worry about the coronavirus thing, tooth fairies don't know anything about science, and magic doesn't cut it when it comes to medicine.

'You know how in the old days,' I explain, 'people died all the time?'

'OK...'

'Well, it's probably because their cures were heavily tooth fairy related. If you think about it, things have really got a lot better since we started doing experiments and stopped listening to magical beings.'

He seems relieved, like a weight has been lifted from his shoulders, and flashes me his charmingly incomplete smile. 'Oh, by the way Dad, his name *is* Goldmember – look.'

He shows me the letter. Yeah, messed that one up. Oh well, I'm sure I won't be thinking about it later when I'm watching some premium rate TV channels that I can still afford.

By breakfast, the tooth fairy issue is all but forgotten and the kids seem pretty keen on doing some April Fools jokes on me.

They start off pretty lame:

'Daddy, Daddy! There's a spider!'

'Where?'

'No, there's not.'

'Oh, OK.'

But it's when I hear that they're talking about putting worms in my shoe, that I realise I have to put a stop to it. Firstly, I don't want them going out into the front garden unsupervised. Secondly, that would be really, really annoying. It's just before I start them off with their school stuff that things take a turn for the worse.

'Dad, can I wear my wellies today?' Carrie asks.

'Fine,' I say, nor really caring either way, and knowing better than to argue with kids when they're being weird. Sometimes they just are.

A second later, she's screaming. 'Aggghhh! Daddy, Daddy! Arthur put worms in my welly!'

'I'm sure he didn't…' I say, walking over and fearlessly putting my hand inside, because of *course* there isn't a worm in there – it'll just be some string or a toy or something – Arthur's not a bloody psychopath.

Except when I put my hand inside, I feel something – warm, wriggling – that seems very much like a handful of worms. I can't quite believe it. Most of all how he got them? Did he sneak out when I wasn't looking? I shake my head, my eyes fixed on Arthur, as I pour the worms out onto the kitchen table.

And they scurry away.

Looking far less like a trio of worms. Than a rat.

'Aggggh!' I scream.

'Aggggh!' screams Arthur.

'Aggggh!' screams Carrie. 'Why are we screaming?'

'It wasn't worms, Carrie! It was a rat! There's a rat in our kitchen!' Fuck! A rat! I just touched it! With my *hand*! I've been worried about coronavirus, and now I've got the fucking plague! I've got FUCKING PLAGUE!!!

'OK everyone – wash your hands! Carrie – did it bite you?'

'No.'

'Good.' I check my hands, I'm good too. 'OK – we have to wash them *now*. This is serious – three Happy Birthdays!'

'Isn't it two?'

'Not with a rat. It's three. Maybe four.'

We wash our hands in the kitchen sink – me holding up Carrie so she can reach the tap after I've done mine. Gradually I start to calm down, but I know the rat is still in the house, having scurried under the fridge. I bend down – I can't see it, but I know it's there. Still, I can't quite believe it – we have a *rat* in our home. In the flat. A flat rat. Give me a rolling pin and come out here, I will make that happen.

'Carrie, where did you leave your wellies?'

'In the hall – they were dirty after our walk, so you said to leave them outside.'

'OK – that's good.'

I feel a bit relieved. We had a rat in the *building*. Not in our flat. That makes us less disgusting. I mean, we have a rat in our flat *now*. But that's only because my daughter brought it in. Yeah, that makes us sound like a model family. Still, there's only one course of action: I'm going to have to put work on hold for a while and deal with this.

'All right, guys – we're going to go down to the shops. We're going to go and buy a rat trap!' I regret trying to make it sound exciting as soon as it comes out of my mouth.

A few minutes later, we're trudging down to the shops, unsure as to whether this counts as buying essentials or our once-daily exercise. I'm thinking it's the former; rat traps do seem pretty essential…

Except clearly they're not. The hardware store is closed, Robert Dyas too. There's not a purveyor of rat traps in sight. What is this post-lockdown world coming to?

We're just about to turn back defeated, when I spot another establishment that might serve as an alternative. The pet shop. The pet shop is open! People have rats as pets! Maybe they can help!?!

The owner greets us warmly as we enter, but before I can attempt to talk to her the kids interrupt; clearly they have an agenda of their own. 'Can we go and look at the animals?' Carrie asks. We've barely even crossed the threshold.

'Sure – just make sure you give people space, all right?'

'All right.'

They run off to the other side of the floor, and I approach the counter.

'How can I help you?' the owner asks, smiling.

'Hi,' I say. 'It's about my… pet rat. It's… escaped, and is hiding under the fridge. Have you got any kind of… rat trap?'

'I don't quite get what you mean.'

'One of those ones that snaps down.'

She suddenly looks wary. 'That would kill it, sir. It would kill your pet.'

'Really? Oh! I thought they just kind of… trapped it… like it says in the title… Well, that is a surprise,' I reply, nodding. 'They should get in trouble with trade descriptions – I'm in advertising so we have to think about things like that.'

'Right.'

'And you're sure there's no possibility that it *would* just trap it? So I could put it back in its cage?'

'No. And we don't sell them.'

'Fair enough… What about poison? Do you have any of that?' Her attitude towards soliciting my custom does not appear to be improving. 'Not… *fatal* poison obviously. Just… a tranquiliser or something like that? So it would fall asleep and I could… rehome it.'

'No.'

'Rat treats? Do you have any of those? So I could tempt it out and… stroke it, you know rat-owner style.'

'We have plenty of rat treats, but I have to say, you don't actually sound like a rat owner…'

'I'm totally a rat owner, I just haven't had it escape before. Because I'm such a *good* rat owner. I normally just let it run round in its little ball.'

'Those aren't for rats.'

'Oh, it's a really big one.'

She shakes her head.

'Definitely?'

No response.

'It's home made?'

She's not buying it.

I go and fetch the kids from over by the cages. There are a couple of pet rats in one. They're actually really nice – not like the pestilence-ridden monstrosity currently residing under my fridge. I wonder if I should get one? Maybe a feral rat would consider a pet rat 'hot'? I could lure it into the tame rat cage for some potential mating, and then I could shut the door behind it? Of course, I'd need to get the sex right and I'm not sure the tamed one would be up for it. Maybe not. Seems a little on the wrong side of consensual.

My concentration is broken when I realise that directly in front of me is a python. In its cage – it's a pet shop, not a jungle – but ideas start to flow. A python would eat a rat no problem. And it's only a hundred quid. That seems very reasonable. I don't have any desire to own an exotic animal, but I do love a bargain. The idea quickly disperses. I bet the cages are really expensive, *and* it might try to eat one of the children. I grab Arthur and Carrie and usher them back to the entrance.

'All right guys, we're going.'

'Are we getting a rat trap?'

'No – sorry.'

They both sigh in disappointment – clearly I did make it sound more exciting than it was.

The shop owner stares at me as I leave – like I'm part of an oppressive regime that has tried to commandeer her business for its own genocidal ends. With very little to lose, I decide to try my luck one last time. 'That python – would you be willing to hire it out…?'

'Please leave.'

'Course.'

And then we trudge home, careful to stay two metres away from people that we pass in the street, to return to our pet rat.

***

I do some research, and it doesn't look like you can catch coronavirus from rats. Phew. Weil's disease, tuberculosis, E. Coli, yes, but not coronavirus. Well, it's not 100%. There is one website that says it's possible, but they sell rat traps, so I'm not sure their 'maybe' can be trusted. Plus, they have a really long delivery time, so right now I don't like them in the slightest.

I consider the possibility of toughing it out over the six-day waiting period – but I don't think I can last that long. I'm going to have to deal with this myself.

I find a video, 'natural ways to deal with rats', and think I've hit the jackpot, only to see a list of loads of stuff I haven't got: essential oils, owl's feathers (I mean, if you've got access to those, surely you can send Hedwig to deal with it personally) – but then one comes up that actually might work: onions. I've got those. But they're not that easy to get hold of at the moment. Besides, an onion is the difference between a pasta al pomodoro and some spaghetti with a tin of tomatoes poured on top… So I decide to keep searching. And then it appears: human hair.

I have some of that. Apparently rats can't stand it (along with humans given my current dye job), and as mine needs removing anyway, a plan begins to form. If I can make a pathway lined with hair from the edge of the fridge to a cardboard box, maybe I can funnel the rat inside. It's not great, but it's better than my other idea of creating a home-made glue trap. Particularly as we only have Pritt stick.

I find a box, and go to the bathroom, kitchen scissors in hand. I've got some hair clippers I ordered coming tomorrow (after a four-day wait – less in demand than rat traps apparently), so I can cut it off now and tidy it up with the clippers in the morning. That's *probably* not a stupid idea.

I start to chop away at it and suddenly it becomes clear why haircuts are so expensive. But I push on, reminding myself that I'll be wearing a hat till the clippers come anyway; the only difference is that it might feel a bit looser.

By the time I've finished, I look like the survivor of a nuclear blast, but I have the required hair, so I trudge to the kitchen and bend down by the fridge. The rat's still there, so I start laying the edges of my hirsute path, trying to ignore the thought that maybe I could have just built little cardboard walls instead. It'd probably just have chewed through them immediately anyway. *Yeah, you keep telling yourself that.*

The path complete, I build a little ramp up to the top of the open box, then Pritt stick some newspaper on top of it, making little slits in the paper so it'll rip and drop the rat through like a pit trap. Finally I put a piece of cheese on top as bait. It's one of the only things I can spare, but I start worrying that I've gone too stereotypical. Because it might not actually work – not because it might offend the rat. Surely, mice and rats like cheese? There must be a reason it's a cliché. Even if not, if might still be effective if the rat's hungry enough… or has a keen sense of irony.

We do the kids' lessons while I work (cap on) at the kitchen table, ready to pounce as soon as the rat hits the box. Two hours later, it's still under the fridge, but the kids have concentrated really well so I've actually managed to get a bit of my own stuff done. It's times like this when you feel really good about putting some effort into raising your children, and not just fobbing them off onto an iPad for ten hours a day. Also, it'll make it really special next week, when the holidays start, and I fob them off onto an iPad for ten hours a day. It's like that wearing a coat indoors analogy that Arthur's so fond of.

By the end of 'school', the rat still hasn't emerged, so I have to stay in the kitchen, working and making dinner, while the kids watch TV. By seven-thirty, it's clear that any human presence is putting him off coming out, so I realise if I want to get rid of him, I might be in this for the long haul. I get the kids to do their own bedtime and then watch TV on the computer until I finally fall asleep on the kitchen floor, a few cushions from the living room sofa, my makeshift bed. It's even less comfortable than a sponge cake.

My dreams are filled with the sounds of scurrying rodents, until at about one in the morning I'm woken by the sound of a bump. I jump up, turning the light on, then look at the box. It's in there! I've caught the rat! I've caught the rat!

I quickly shut the box, taping up the top so it doesn't escape, and run to the front door, almost forgetting the keys as I leave. Jumping down the communal stairs a few steps a time, it's only moments until I'm at the door of the building. Pushing out into the road, I pound down the street like a madman, suddenly realising I've forgotten to wear a hat and that I'm barefoot. Jesus, I must look like I've escaped from a lunatic asylum! I don't think this would look worse if I was shouting 'rat delivery!' as I ran. But I just need to get to the main road and chuck him out there. Then he can jump into a sewer and live there. If anything what I'm doing is a kindness. From what I've heard, rats *love* sewers.

Inside the box, I can hear the rat scurrying around trying to escape. I'm about five doors away from my building when I realise it's not just scurrying – it's chewing. And its pointy little nose is poking out of the bottom corner of the box. Facing towards me. Aggh.

I start sprinting as fast as I can (which admittedly isn't that fast), as I see its revolting yellow incisors chomping through the cardboard at breakneck speed. I only have a few seconds to get rid of it before it jumps out and probably infects me with coronavirus *and* TB. Suddenly the rat trap manufacturer's 'maybes' are starting to sound a lot more convincing. I'm not going to make the main road, so I look round for a drain to let it out into, but it's too late – half the rat's body has already squeezed through the hole.

I scream in panic, bringing the box up in an arc that flings the rat away from me towards one of my neighbours' houses. The rat flies through the air colliding with their downstairs window. The lights are still on. Shit – they're awake. I think some middle-aged man lives there alone – this is terrible. I watch, stunned into immobility, as the rat escapes into the house through a broken airbrick, and then I shake myself and start back towards my flat, dropping the box, before going back for it – remembering that it probably still has my address on it. And how important it is not to litter.

The curtains twitch before I'm on my way again, but I shoot off up the road, unsure as to whether the owner saw me. I feel really bad. I just hope if he did get a glimpse, he doesn't make the association with his upcoming rat problem. It's definitely good that I didn't go the route of shouting 'rat delivery'...

Thursday 2nd April

I awake refreshed, feeling genuinely elated not to have a rat in the house, and not having had to spend the night on the kitchen floor.

'Did you get it?' asks Arthur, coming in.

'I did,' I reply.

'Did you kill it?' asks Carrie, following.

'I didn't. In fact, I gave it a new home.' The words make me wince as they come out.

'Daddy? Are you ill?' asks Carrie.

'No,' I say confused.

'You look like Sherry's mum when she had keem… keem…'

I suddenly realise she's talking about my hair. I put my cap on straight after I cut it yesterday. But wow – chemotherapy? God. They must think I'm *really* ill. 'It's not that,' I say, trying to reassure them. 'Don't worry about that.' But then something else strikes me. 'What are you talking about? Sherry's mum didn't have chemotherapy.'

'Not keemothairapee – it was a type of bread she had when we went out for a curry with them. It had meat in.'

'Oh – keema *naan*.' Phew. That's a lot less dark. Thinking back, I do remember that evening – Sherry's mum had had a really bad haircut.

'Well, it's nothing to worry about – I had to cut my hair off to trap the rat. That's where I got all the hair from yesterday.'

'Oh!' says Arthur, laughing. 'We thought you got that from your back.' Ah! Some more positive news to begin the day…

The clippers don't arrive until six, which means I have to do a Zoom meeting with the sofa client in a hat. Larousse tells me it's unprofessional before the client joins us, so instead I tilt the camera down, so they mainly just see my chin. Luckily, they come online before L can object, and they don't ask, just assuming I'm incompetent with technology. Which is a relief. I doubt they'd have believed that people found full-face Zoom meetings with me difficult because of my distractingly attractive eyes.

At six fifteen, I shave in a grade four all over. It's definitely better than it's looked all week, but it's a bit of a shock being confronted with my actual hairline. I mean, it still comes to my forehead, but it curves more than a *Playboy* centrefold.

But generally the day passes without incident, and it's a welcome bit of downtime following the crap I've had to deal with all week. Until Arthur comes into my room at 4:00 am, after having a nightmare about Pip coming in and grinding up one of his teeth in situ. Think the pestle and mortar might have been too visceral an image. Oh well, looks like I'm sharing my bed for a night. Hey ho, at least I've got another kid.

Maybe I can do better with her…

Friday 3rd April

So it's here. The last day of school-not-school. This is it – my last chance. From tomorrow onwards, I can't even make the kids do worksheets while I stumble through what currently passes for my work. So I've got to make today count. I've got to find a way to sell sofas to people that can neither try a sofa nor even *want* a sofa; a way that doesn't involve baking, and, more specifically, sitting on a cake.

I sit at my desk, feeling the stress bearing down on me with the weight of a thousand cushion shaped moulds… that will probably go into production in about a week, if I can't find a better alternative.

Right – how can people experience a sofa? What else would be comfortable and plump to have beneath you? Shit. All that's coming into my mind is a really big butt. I don't think 'as comfortable as if your bum was bigger' is going to sell *anything*. Come on: comfortable things… Jogging bottoms … 'Even when you're doing dress up Fridays – you'll still feel like you're in loungewear…' Nah – that's a trend that no one's going to be bothered with for more than a couple of weeks. At best it'll keep going under a more realistic name: *dress-up-and-post-a-picture-on-Instagram-before-changing-back-into-your-pyjamas-Fridays.* Maybe I shouldn't knock it till I've tried it – perhaps I'd be more creative if I wore some of my office clothes…

After forty minutes of sitting in the clothes I would have worn to the office, with the addition of a neckerchief that I would *never* wear to the office (I ordered it thinking it'd help me get in with the office hipsters, needless say it has yet to leave the house), I change back into something more comfortable, still as far from an idea as the world seems to be from a vaccine.

I can't help wishing Amanda was here. Not in her role as my boss, but as my girlfriend. To just wrap her arms round me from behind and tell me I can do it. That I'm great and can come up with something that will blow people away. At least, I *think* as my girlfriend. I imagine my old boss JC doing the same thing, and yeah, definitely as my girlfriend. But that's what I need the *sofa* to feel like – like a hug from someone you care about. A warm, lying-under-you, flat hug… but a hug nonetheless.

Unfortunately, the sofa people don't want that. They want people to know how *different* their sofas are. To give them individual personalities. Individual hugs… Tsch!

And then it hits me: celebrities.

I can use celebrities! Not actual celebrities – they wouldn't be seen dead endorsing mid-range sofas – but their *surnames*! They're the archetypes of our age, right? I just have to associate each sofa with someone famous, and get people to imagine getting a hug from *them*… Just need to make sure I choose some that haven't done anything obnoxious and annoying in the lockdown yet…

Right… soft, plump cushions. Got to be a man… I don't think people would take too kindly to a sofa like that being called the 'Rebel Wilson'. *And* she's not very cuddly… kind of a female Jack Black… someone else… 'The *Corden*'! That'll do it. Yeah! I look him up: he doesn't seem to have done anything *too* irritating yet. Also, I find it inexplicable that anyone would like him in the first place, so clearly he's pretty much bullet proof.

Cool – done! OK… the Chesterfield. I need a firmer celebrity. Again, can't be a woman. Too objectifying… Who's muscley? Could I go with 'The Jackman'? No, I don't think that's quite right. Sort of suggests: 'firm, but older than you'd expect.' Plus people associate him with Wolverine. It'd probably seem like the sofa's a bit hairy. And that you'd occasionally get sharp springs randomly shooting out into your back… 'The Hemsworth'… that'll do it. Their Chesterfield's yellow – he's blond, he's tough – this is good.

OK – the corner sofa. Who can bend round corners? Hmm… Darcey Bussell maybe? But 'The Bussell'? Just sounds like lying on it will be a bit hectic. What about Jackie Chan? 'The Chan'? He's super flexible. But a hug from him sounds like it might be a bit punchy. Plus it'd also suggest the sofa is quite small. Not that I'd say that to his face… Sting! Yes that's it. Everyone *knows* he's bendy. Perfect! Plus it has the added advantage of suggesting that the sofa can last for *ages*.

I feel pretty confident there's some mileage in this and I send what I've got over to Larousse and Amanda. I'm sure there are equivalent celebrities that appeal to young people that we could use for that demographic. What am I talking about? They can only afford futons anyway. We just need someone who sings a bit flat. Maybe call it 'The Bieber'? Jesus, he's probably in his mid-thirties by now. Talk about the cutting edge. Strange that my knowledge of who's hot in music seems to stop around the same time that Arthur was born…

The presentation sent off, I take the kids out for a walk. It's nice to get a bit of fresh air – we didn't leave the house all day yesterday. I think I was worried that the guy whose house I threw the rat at might see me. Or the pet shop owner. Or the person who keeps accusing me of hoarding. But, as we stroll around our local neighbourhood, we don't see *anyone*. The streets are empty. We don't even have to go off the pavement to let anyone past. It's almost relaxing.

That is, until we make it home, and, just as I'm opening up the door to our building, I hear a voice behind me.

'You didn't clap.'

I turn round to see Paul Perry, the guy who lives opposite. He's late 50s, maybe sixty, and has a face fixed in a permanent squint. He's lived there since he was twenty-five, when buying a whole house was actually affordable and now he runs the local neighbourhood watch. Not because he cares about everyone's safety – he just wants an excuse to surreptitiously look out from behind his curtains – which, it seems, if he ever made a CV, would be the only thing written under 'interests'.

'You didn't *clap*,' he repeats. I have no idea what he's talking about. Did he do some particularly good staring out of his window at passersby earlier? Maybe he rolled his eyes in a way that he felt was worthy of applause?

'*For the NHS*,' he explains.

'What?' I ask, and then the pieces suddenly fall into place. It's Friday. Which means yesterday was Thursday. 'Did that happen again last night?' I ask, genuinely. I thought it was a one-off. 'I didn't realise. I tried to take a day off the news.'

'Did you take a day off supporting the NHS?'

'No – I always support the NHS. Who doesn't support the NHS?'

'People who don't clap.'

The accusation puts me on edge, and excuses start tumbling out of my mouth like travelling acrobats.

'I was… I was putting the kids to bed. They're in the back bedroom – I didn't hear.'

'Well, that's surprising.'

'What, putting the kids to bed?'

'No – not hearing. Everyone else on the street was clapping. Most of them have their bedrooms in the front as well – they didn't seem to miss it.' *Not sure he should know that about the bedrooms…* Maybe they should just change the moniker 'Neighbourhood Watch' to 'Neighbourhood Perv'.

'Look – I didn't know,' I insist, turning to the kids to back me up. 'We didn't know, did we?'

'*We* knew,' says Carrie, nodding. 'Granny told us on the FaceTime.'

'You knew…? When did you FaceTime Granny?'

'Yesterday. We did it ourselves while you were doing your hair.'

Great, now I'm the non-NHS supporter, who spends his time preening in front of a mirror while his children make unsupervised video calls. I can't quite believe they used FaceTime without my permission. I need to put a code on the iPad. Hopefully, there're no internet predators out there with high quality Grandma disguises. That said, I've read Carrie *Little Red Riding Hood* a *lot* – that should have made her suspicious of grandparents who look slightly off. Not *too* suspicious hopefully – Granny Jan definitely isn't at her best at the moment.

But, I can still feel Mr Perry staring daggers at me – I have to emphasise this is the first I've heard of it. 'Well,' I tell the kids, uber-serious, 'you should have *told* me.' I look back up to Mr

Perry with an *I'd-forgotten-you-were-here* expression. 'They didn't tell me,' I explain. He looks sceptical.

'I just think it's important to show our support in times like this,' he replies. He's so smug. I want to punch him. I won't – obviously – it'd just make more work for the health service, and he'd think I'd proved his point. But it's *annoying*. I mean, he's never done anything good or helpful for anyone. All he ever does is stay at home. Shit – maybe he was just ahead of us on that one. Turns out he's been helping flatten every disease curve for the last twenty years. I thought he was boring – turns out he's just a fervent suppressor of illnesses.

But he's not finished – there's more to come. 'The NHS are the backbone of this country. It's people like you who undermine their morale.'

'People like me? I didn't know it was *on*,' I splutter. 'I would have *liked* to have done it. And "undermine their morale"? *Come on*! I doubt anyone would have noticed. It's not like the street is awash with NHS workers!'

'Um… Annie. She lives four doors down from you. She's a nurse.'

Really? I know Annie. I didn't know she was a nurse. 'Are you sure?'

'Yes. I've seen her in uniform.' *Well, that doesn't mean anything. Maybe she was just doing a bit of roleplay with her husband while you were staring through her bedroom window.*

'Look, I'm sure Annie knows I'm very behind the NHS. And I agree it's important. But I was also doing something important as well – looking after my children. It's paramount…' *Huh? There's a word I've never said out loud before,* '*paramount*… to make your kids feel reassured and safe at bedtime… Plus, as I said, I didn't know.'

'We did try to tell you, Daddy…'

'Shush. You didn't.'

'We did,' says Arthur. 'You said to stop talking or you'd get angry. Then you went out of the room, dropped something and said the f-word.'

There you go: calm and reassuring.

'Not the f-word,' Carrie contradicts, '"*Fokk*". He said "fokk".' *Well, thanks for making that better.* I should point out, I stupidly told Carrie not to use the f-word when she said 'fart' one time. Now she's convinced that *that's* the f-word. Nothing better than having a self-censoring child telling their grandparents 'Excuse me I did a… noisy bum. Whoops! I nearly said the f-word…'

'Seems like your high-quality parenting is paying off,' sneers Perry from behind his front gate. 'I hope you'll remember you prioritised swearing at your kids when you're next in hospital. No doubt being cared for by some NHS staff that you failed to support.'

'I didn't *swear* at them!' I snap. Carrie looks at me, dubious. '…I swore after I'd left them and shut the door.' *The same as I'm going to be doing with you, Mr Perry, as soon as I'm inside…* (I'll get the kids to run ahead of me upstairs before I really let rip.) 'And I won't have you saying we don't care! We clapped a *lot* last week, didn't we guys?'

Finally, fishing for the kids' support pays off. 'Yeah, we clapped really loud,' says Arthur.

'Exactly, really loud. If anything, we were worried we'd overdone it a bit, that Annie, as the street's only NHS worker…'

'Rebecca Cass is a doctor too. She lives three doors down in the other direction.'

'And Rebecca who is a doctor which I knew… We were worried that they might feel a bit embarrassed. But I think from now on, we'll ignore that, and just go at it full pelt. Anyway, if you'll excuse us, we were just about to make a banner, so we shall have to take our leave. Good day to you!' *Take our leave?!? Good day to you?!?* Where did that come from? Why did I suddenly decide to exit arguments like I was in a period drama?

I usher the kids inside and shut the door, muttering 'twat' under my breath. Hmm… forgot to tell them to run ahead, but making something inaudible is probably a close second. God, that was embarrassing. I really should get to know my neighbours. The NHS ones at least. Not Mr Perry. He's a twat.

After lunch, I get the kids to make new rainbows for the front window. It puts our total up to four. These ones also have the letters NHS emblazoned over them to make it clear we're supporting the health service, and not just showing some belated solidarity with last year's Pride. Actually, when I check Carrie's, it says N*N*S rather than H – her 'h's and 'n's are pretty much the same – but I think that's OK. I look it up and it doesn't seem like any of the interpretations are offensive: 'Nearly New Sale', 'Non-Native Speaker', 'Nigerian Navy Ship'… Yeah, they're all good. Well, as long as the Nigerian Navy doesn't get ideas above its station and attempts an inland invasion via the Thames. Worth checking though. I did have a slight worry that 'NN' might stand for 'Neo Nazi'…

But it puts us in a good position. We're two posters ahead of Mr Perry. And his are both print-outs. No love/felt tip has gone into them. Eat it, Perry. Bask in the shadow of the die-hard NHS fans that live opposite.

Who is it that doesn't support the NHS now?

Saturday 4th April

We've entered into an NHS supporting cold war.

Mr Perry has printed out and put up four more posters. But

I'm not prepared to let him win, so I get the kids back on the colouring. It's Saturday, so I even do one myself. Carrie manages to write NNS on hers again, although this time she puts on a second S. I give it a bit of thought before making an executive decision she has to redraft. The Neo Nazi interpretation was a long shot, but combined with the letters SS it's definitely not something you should be displaying outside your flat.

I stick them all up onto the windows. There're so many now it's starting to block the light. But we're ahead. Only one ahead, but still ahead. As I finish Blu-Tacking the last one up, I notice that Perry is at the window as well – and he puts up *two* more. It's not fair. He just has to press 'print'. We don't even *have* a colour printer anymore – ours would be in boring-as-hell (but surprisingly economical) monochrome. Nothing more hopeful than a rainbow in various shades of grey.

'Can we watch TV now?' asks Arthur.

'No, we're not done yet. Back to the table. We've got more colouring to do.'

Trying to ignore their groans of disappointment, we get back to it. By 11:00 am, we have another eight posters done. It feels good. *Try shaming us about not supporting the NHS, Mr Perry? Well, look at us now. We're winning. We're beating you!* The only question is whether our felt tips will dry up before his printer ink does. But I feel a rush of self-satisfaction as I stick the posters onto the glass. Is this what smug people feel like the whole time? It's nice. Maybe being conceited and self-satisfied in life is something worth aiming for…

'Right kids – great job. Let's make a mid-morning snack as a celebration.'

Sitting on the floor of our living room (*which is what's actually at the front of our flat, not my bedroom, Mr Perry.* He thinks he's so clever. If only he knew how much time I spend watching TV in pyjamas), we eat our cinnamon bagels. The room is depressingly dark. It feels like we're living in a squat.

'Daddy, can we let the light in?' comes Carrie's plaintive cry. She looks a bit weak and pale, as if, over the time it has taken to eat a bagel-half, she's already managed to develop a vitamin D deficiency.

'Well,' I reply, 'maybe if we'd shown a bit more solidarity as a family yesterday, this wouldn't have been necessary.'

'I don't know what that means,' says Carrie. *I know you don't know what that means. Otherwise I wouldn't have said it.* Sometimes, as a parent, it's important to take advantage of your children's lack of vocabulary to vent.

But she's right. We can't live like this, in a flat with no light. I love the NHS, but I'm turning my children into veal. It's not sustainable. This could go on for weeks.

'You're right – we need to find another way.' One by one, I take the rainbows down. I see Perry's upstairs curtains twitch, and I imagine his smug gloating face hiding behind them, thinking that he's better than us. That we're weak.

'Shouldn't we just leave one or two up?' asks Arthur.

'Oh, we're not taking any down.' I reply. 'Get the Sellotape. We're making a banner.'

After deciding it'll probably fall apart if I attempt to laminate the sheets, we stick the rainbows together and add a few more to make a massive 5 by 4 grid. It looks ridiculously amateur. But damned enthusiastic. I put some string on the top, and thanks to some clever engineering manage to suspend it between the two openable windows of our front room, so it hangs down the front of our building. There you go – Mr Perry. Let's see you spunk one of those out of your printer.

It also means we now have access to natural light for more than a single hour a day. And, that I get a perfect view of Mr

Perry, when I see him, twenty minutes later, standing in his front garden shaking his head, pretending that we're lowering the tone of the area.

But clearly just jealous as hell.

***

In the evening, I'm reading the news when I hear that a kid died today. It really throws me for a loop. Those poor people, that poor child. It makes me realise something – the whole kids-don't-get-it thing has really insulated me from a lot of the worst aspects of what's been going on. It just gave me something to hold onto – that even if I get it, my parents get it, if something happens to *all* of us – that at least the two people I love most in the world would be all right. That they'd be safe. But now, I don't even have that, and suddenly I feel adrift in a world of uncertainty.

I'm sure the kid was an outlier, a one-off, but that doesn't make things better for the parents that have been left behind, the family who feel like the light of the world has gone out. When you're going through the frustrations and difficulties of lockdown, it's easy to forget that people are dying out there. It just doesn't seem real. But something closer to home – it makes you think. And it makes me realise how selfish I am.

Perhaps that's all that empathy is – imagining that what has happened to someone else has happened to you? A mechanism to harness your own self-centredness into finally appreciating another person's pain?

As I fall asleep I can't stop the thoughts going round my head. Of that child, of those desolate parents. But I can't help playing the same thing out in my own little world. And asking: what if it happened to me?

Sunday 5th April

Being divorced during lockdown isn't great at the best of times: having to FaceTime your ex-wife every day so the kids can talk to her, having no one to talk to around the house, being landed with everything bloody else, but today things reach a new low.

Today I have to FaceTime Sally's mother.

Sally's mum is right pain in the butt. Her Dad was nice (apart from his embarrassing forays into performance poetry) but her mum – well, she hates me.

She thinks I treat myself too much, whereas in reality she's so aggressively down to earth, it's almost pretentious. I mean, she washes her hair with a bar of soap. A BAR. As far as she's concerned shampoo is a luxury of the decadent bourgeoisie. She doesn't live that far away, but I've managed to avoid bumping into her so far. One of the few pluses of social distancing. It's not only your friends who you don't get to see anymore…

We have a brief phone call to arrange the FaceTime, and during the one minute we spend talking, I get the impression that she's actually *enjoying* what's going on. As if she's finally getting the wartime experience that was denied her by being born too late to miss the glory years of World War II. Perhaps it's for the best; perhaps she can finally move past her resentment at having been cruelly forced to live through the most peaceful and stable period in world history.

I set the kids up on the table with my iPad, and open FaceTime. Just before it connects, Arthur has a thought. 'Oh! I want to show her my drawing!'

'I want to show her my drawing too!' says Carrie, and then they both run off. Leaving me to talk one-on-one to someone I thought I would never have to speak one-on-one to again for the rest of my life.

Granny Daphne appears on screen, with nothing but a look of

disdain on her face. Marilyn Monroe said 'a smile is the best makeup a girl can wear' – well, Daphne never has liked makeup. Unlike my mother, I doubt she's feeling the sting of cancelled hair appointments. She seems to take pride in looking old. Like any attempt to improve her appearance might make it look like she gave a shit.

'Hellooo Tommm,' she says, elongating the words as if it helps her get through the sheer tedium of having to talk to me.

'How are you, Daphne?'

'I'm keeping well, I'm keeping well,' she replies. 'Yes, I'm getting by. It's hard of course, but you just have to just push through.' There's a glint in her eye, as if pushing through is the most fun she's had since getting a deal on cheap mince during the height of mad cow disease. 'I'm sure a lot of people are finding it very stressful, but me, I manage to just keep calm. To just… keep calm and carry on.' *A war quote, an actual war quote.* 'I imagine *you're* finding it very difficult, Tom.'

'I appreciate you saying that, Daphne – it's tough looking after the kids and working at the same time…'

'Oh, I didn't mean that. I just meant… you. With your *lifestyle*.'

'My "lifestyle"?' The way she says it, it's like I'm part of a Baphomet worshipping S&M scene in 1970s New York.

'All your *extravagances*.' Here we go.

'What extravagances?'

'Well, you *do* love your cappuccinos, you're always drinking *cappuccinos*,' she says. Yeah, I love cappuccinos – well, flat whites – but I have *one a day*. She owns a *house*. What's a little bit of microfoam compared to the title deed of a building? 'And that bread you buy – you must be missing that. That *sour*bread.'

'Sour*dough*. And we only bought that once. And that was *Sally*. When you came to stay.'

'But I imagine it must be difficult for you to go back to normal bread. It's probably easier for people like me who eat normal bread the whole time. The supermarket still has that.' It also has 'sourbread'... They just put in slightly open bags so that people can cough all over it. But I try to ignore her dig, putting on my concerned your-daughter-was-a-fool-to-divorce-me face.

'Maybe you shouldn't be going to the supermarket, Daphne? You might be able to get priority for an online shop.'

'I don't see why. I'm not "*vulnerable*".' She says the word as if she's straining to lift a mangle (which I'm sure she's using, preserving her washing machine's spin cycle for 'vulnerable people'.) 'I just make sure I'm careful. I put on three pairs of gloves and a facemask that I made.'

'Oh, OK. I think one pair of gloves is probably enough. It's what protective gloves are meant for.'

'Oh, they're not *protective* gloves. They're just gloves. Normal woollen gloves. Nothing fancy. I put on a pair of mine, and a pair of Kenneth's over the top. They're a bit holey, so I wear rubber ones underneath.'

'Right...'

'The only downside is that they're giving me a lot of sores. But I don't complain. It's important to do your bit. Look – I've developed a fungal infection.'

She holds up her hand and it makes me wish video calling had never been invented. Her hands are cracked like barren ground in a drought, if it was red and a bit weepy. It's all I can do not to visibly flinch. 'They've cracked from all the washing and anti-bacterialising,' she continues, displaying them like she's in a hand cream advert, 'Of course I'm not worried about myself, but I don't want to be a *carrier*.'

'Maybe you should get some moisturiser?'

'Don't be silly, Tom. I need to leave that for the *vulnerable* people. You're not hoarding that as well as sourbread are you?'

Her hands remain up by the camera for far too long, and I can see exactly what's going on behind her eyes – this is probably the type of fungal infection people had during the Blitz. I'm surprised she hasn't sprinkled some rubble over herself to give the impression that coronavirus has led to the partial collapse of her home.

'Oh, and here's the mask I've been wearing,' she continues, holding up the cut off corner of a plastic Waitrose bag with rubber bands on it to attach it to her ears. 'It doesn't fully cover my mouth of course, it sags a bit – but I make do, Tom. I make do.'

'Would you like to talk to the kids now, Daphne?'

'Anyway, I think Sally's coping *very* well,' she replies, completely ignoring my attempt to leave. It strikes me she might not even *want* to talk to the kids. They probably wouldn't appreciate her attempts to stop the spread of a deadly virus with seniors' craft projects. I'm surprised she hasn't offered to supply hospitals with hand-operated ventilators she makes out of pigs' stomachs. Probably has a few in the freezer for just such an occasion. 'She's missing the children of course, but she's like me – able to cope with anything. A *practical* person. Perhaps that's why it didn't work out between the two of you.'

I've got a good mind to show her my fucking banner.

'Carrie and Arthur are just here – I'll put you on.'

'I'd appreciate that – I'm only leaving the house once a day for my walk – I go very early to avoid the crowds. It'll be nice to see a human face.' *As opposed to my non-human one?!?*

'Is it pretty busy in that park near you?'

'Oh, no, I don't go there. I walk around the car park. There's a multi storey that's empty now the shopping centre's closed, so I just go up and down the levels for an hour and a half.'

'Probably a nice view at the top.'

'No, I don't look at any of that, I just do my exercise and go. It's the only place that's properly quiet.'

'Well, that's good you're being careful.'

'Oh, I'm not going to be careful. I just like it there.' Of course. Nothing like a bit of Brutalist NCP architecture to clear the head during a pandemic. I really have to get off this call as quickly as possible before I commit the world's first video chat suicide.

'Sorry Daphne,' I say, pulling my phone out of my pocket. 'I've got a work call coming through.'

'Work? On a Sunday?'

'Yeah – weekends don't seem to mean as much at the moment, do they!?!' I say, trying to feign a sense of humour about something that isn't actually happening. She looks sceptical before a look of understanding flashes across her face. 'If it's one of your girlfriends, there's no need to be embarrassed, Tom. Sally's moved on, it's only fair you should too.' Thanks Daphne – and, FYI, Sally moved on while we were married, so let's not give her too much credit for her ability to pick herself up afterwards. When getting back on your feet, it's usually good manners to first wait until you've fallen down.

'Kids – take over!' I shout as I walk off, feeling the heaviness evaporate with every step I take away from the monitor, until soon I feel as light as a well-risen sourbread. I head into the kitchen, annoyed that I can't shake my plan to make a cappuccino. There'll be hell to pay if she finds out. I wonder if she's been talking to Larousse…

***

Just after lunch, I spot that Perry has put up a banner.

It's bigger than mine. I never thought this lockdown would have ended up in me comparing banner size with a man in his late 50s, but hey, that's what's going on. Life is what happens when you're making other plans.

I should have been suspicious first thing when I saw him receive an order from Amazon and open it up outside his house. He caught me looking out of the window as the van drove off, and he was pretty ostentatious in revealing its contents. He looked annoyed when I couldn't see what they were because they were too small, but now I know exactly what was in there – poster paints. Poster paints that come in smaller tubes than you'd expect. But still, that's an impressive delivery time – he can only have ordered them yesterday. Considering how long it was going to take me to get that rat trap, it's damned impressive.

Anyway, he must have dropped the repurposed bed sheet out of his window while we were eating, because it's there waiting for me when I walk into the living room, yoghurt pot still in hand: a seven foot wide rainbow, the colours of which seem to morph as they go move along its length. I guess what the poster paint pack lacked in the size of the individual tubes, it made up for in the wide range of shades included.

I consider whether we should do a sheet ourselves, but, to be honest, none of ours are in the best shape. One of the downsides of having kids is that your bed linen doesn't always make it out the other side. Pretty much everything has got little stains on it from various accidents or spillages – tea they've knocked over, accidents they've had in the night, and I don't think a banner made from a soiled bed sheet is going to cut it. Plus the reality is: we can't even spare one. I suppose I could do an Instagram post where Arthur's sleeping on a bare mattress to 'support the NHS', but it doesn't really seem fair. I think I just have to accept I've lost.

But then I spot Annie, getting onto her bike outside her house. And I see an opportunity. I almost spit out a mouthful of yoghurt in excitement – *almost*, thank God – dairy's one of the things you have to try and make last for the week.

I open the window as quickly as I can, putting down my bowl in the process. And then I begin to applaud.

'Go Annie!' I shout.

'Thanks,' she smiles, as she cycles past. And she seems to hold herself a little more upright as she continues on down the road.

Woo-hoo! THAT's some supporting of the NHS. Supporting an *actual* NHS person. Making them feel good…

I feel a bit ashamed when I realise it was 100% motivated by me trying to get one up on Mr Perry. That is, until I see him running out of his front door about ten seconds later, tripping over and falling on his face, then getting up and clapping as loudly as he can. When he realises she can't hear, he starts running down the street after her, cheering. She doesn't turn around. The look on his face is priceless. He realises he hasn't got any shoes on and turns back, trotting back to his house on tip toe. He really should be more careful. If he ends up with a foot injury it's just going to be making more work for the health service…

Monday 6th April

I can't believe it's the holidays. Because, I guess, it's not.

Everyone from the office is stressing as the company's started furloughing workers. John, my office nemesis, has already gone. Annoyingly, he's probably really happy about it as he doesn't have kids and I doubt his finances are on the same knife-edge as mine. Sitting at home watching YouTube videos will probably suit him fine. Apart from the 80% salary, it'll be pretty much the same as what he does when he's actually working.

But I can't risk the same thing happening to me. As much as I'd like to be able to just focus on the kids for a bit, things are really tight now I'm doing this alone, and losing any income could screw us. I chatted with Amanda last night, and she said they're doing a second round in a couple of weeks, so, even though I'm meant to be abroad sunning it up and eating food that the Covid-19 symptom of 'taking-away-your-smell-and-taste' would probably improve, I've decided to move my days off to an unspecified point in the future. Hey, if the holiday company who's still got my money doesn't go bust, I might even be able to spend what they owe me on travelling to the very place I was meant to be going. In 2025.

I feel guilty about shoving the kids in front of the TV while I work, but I don't have a choice. We've got a Zoom meeting with the sofa client and I can't have them coming in and telling me they're bored and asking what to do. I sit down in my bedroom and set myself up at the computer. I bought a headset with a microphone that came through this morning. I listened to a podcast saying they were going to be the key purchase in this new remote-working world, but seeing my reflection in the black mirror of my dead monitor, I've got a suspicion it's just going to make me look a bit stupid. Maybe I'm just a bit paranoid about my appearance at the moment as I haven't really got used to my hair yet. My short, extremely dark hair. Especially as the kids told me yesterday that, after I left the FaceTime, Granny Daphne said I looked like an Action Man toy…

I try to reassure myself, but, when the meeting starts, it turns out I was right to be paranoid about being on camera. I don't even just look like an Action Man. More like an ageing Action Man who works in a call centre… I suppose it *can* be difficult to find work after you leave a career in the army. The headset's a nightmare. I can't even get the mic to register for the first three minutes. It's embarrassing. And then I'm just stuck with staring at an image in the corner of the screen of my ridiculous little head staring back at me for the next forty minutes – stupid mic stuck in front of its stupid face. Maybe next time I should just go the whole hog and wear a Madonna style cone bra.

But the meeting itself goes well, and, at the end, everyone's telling me how much they love the idea as well as complimenting me on the clarity of my audio. Maybe it wasn't such a bad investment after all. I'm actually feeling a bit better about myself when I go into the living room to tell the kids to turn the telly off. That is, until I hear something. Some clapping from outside. What the hell is happening? I go to the window only to see all my neighbours lining the pavements, applauding and cheering. Further down the street, Annie is on her bike – getting an ovation from EVERYONE.

Everyone that is, apart from us. Across the road, Mr Perry stares up at my window, a smug smile on his face. He's coordinated this. He must have got hold of her work schedule, and decided not to tell me.

He drops his smile, and glares at me pointedly, shaking his head in disgust. A few others follow suit. I'm in shock. I've got a banner – I've got a *massive banner*. I look down from window, to be confronted by a blur of smudged felt tip. It must have rained a bit in the night. There's still the *vague* sense that it's pro-NHS, but it's a little underwhelming. Like having a cheerleader who's a bit too drunk to pronounce the words properly.

Damn it. I was right – I should have definitely laminated.

Tuesday 7th April

After another morning of working while the kids watch TV/go on the iPad (I'm beginning to realise that what the school was providing *was* actually quite useful), we're back at the shops again.

I've decided to reframe my inability to get an online shop as a moral stand. It's not that I'm somehow incompetent at using their online queuing system, simply that I wasn't trying as hard lest the 'vulnerable' suffer. Turns out at least I've learnt something from my ex-mother-in-law.

I have to admit I'm beginning to feel a genuine respect for the supermarket staff. They're really rising to the occasion. I mean, if you're a doctor or a fireman, you know you might have to deal with some difficult shit at some point, but a *cashier*. No one goes into that thinking it might go pear-shaped – surely it's not *that* much of a calling, applicants thinking: 'I want to scan items for a living – maybe it'll be in a burning supermarket, maybe it'll be in a warzone. Doesn't matter to me – all I care about is helping people pay for their shopping.'

But now the cashiers are on the front line. I'm sterilising my trolley handle when I go to the supermarket, despite the fact it's ALREADY BEEN DONE, keeping my distance, trying to avoid touching anything, while they're touching EVERYTHING. And smiling while they do it. It's incredible.

But there's one person who is above them all; braver, stronger, with even less thought for his personal safety.

Queue guy.

Queue guy is normally a cashier, but has now been pro/demoted to a new role. This poor teenager (who I'm sure is now regretting not staying on for sixth form), has been given the task of walking up and down the line of customers, and asking people if they're over 65. Even watching him from afar mortifies me. It's like he doesn't even realise the danger he's in – the fool's got a smile on his face – I feel like I've just watched someone push a turkey out into a grain field to see if there are any landmines.

'Excuse me, if you're over 65, you don't have to queue,' he says, approaching a woman who I think is *very* borderline.

'Oh, thank you!' she says. 'I didn't realise.' She smiles, and makes her way to the front. Queue guy seems pleased with himself, but it scares me. His early success is lulling him into a false sense of security.

'Excuse me, if you're over 65, you don't have to queue,' he says to another woman.

'I'm 47,' she spits back.

'Oh, you'll have to queue then,' he replies, before moving on, water off a duck's back. I'm almost impressed – the guy's invulnerable. But as he continues onwards, moving from person to person, he leaves a trail of outrage in his wake. Who even thought to do it like this? Put up a sign, give someone a megaphone – don't ask people *individually*. It's like the reverse of the Think 25 policies. If they ask you, and you're a day over 30, you're walking on air for the rest of the day. Here, if you're a day younger than 65, you're going to think you've failed at life. But no one seems to be doing anything. I realise I have to take a stand.

I tell the kids to stay in our space, and hesitantly approach him.

'Excuse me...'

'You're not over 65!' he announces in a nasal squall. 'Please maintain a two metre distance – please join the back of the queue!' I don't like his tone, but phew! I may look like an Action Man, but at least I haven't been tarred with the pensioner brush yet.

'I'm not trying to skip the queue – and I'm going to maintain a two metre distance.'

'Then what do you want?' he fires off accusatorially.

'I just think – that maybe you're offending a few people.'

'Offending? I'm just doing my job.'

'It's just... a lot of these people – they're quite a lot younger than 65. They might feel a little upset. I mean – how would you feel if people starting asking if you were eighteen yet?'

'I'm not eighteen yet.'

'Oh, OK, but you're implying they're *older* than they are.'

'You're implying *I'm* older than I am.'

'That's not the same – you're seventeen – '

'Doing it again–'

'OK – *sixteen*. But everyone *wants* to be sixteen. There's a real sweet spot between sixteen and thirty that we all want to be part of. No one wants to be 65. It's awful.'

A passing woman, skipping the queue, gives me the evils.

'There's nothing wrong with being 65!' she says, scolding me.

'Of course there isn't,' I reply, 'but no one wants to *look* 65…' She isn't thawing. 'Which you don't,' I explain, trying to finagle my way out. For the record, she definitely does.

She tuts then moves on. I turn back to Queue Guy.

'I just think it would be better to do a general "anyone over 65 can skip the queue", and then see if anyone takes you up on it.'

He thinks for a few seconds. 'I suppose I *could* do that. But what about if people who I *don't* think are 65 start skipping the queue. All I have is my instinct here. I have to rely on my instinct.'

Please never rely on your instinct. You're like a guy at a fairground playing whack-a-mole. Except you're at the wrong stall, attacking a petting zoo with a hammer.

My expression prompts him to reconsider. 'Well… do you think it would be OK to ask them for ID?'

'I think it would be best not to.'

'All right – well… thanks for the heads up.'

I go back to my place in the queue, and watch as a few of my queue-mates breathe a collective sigh of relief. My good deed for the day is done.

I see him again on the way out. And Queue Guy is doing just great – old people are getting in, old*ish* people are still holding their heads high, everything is once again as it should be. But then, at the back, I see a woman pushing her way to the front. I don't recognise her to begin with because of the facemask, but then I realise it's made out of a carrier bag. The woollen gloves confirm her identity. It's Daphne. I can't quite believe it – all this time protesting about how she's not vulnerable, about how she doesn't need 'special treatment'… and then she accepts it hook, line and sinker. I mean she *should* get special treatment, but still… It goes through my head maybe I should tell Queue Guy to ask her for ID. She hates it when people think she looks younger than she is…

On the upside, I remembered to get the kids Easter eggs; oh, and the other cool thing the supermarket have introduced is that they'll now help you carry your shopping! I tried doing my normal, 'No, really – help someone else,' when a guy came up to me, but they insisted.

We were halfway home before he realised I didn't have a car.

Wednesday 8th April

Mark sent me a video this morning. It was all these 'inspiring' images, with a voiceover telling us how all this will one day be remembered as a 'golden time', where we learnt to 'stop and be present', a time when all that the children will remember is 'all the mums and dads at home drawing and playing ball games'. That we shouldn't stress, that we should 'focus on the silver lining'.

We both agreed whoever made that video should be shot. But the video made me feel really guilty. If *my* kids remember this as a golden time, it'll be because they finally got to watch TV and play on the iPad for the whole day. The time they suddenly realised how much fun they could have had in the rest of their childhood if their designated guardian had been more neglectful… It makes me feel rubbish. The only drawing we've been doing is these bloody NHS banners – and that's to one-up a quinquagenarian – the closest we've got to playing ball games is me dropping a bag of peas onto the floor. I doubt them helping me pick those up will be emblazoned on their memories.

I decide I need to make a change. I need to make sure I don't lose my job, but I also need to make this time with the kids count. I can't do *much* – I'd be fired – but once a day I'm going to start doing stuff with the kids. Starting tomorrow.

We stand by the window at eleven, ready to 'cheer Annie to work', only to find no one else is there. Even Annie. I spot Mr Perry smirking as he watches us from his window. We're caught short a couple of hours later when we're in the kids' bedroom, suddenly hearing cheering coming from the front, only to get there too late to join in. Perry *must* have a timetable. How else could he know? He's such a dick. It's feeling vindictive how much effort he's going to to make us look bad.

It's not long after that we go out on our daily walk. The street's a bit busier than normal, so we walk to the main road down the alley than runs behind the back of the houses on our side. Ahead of us, I see someone. I hesitate, spotting a potential alley blockage, but she seems to be going into her house, so we push forwards. It's only when we get closer that I realise who it is.

Annie.

'You caught me,' she says, seeming a bit worried. Then she recognises me. 'Oh it's you! Phew! Hey, Tom!'

'Hey, Annie,' I reply, confused as to why I 'caught her'.

She continues unlocking her gate, before she looks back up, as if she's remembered something. 'Thanks for not cheering by the way.'

The sarcasm cuts like a surgeon's knife. But her tone doesn't *seem* sarcastic. It's almost like she's… being genuine? She carries on before I can try to justify myself.

'It's doing my head in,' she continues. 'The banners and

Thursday night thing are nice, but *every* day on my way to work. I can't stand it. It's killing me. I feel like utter crap at the moment. I don't want everyone staring after I've had four hours' sleep.'

Not sarcastic. Not sarcastic! I feel like giving her a hug. Probably not a good idea.

'Well, I don't want to big myself up for not clapping,' I reply, trying to sound modest, skirting over the issue that I totally would have joined in if I'd known about it.

'Well, it's appreciated,' she says. 'Can't believe my bloody husband gave that Mr Perry my timetable. I hate that man. I wish he'd stop.'

It's music to my ears. Sometimes the NHS doesn't just heal your body. Sometimes they heal your soul.

'Would you like me to have a word?' I ask.

Annie looks at me, her faith in the kindness of strangers restored once more. 'Would you?'

'It would be my pleasure…'

***

Knocking on his door on the way home feels like the highlight on my week. The kids and I take a few steps back so we're on the pavement while he makes his way to the door.

'Oh, Mr Perry, hi,' I say, rubbing anti-bac into my hands after touching his door knocker. 'Really sorry to bother you, but… I was just talking to Annie.'

'How were you talking to Annie?' he snaps. 'She's at work – you can't have been talking to her. I have her timetable.'

'She had to come back for something. The weird thing is she was sneaking in round the back of her house.'

'What are you talking about – sneaking round the back of the house? That's nonsense.'

'Turns out – she's not exactly enjoying your daily "send-offs".' I'm feigning a tone of utter seriousness, but finding it hard not to smile. 'She told me to ask you if you could maybe… stop them.'

'How does she know it was me?'

'Well, you did ask her husband for her timetable.'

A look of panic transforms his face into a cartoon of desperation. 'I… I… You need to tell her it was you.'

It's nice to be able to laugh once in a while. Talk about clutching at straws! 'Why would I do that?'

'Because I *know*…'

'What do you mean "you know"?'

'I know…' he says in an exaggerated whisper, 'about the *rat*.'

'I…'

How the hell does he know about that?!?

A victorious smile cuts across his pudgy face. 'I saw you running down the street with a box last week. Wednesday evening I think it was. I saw you panic, and then something – I didn't know what at the time – flew out of the box. But two days later, I'm chatting to Mr Cook down the road, and I hear he now has a *rat* in his house. Well, I start to put two and two together…' He changes tack. 'You probably wouldn't know this (as you don't seem to take any interest in who lives on our street), but I'm a big fan of the literary detective genre…' I'm not sure that means anything. I'm a big fan of fantasy books, but I don't think I'd have a lot of luck fighting a mage with a broadsword. 'And I realised that the aforementioned 'thing' that flew out of your box, was that… very… rat. It was just a theory at first, but your reaction has confirmed it.'

Damn. Damn you, reaction.

I let out a sigh worthy of a man with a far greater lung capacity. 'Shit.'

'And so the game is afoot, the tables have turned. Either you tell Annie that the clapping was your idea, or I tell *everyone* about the new rat scam you're operating… attempting to drive people out of their houses so you can buy them cheap. It's despicable.' Huh! He really does read a lot of detective novels. *Buy them up cheap*? I can't afford to buy the flat I *live* in. Maybe I'm planning to force people out of their homes and attempt to rent them at a slightly reduced rate…

But I can't have everyone knowing about the rat.

I don't have a choice but to do exactly what he says.

***

That evening, depressed, I write Annie a note wearing rubber gloves, and drop it into Mr Perry's house. He wants to deliver it himself so he can make sure that I've followed his instructions. I'm almost tempted to write a secret message in between the lines in lemon juice (the closest I get to the 'literary detective genre' is reading Enid Blyton to Arthur at bedtime) but I doubt she'll know to iron it/put it in the oven. We're also down to one lemon and I said I'd make the kids pancakes at the weekend.

It looks like shame is going to win out.

Thursday 9th April

As it's looking like we're going to be leaving the house even less than normal, this morning we do our first PE with Joe Wicks. It's also part of my attempt to do more things with the kids. Turns out it may be the first nail in the coffin of me abandoning that attempt entirely.

I press play on the iPad, and Joe appears onto the screen with a forward roll. It gets my back up immediately. What a completely unnecessary way to get around. I don't want to take instructions from someone who thinks gymnastic moves are an acceptable way to travel. What if it rubs off and I start cartwheeling to the bathroom?

The room he's in makes me wary as well – it's suspiciously empty, there're not even any marks in the carpet where a sofa used to be... *and* he also seems to be wearing some kind of wrist support. Has he broken his arm or something? How dangerous *are* these workouts? He hasn't even got a table to bump into.

He starts off the session with a 'spot the difference' around his flat. I've never seen his place before, but I can spot the difference to *my* flat – his is tidy and doesn't have any furniture in. There's also probably a higher likelihood he'll be living in it in three months' time because he's not been furloughed and can still pay his rent.

Then he begins the workout proper, starting with what I assume is his usual five minute warm up. Carrie, Arthur and I all try to join in, squatting down and twisting from side to side in a kind of crab posture.

'I feel stupid,' says Arthur.

'Me too,' replies Carrie.

I feel stupid as well, but it's my job as a responsible adult to pretend that I don't. 'Kids – you can't overestimate the importance of exercise. And if you don't warm up properly, you could hurt yourself – ow!'

I smash my hand really hard into the underside of the table. If you *do* warm up properly you can hurt yourself too. But I stay on track. 'We need to do this so we stay fit as family.' As if the hour long walks we're doing every day don't count.

And they clearly don't. By the end of the warm up, my body's already beginning to hurt – and not just the bits that have collided with furniture. We're only five minutes in and already I want to give up. Luckily, Joe reads out a 'poem' that someone has written to inspire us. This 'poet' claims the workouts make you feel like a 'shooting star' afterwards. Despite their lack of rhyme scheme or meter, I decide to give them the benefit of the doubt.

I shouldn't have. By the end of the workout I do feel like a shooting star, but one that has burnt up in the earth's atmosphere, and is now merely a few grains of rubble that have made it through.

'That was horrible,' says Arthur, lying on the ground next to me.

'Yes it was,' I reply.

'I don't like Joe Wicks,' says Carrie.

'I don't either,' I reply. Shit. I think I've actually twisted my back a bit – I'll have to take a couple of ibuprofen to take the edge off. Finally a positive to stocking up on the wrong kind of painkiller pre-lockdown. 'Don't worry, we won't do it anymore.'

'Tomorrow's the fancy dress one though,' says Arthur.

'Oh yeah! Can we do that? Can we do that!' says Carrie, suddenly overbrimming with enthusiasm. I feel really annoyed, but I don't have a choice – if the kids have a chance to dress up for something in the midst of all this, you can't really deny it to them. This has probably always been the case. It doesn't matter how unpleasant a task is – if they get to do it in a costume it's all good. I imagine it's how the Hitler youth started. *Yes kids, we* know *you don't want to be fascists, but look how fancy the uniforms are!*

***

My body is still aching when I go to bed. I'm in so much pain that doing the evening NHS clap hurts. It's one thing to go to a gym and ache a bit afterwards, but doing a bit of jumping up and down in your living room and barely being able to function… well, it just feels embarrassing.

Lying there, I make a decision – I'm going to let myself go. Isn't that what we're all meant to be doing during lockdown? Not trying so hard, accepting this is a once in a lifetime situation – no one's going to be being their best selves. We've just got to survive, to just try to make it through in one piece.

I'm eating crap I wouldn't normally eat anyway, so I'm hardly going to lose weight. Now that pasta's back in stock, we're often having it twice a day, I'm eating about 50% of my normal fruit and veg, very little protein, but I just need to accept it. I've already put on a few pounds. I have no idea how many as I don't have any scales, but I'm done with all this stupid exercise; I'm done with trying.

I feel like I have reached a new level of maturity, having transcended vanity and worldly pursuits when a message comes through from Amanda. I haven't talked to her yet this evening as she's been putting the finishing touches to our sofa campaign, so I'm pretty pleased to get something through from her.

Until I see what it is.

She's sent me a photo. A very sexy photo. Oh my GOD, it's a sexy photo. Having lived in a world exclusively populated by me and two under-tens for the last three weeks, it takes me a bit by surprise. Hope-my-kids-don't-come-through-and-try-and-get-in-the-bed-with-me level surprise.

Of course, that's not what bothers me specifically. The photo itself – I'm very pleased to receive. What bothers me is the message I get a few seconds later… 'Am I going to get one too? ;)'

Um… I'm pretty sure you're not.

She's in incredible shape, and amazingly beautiful, and I'm… well – not. There's *no* way I'm sending something back. But somehow, in a moment of blind optimism (and fully-sighted obligation), I begin to convince myself that maybe I can fool the camera; that if I get the lighting and angle right it might look OK.

I take a shot. Wow. If she's Venus sculpted from marble, that is definitely not David. I can't quite believe what I'm looking at. If this photograph was in an art gallery it would be called 'Man in Pants'. Well, if the artist decided to abandon his first title of 'Man in Slightly Old Pants'. Let's be honest, this would never be in an art gallery. Maybe if the Tate had a new exhibition called 'The Human Body in Decay'.

I'm also worried that the kids will burst in. I didn't think I could top my previous photographic effort, but 'Man in Pants Surprised by Children' might just do it. On the upside, it's times like this when I'm glad I never paid up for extra cloud storage. This exists on my phone and nowhere else in the world. And now, not even there.

I shake my head as I wonder what to do. I'm far too old for this. Things weren't great with Sally and me, but at least I never had to sext her. That's one of the positive things about marriage that no one ever tells you about – being on permanent hiatus from having to look good in erotic photographs.

My phone beeps – it's Amanda again. Another winky face. This time accompanied by '?'

I go into complete panic mode. 'Sorry – phone camera is broken. Sent normal phone away earlier – got SIM in really old phone. Sorry – said it'll be a week till back :('

I hate lying to her, but what can I do? This is no way for a relationship to end. The situation gives me a sudden flashback to the time I once found some porn that Sally had been watching. I sat on the bed, turned the iPad on and found myself in the middle of some seedy video with a POV shot of this disgusting man in his underwear with hairy thighs and I just thought, 'Yuk – I can't believe my wife is into this.'

That was when I realised it wasn't a porn video – the iPad's camera was on and I was filming my own legs… Although it did turn out she *wasn't* into that, so I can't fault her on her taste.

But the memory reassures me – lockdown or no lockdown, I'm doing the right thing by not sending anything to Amanda. I'm not lying to her, I'm protecting her, protecting *us*. I feel a bit better when the phone beeps again. Only to read her message, and suddenly realise exactly what I've done.

'The countdown begins. Looking forward to next week… xxx'

Oh God.

I think I just gave myself a one-week deadline to get in shape for an erotic photo.

Fuck.

Friday 10th April

I begin my morning reading a Wikihow on how to take a sexy photo. It's not the way I'd envisaged starting the day when I got into bed last night, but sometimes fate makes your decisions for you.

I scan through the tips. 'Apply makeup to give yourself a dramatic look', 'Make your hair voluminous and sexy'… Why do I feel this isn't meant for me? Even if my hair was longer, I doubt a 1980s David Hasselhoff with a side serving of Instagram-level mascara would increase my sex appeal. On the upside, the site does remind me that 'you don't need to do your make up if your face won't be in the photo'. It's a relief. I was thinking of going full drag queen, then snapping a shot of my penis.

The more I read, the more depressed I get. Clearly men who are hitting middle age aren't meant to be doing this. Just to experiment I try a few of the other tips on for size: 'take a photo making the S-curve to accentuate your chest', 'relax your face and breathe through your mouth'… I look like I'm having an attack. I'm pretty sure that if I threw my back out after emerging from the shower you could snap the exact same shot. It doesn't help that I'm currently leaning against my door so the kids can't get in. I can almost see the newspaper article now… 'Found naked and helpless, his children were unable to rescue him after his spasming body blocked the door. The only evidence as to what happened is the photograph that remains. We can only guess that, unable to speak in the throes of his episode, he had the wherewithal to photograph himself to communicate his situation to a loved one. If only he had managed to press "send"…' They'd probably include the photo as well. Maybe with the question '*If a friend sent you this, what would you do?* Four more signs that an elderly person is in trouble.'

The only thing on the site that actually seems applicable is 'highlight your best features'. That makes sense. I just need to work out what they are. I look at myself in the mirror. My eyes are a bit baggy, my nose is a bit big, my lips could be fuller, I've got pretty unimpressive cheekbones. Ears, maybe? Maybe slightly too much lobe. It almost seems that it's the bits in between that are the best. Reasonably smooth cheek skin? Could I go with that?

I don't even consider my body. I've got no abs, weak muscle tone – I doubt I can get that sorted in a week. You'd really think that considering how disappointing everything is, something would stand out, but no, I've been consistent in my mediocrity. Maybe that's my appeal. I think I read that interior designers advise you to never have one room that's bigger and better than the others, 'cos it'll make the other ones look rubbish. Maybe that's what I'm achieving here. Not great when the body you're inhabiting is the physical equivalent of a well-balanced house owned by a slumlord.

It doesn't take me long to realise that if my uncut body's not going to cut it, I need to think about my mind. Again, it's not the best, but it's in the top fiftieth percentile. Probably. I'm pretty sure there's some *really* stupid people out there, so if anything it might be even higher. Although it's counter-intuitive, averagely intelligent might actually be quite something.

An idea comes to mind – me, lying on the bed, draped in books. Sexy, but *intellectual*. 'Me? I'm just reclining here wearing nothing but a copy of James Joyce's *Ulysses*… If you'd caught me while I was still reading, imagine *what* you might have seen…' I'll have to remember to turn it to the middle – I don't want people to think I got stuck on 'Stately, plump Buck Mulligan'. Not a good phrase to associate with a covered penis at the best of times. But this could work. I could even borrow some of those toy glasses Arthur has, looking over the top of them towards the camera in a sultry fashion. Actually, I think they might be part of a Harry Potter costume. It'll look like I'm sending through some deepfake porno of Daniel Radcliffe.

I head over to the living room, and look through the bookshelf. No *Ulysses*. Arse. That must have been Sally's. What else have I got? Scanning through my shelf, I suddenly realise I don't possess a single book that isn't in the sci-fi or fantasy genre. I can't drape myself with *those*. Seeing the naked male form adorned with nothing but three volumes of *Lord of the Rings* wouldn't turn on a hobbit. Even the books whose title she wouldn't know have covers advertising their geekiness. I can't hide my junk with a picture that looks like it's been drawn by Napoleon Dynamite on a good day. *Yes, it's a paladin who's half-hawk, but what is behind that semi-avian warrior priest? My disappointing penis, that's what.*

I head back to my room and the drawing board (having also spotted a lone copy of *Great Expectations* and decided that's asking for trouble). I scroll down to the bottom of the Wikihow page, in the hope that I'll find that magic ingredient, that secret angle or lighting trick that makes even the most physically unattractive person look sexy, but there's nothing.

What makes the page even more depressing is seeing that all the comments at the bottom are from thirteen/fourteen-year-old girls, whose boyfriends have asked them to take a naked picture. It really upsets me. I'm going to have watch out for Carrie when she's older, as well as making sure Arthur isn't one of these dickhead boys. I literally don't know how these kids can have the confidence to ask that at thirteen? I used to get nervous asking a girl if I could borrow her sharpener. The amount of times I tippexed out pencil because requesting a rubber seemed too suggestive...

But it just reminds me that this isn't my world. In fact, the only thing I do have in common with the thirteen-year-old girls is the answer that would be provided if I asked in the comments if I should be taking this: *Don't do it. The pictures will end up everywhere and you'll be ridiculed. You think it will make you popular but it won't.*

There's also a good chance my photo would break multiple obscenity laws.

***

The fancy-dressed Joe Wicks workout is even worse that the normal one. The only plus is that wearing a cape and pirate's hat might make it into the equivalent of hot yoga. Surely, I must be burning more calories? Hope makes me believe it, because burning more calories is the best chance I've got of staying in my relationship for more than another week. Well, unless I dramatically increase my library size. Maybe that way I can create the bibliographic equivalent of a burka.

I really push myself, trying to avoid any distractions. I mean, I do feel slightly put off when Arthur enters the room halfway through in full on Hogwarts gear (glasses included), but the vision of my upcoming photo shoot helps me push forward to a second wind. I. Will. Not. End. Up. With. A. Hufflepuff. Bod…

***

My day ends with a phonecall to Mark. I don't tell him about the photo, more through self-preservation than embarrassment. Telling Mark about something compromising is like saying to a torturer, 'Don't go near my belly button, it makes me feel really weird when someone touches it. *Definitely* not with anything sharp.' Not a good move.

Although, this once I think I could get away with it. Mark's not in a listening mood. He's calling from the ensuite in his attic so Karen can't hear him. He wants to discuss what he's already calling his 'upcoming divorce'.

'How is it though? Really?' he asks. 'Being divorced?'

'Awful. It's totally awful.'

'No – but, *really*? Karen can't hear. We've got a whole floor between us.'

'Mark, I know you're having a shit time, but look at what I'm going through. I do nothing but look after the kids and work.'

'Yeah, but that just means you shouldn't have pushed for custody. And I've only got one kid. I reckon I'd be fine just seeing her at weekends.'

'You wouldn't be. Look – getting divorced just makes everything worse.'

'But you met Amanda. She's better than Sally.'

'Not better per *se*,' I say, trying to be political. 'I like her more now. But I thought Sally was great when I married her.'

'Nah, Amanda's better.' For fuck's sake.

'Mark – you've got Karen – she's already amazing,' I say, before swerving in an attempt to appeal to his baser instincts. 'Do you not think *she's* better than Sally?'

'Oh, she's better than Sally, sure. But that just means I could get someone better than Amanda afterwards. Sorry to break it to you Tom, but I'm more attractive than you.' Visions of the day's previous activities put me in a position where I don't feel I can argue…

'Trust me,' I reply, 'you've forgotten what it's like to be single. I mean, when was the last time Karen asked you to send a sexy photo?' I regret letting it slip as soon as it's out. Mark doesn't even seem to notice.

'Karen used to send me sexy photos…' he reminisces. 'I'd be sitting at my desk, and suddenly some boobs would appear on my phone. I miss that. She doesn't send me pictures of her boobs anymore…'

'She's homeschooling, Mark. You can't whop 'em out when you're teaching a six-year-old diphthongs. You're going crazy. This is just lockdown talking.'

'I dunno…'

'Come on, Mark: you're not going to leave your wife.'

He doesn't answer for a few seconds and when he does he seems to have lost all his momentum. 'No, I'm not…' he replies, sounding as if somewhere deep within, he's just profoundly tired. 'I'm just worried she's going to leave me…'

'That's ridiculous – she really loves you.'

'I'm not sure she does. She's always shouting at me, Tom, getting angry. All I ever seem to do is annoy her. For a while I was worried she was having an affair.'

'Affair? She's not having an affair. For one thing it would be breaking every rule of lockdown, and she's very conscientious.'

He sighs. 'I think I'm going to go to bed now. Maybe I'll sleep up here. Give her a bit of space. Talk soon, yeah?'

'Yeah, talk soon.'

He hangs up, and I sit there on my sofa actually feeling a bit worried for the two of them. They're my two best friends; it'd be awful if they broke up.

But I guess lockdown is driving us all a bit insane…

Saturday 11th April

There are certain things you shouldn't do in the street: peeing, nakedness, rehearsing a best man's speech (believe me, I've tried it)… Well, turns out there's a new one to add to the list: exercise.

I'm lying in bed, trying to get another hour's sleep, when I hear the doorbell ring. I head to the front window, thinking it's a parcel I'd forgotten I'd ordered; my intention being to wave the Amazon person away, all relaxed and cool, before running down in my pants desperate to tear open whatever junk I ordered in a fit of depression at two in the morning a couple of days ago. After spraying the box with Dettol of course. I'm not an animal.

But instead of the Amazon delivery driver, I'm confronted by Lizzy from number fifty-nine.

'Hey, Tom. Just letting you know we're doing a street workout if you want to join?'

If I want to join? *No, I do not want to join.* The last few days have reminded me how much I hate exercise. And, now I've been confronted with the possibility, I've come to realise that what I would hate even more than working out is working out in the street. However, Lizzy seems to interpret my expression of abject horror as a question concerning what form the upcoming routine will take.

'I'll be leading the first few numbers, and then Katherine from fifty-seven will be leading the next. She's a dancer.' *No, I'm pretty sure she's a management consultant.* I keep it to myself. Besides, if she wants to identify as a dancer, who am I to judge?

'So are you in or out?' *Out, most definitely out.* But before I can answer, she attaches a small addendum. 'You look like you need it.' For the first time since I opened the window, a gentle breeze reminds me I'm only wearing my pyjama trousers. She's getting the top half of 'erotic photo – the live experience', and her response is telling.

'I just mean because you look a bit sleepy,' she blurts out, having recognised the neighbourly faux-pas she's committed. But the words have been said, and are echoing round my head like a pinball machine that's gone for the theme of fat-shaming. Is this what naturally comes out of people's mouths when I have my top off? The response I'm going to be getting to the photo I send Amanda? *Did you not do the street workout, babe? You look like you could have used it.*

'Cool. I'll be down in five.'

I put the kids in front of the TV to watch Netflix (well, walk past the kids who are in front of the TV already watching Netflix and don't tell them to stop), and go to my bedroom to dig out the workout gear I bought for last year's Spartacus Race.

Eight minutes later, I'm standing in the front of our building looking up and down the empty street. Lizzy comes out of her front door and gives me a wave. She's holding a little speaker. Part of me dies a bit more.

'What time are we starting?' I ask.

'Now,' Lizzy replies.

'Aren't we going to wait for people?'

'No, no one was in the mood. Street full of grumpy guts we've got here. Apart from Annie of course – she's a nurse.'

'Yeah, I know.'

'Can't blame her for having a lie in!'

God, sometimes I wish I'd got a job with the NHS.

As Lizzy puts the speaker down on the edge of the pavement, it starts to dawn on me that I'm going to be doing this completely alone. Well, Lizzy will be here telling me what to do, like I'm paying her or something, but that just makes it worse. It'll look like I've decided to engage a personal trainer but couldn't afford a proper one.

'Right,' she begins, getting her phone out. 'How about some Abba to start with?' *Please no.* 'And remember to stay a few metres away. We're doing a responsible socially-distanced workout.' It's Abba. I'd rather be doing this a few streets away. I was socially distancing from Abba way ahead of the curve.

'Could we not do some other music?'

'Trust me – this is a crowd pleaser.'

I don't want to have to point out why that might not be relevant here. Not only is 'pleaser' part of the phrase, but I have a nagging feeling there's something else she's overlooking. Maybe she should be playing to her very exclusive audience here. I don't want to be selfish, but how about a me-pleaser?

Lizzy presses play, and *Dancing Queen* starts pumping out into the air. I literally can't think of a less masculine song. At least if she'd gone for *Gimme! Gimme! Gimme!* I could have sung along with the 'man after midnight' bit and pretended to be a straight-acting gay guy, but this really doesn't let up. Lizzy turns her back to me and starts to move, calling out instructions. The turning-her-back thing just seems rude. I hope she wouldn't do this if we ever grabbed a coffee together.

'OK, step to the right, one, two… to the left… one, two…'

I follow in as half-hearted a fashion as I can get away with. Which is very much around eighth-hearted given that she's facing in the other direction. She seems to be far less self-conscious than I am about doing low-level aerobic activity in the middle of an empty street. Maybe she's hoping it will inspire people. If you build it, they will come. She's built it. They're not coming.

A few more 'bend-over-reach-arounds' (which I can't help getting a *Full Metal Jacket* vibe from) later, and she's putting on another track. She turns to me and flashes me a smile.

'You feeling good?'

'Yeah!' I reply. 'In fact I think I've probably done enough.'

'What are you talking about?!?' she laughs. 'We've done three minutes! You're not going to shift that… sleepiness… with three minutes.' *Bad attempt to cover. Very poor attempt indeed.*

We start again, this time to *Macarena*. A song that I hate significantly less that *Dancing Queen* when it comes on in a nightclub. But not in a street apparently. I really need to get back inside – this is like Joe Wicks without the dignity. And yesterday I was doing his thing as a vampire pirate.

Halfway through the new track, I hear a door down the road opening. I don't even bother to look over, thinking it's bound to be someone going to the shops, keeping their head down like they haven't seen us – but no, it's another exerciser! We've got another idiot willing to join in! That's great! That definitely dilutes my contribution.

It only takes me a few of his perky little steps to realise that the aforementioned idiot is Lizzy's husband, Carl. He's a complete tool. He's wearing a headband like he thinks he's in a Wes Anderson movie, but the rest of the outfit (along with his spherical noggin) puts him firmly into 1980s *It's a Knockout* territory. At least he's coming over. When he's performing this ridiculous spectacle standing next to me, I won't look quite such a tit.

Except he doesn't stand next to me. He stands next to Lizzy.

And starts jigging up and down alongside her, also with his back to me. What's happening? I'm in a class with more teachers than students. It's like a couple were doing something together, and I tried to join in because I liked looking at their bottoms. This is awful.

'Think you can give me a little bit more?' Lizzy says, turning.

'No,' I reply. 'I'm really out of breath.'

'You're not,' says Lizzy, seeing through my put-on panting.

'You're not in the slightest,' says Carl in a ridiculous sing-song-y voice that sounds like a baritone slide whistle.

And they're right. I'm not in the slightest. I've clearly just been standing there. If anyone's been watching, it really will have looked like I've been staring at their bottoms.

Two tracks later, and I've managed to warm up a bit (figuring I should at least try to get something out of this if I'm going to be embarrassing myself so profoundly), when Katherine from number fifty-seven turns up. As everyone is very well aware – she's a dancer. But on the offchance that someone *didn't* know, she's decided to wear a Pineapple Dance Studio hoodie cropped above the navel along with leggings.

She takes her place at the front, and I assume the others are going to finally fall in with me, but no. They just stand there as well, all three of them doing it in a line, with me behind them like a moody child in the back seat. Katherine's actually in really great shape, so, it is actually tempting to look at her bottom. In an effort to avoid it, I decide to focus my attention on Carl. His bottom is horrible, but at least I won't end up the street pariah for objectifying our local dancer. Instead, I'll be the pervert with a fetish for the rear ends of disgusting men, but that's probably better.

Thirty minutes later, the ordeal is almost over. I don't know if it will have helped my fitness more than doing the same thing with the kids, but, if it turns out you can burn calories through embarrassment, I'll have dropped a size.

'One final song,' says Katherine, a dancer. 'I took everyone through this routine at an awayday for my firm – I'm a management consultant, you know.' What? *Not* a dancer? Mind… blown… 'It's *Dancing Queen*!'

'Didn't we already do that one?'

'Oh did you? Well, never can have enough *Dancing Queen*!'

And so I find myself in the middle of my street at 10:00 am on a Saturday morning, standing alone behind a row of three people I barely know, dancing to Abba's *Dancing Queen* for a second time. It's not something I'd ever really envisaged happening.

That's when I hear the engine of a truck turning down our street. I breathe a sigh of relief. Thank God. Thank God it's over. Oncoming traffic equals crowd dispersal. This dancing queen's days are numbered.

Except they're not. Carl breaks formation and heads into the centre of the street putting out his hand to halt the vehicle. For God's sake, you can't do that! It's an Ocado van! You're stopping someone from eating in the middle of a pandemic so we can finish our embarrassing dance routine? I can't believe I'm associated with these people.

'Carl, I think we should stop, and let it past,' I say approaching the front line.

'Maintain social distance!' he replies, rather too forcefully.

I look over at the van driver to apologise, but she doesn't seem annoyed. No, she's laughing. And not a 'why has that poor man been led astray by these three nob-ends?' laugh, more an 'isn't-this-fun?' laugh. What is this lockdown doing to people?!?!? I'd heard Covid removed your sense of taste, but this is ridiculous.

The cab door opens, and the driver gets out, so she can admire us without a windscreen to obscure her view. And I think that's the end of it. But it's not. A few seconds late, she joins in – tagging on at the end of the front row so I'm still bloody behind them. Alone. I go back to the routine in an attempt to keep a semblance of dignity, but it's no good. I feel like such an idiot.

They finish and everyone starts laughing. What a great time they're having. Everyone apart from me. The hilarity subsides and they head back to their respective homes, while the driver makes her way back into her cab. As she passes me, she looks over like she's noticed me for the first time.

'What were you doing back there?' she asks. 'You should have joined in. It looked weird.'

'Yeah,' I reply, lacking the energy to come up with a decent response.

And then I'm pretty sure she mutters the word 'pervert'.

Sunday 12th April – Easter Sunday

Coronavirus is completely rewiring my brain. Last night I was watching TV and every time I saw two characters interacting, I'd go into a panic about how they weren't social distancing properly. Well, today is Easter Sunday, and I can't shake the feeling that even if Jesus did rise from the dead, he should have stayed in his cave, and only left once a day rather than flaunting it about in front of 500 people. Sure, resurrection is important, but what about flattening the curve?

But I'm feeling good. At least I'm with the kids. If Sally hadn't got trapped abroad, she'd have them right now. As she will for every Easter, Christmas and summer going forward. So in a way I'm lucky. We may be doing our Easter egg hunt inside today, but at least I'm there with them. And, as this is probably the last time we'll ever do this together, I need to make it count.

Anyway, my plan for 'making it count' has been to buy an absolute clusterfuck of chocolate. I started nibbling at the eggs I bought them the other day, and thanks to the pleasures of homeworking, they were gone by the afternoon; so, fuelled by guilt, I went a little overboard when it came to replacing them. The supermarket had two giant-sized eggs which I'm giving the kids as their main ones, which means the full-sized eggs I'd *normally* buy are getting treated like *little* eggs – four each, and the little ones as... well, those I ate. Any more chocolate wouldn't be good for them.

After waking up, they're begging for the hunt to start faster than you can say 'diabetic coma', but the responsible adult in me realises I've got to start the day on a more even keel. With a nutritious breakfast.

'Why can't we just do it now?' Carrie whines.

'Because breakfast is the most important meal of the day.'

'Only because breakfast is the first thing you eat, so you can't *not* have breakfast,' says Arthur.

'Well, why can't we have chocolate for breakfast?'

'Because I need you to eat something sensible first.'

'But what if we don't have *room* for the chocolate after?' Carrie asks.

'Then you can save it for later,' I explain. Carrie looks at me with the kind of expression normally reserved for people in the process of strangling a baby bird. 'You're not going to be able to eat all of it anyway,' I continue. 'The Easter Bunny has been very generous this year!' As generous as a recently divorced parent trying to buy their children's love.

'Well, I'm not going to eat any breakfast,' Carrie protests.

'Then you won't get any eggs.'

'That's not up to you, it's the Easter Bunny that brings them.'

'There's not really an Easter Bunny,' Arthur explains. 'Daddy just buys chocolate and hides it.' Carrie looks upset.

'You were *with* me, Carrie. You literally saw me pay for it. The Easter Bunny is just a fun thing that's not real like...' *don't say Santa...* 'like...' *don't say the tooth fairy...* 'like... the deities of ancient Egypt.' Congratulations, you have managed to find a solution that doesn't take away their belief in magic, or discriminate against any current world religions. 'Yeah, he's kind of like Thoth. Ra, maybe. Technically Unut would be better, but that's kind of a deep cut.'

'I don't know what you're talking about,' Carrie replies. Clearly she hasn't done Egypt yet at nursery – I'm surprised how much that useless pantheon of knowledge seems to have stuck with me.

'Look – just *pretend* to eat breakfast,' Arthur tells her. 'That way he won't know.'

'I don't know if you know the phrase "I'm right here"?' I ask, 'but, I am. Watching on like the all-seeing Eye of Horus.' *Anything?* No. Nothing.

Breakfast is like the world's worst theatre production. We did an ad for a cereal brand just after Christmas, and I was more convinced at the auditions when the actors pretended to eat than this. And they were literally miming with air.

'Carrie, I can tell you're not eating anything. Eat your Rice Krispies. You like Rice Krispies.'

'I am eating them.'

I sigh, then go to the kitchen cupboard to pull out the weighing scales.

'Carrie – what I'm going to do now is weigh your bowl with the cereal in. That way, if you don't eat anything I'll know.' I put the bowl on the scales and take a reading.

'Why aren't you weighing Arthur's?'

'Fine. I'll weigh Arthur's too.'

'That's not fair,' Arthur objects.

'What do you think fair means?!? That's literally the definition.'

I put his bowl on the scales as well, then go and make myself some toast – trusting that the gaze of objective measurement will be more or a deterrent than that of my eyes, while at the same time keeping a close watch on the bin.

I sit at the counter, eating my toast, looking through my phone, pretending I've forgotten what they're trying to do. I see Carrie crush a few Rice Pops with her spoon.

'You do know they contain air, Carrie?'

'Do they?'

'Yeah, air doesn't weigh anything.'

'Then why doesn't it float off?'

'Even if it did it wouldn't matter, because it doesn't *weigh* anything. That's what I'm trying to say.'

'Look! I'm eating them! You said you wouldn't watch me! Why are you still watching me?!?' *I dunno? Because everything you do is an attempt to deceive me?*

'Sorry. Go ahead,' I reply. I really have no authority over these children.

Five minutes later, I return to the table, feigning surprise that I've recalled the weighing plan, acting like I've bumped into a long lost friend who I'd forgotten I was sponsoring on a twelve-step programme for weight-loss.

'Oh! I've just remembered! We need to check your bowls!' Carrie looks up concerned. 'Time for the weigh in! Isn't this fun? It's like a boxing match! If your cereal bowl weighs too much, you won't be allowed to fight.' Her expression shifts to confusion.

'Is this to do with the eye of Whorey?' Not quite, but both are members of the category 'things that shouldn't be talked about to under tens'.

'No, love – come on, let's weigh the bowl.'

I weigh it. It's lighter, thank God. Also, I was kind of expecting it, as it's virtually empty. But still, it's good for them to know about the idea of 'objective facts'. Science and all that.

'Good girl, Carrie. You're definitely getting chocolate. Both of you wait in here, I'll set up the hunt,' I say smiling, and, to be honest, I'm bloody relieved that my attempts to purchase my children's affection have not been shut down by non-compliance.

'Wait a minute – you said you'd do Arthur's,' Carrie interrupts.

'No, you idiot,' Arthur spits back.

'Arthur! Don't call your sister an idiot! That's terrible behaviour. It's only fair that I do yours too,' I say, giving him a wink.

Arthur hesitantly hands me his bowl. I can tell by his expression, he hasn't eaten a thing. There I was thinking, I can trust my eldest. He won't try to deceive me.

It saddens me, as I put it on the scale, knowing that it will weigh exactly what it weighed five minutes ago. Oh, Arthur, what hope do you have for the future if you don't understand the rigor of experimental methodology?

But it doesn't weigh the same.

It weighs far more. Almost, I'd guess, if I were to do the calculations (which I do actually do, subconscious accountant-brain kicking in with full force), *exactly* the same amount as Carrie's does less.

I look at them both, utterly disappointed. I have to agree with Arthur – Carrie was being a complete muppet. When we get back to home schooling, I really need to show her some basic maths.

It's over. They failed. Easter is over. But, as I stand there, looking down on the two children who have just deceived me, I realise that this teaching moment will soon be lost forever; yet the Easter Sunday morning that follows (the last one they will ever spend with me), will be always mired in our collective memory with sadness, disappointment, and a distinct lack of chocolate. And I know I have to make a decision.

I can tell the truth and wreck what could be a really special day. Or lie and completely undermine the idea of the scientific method.

I really have no choice to make.

'It weighs less!'

They both cheer; running into the living room to go and find the eggs I haven't yet hidden. But what does it matter? Carrie still thinks there's a giant rabbit that has duplicated the exact contents of my shopping basket from three days ago. And they're happy.

Far more so than they'll be when they've consumed 3kg of chocolate (in about half an hour's time). But what do I know? It might be less than a hundred grams. After all, weight isn't real.

Monday 13th April

I was feeling pretty confident that the workouts were going to do some good. No matter how embarrassing/ridiculous/annoying they were, at least I was doing them, taking them seriously. But, following on from yesterday's chocolate binge (turns out when you buy kids an industrial amount of chocolate, they're more willing to share), I'm beginning to lose hope.

It's becoming clear that no matter how much I exercise, it's not going to do what I need it to. Besides, if there's a theme to this lockdown for me, it's unnecessary eating. If I need a work boost – I eat; when I need a childcare boost – I eat; if I want to take a break – I eat. The only time I'm eating less than before is when we have meals. To be honest, a lot of the time, I'm a bit full.

So I'm going to have to find another way to take a sexy photo. I'm a creative. I just have to *be* creative.

I sit at my desk and try to think it through. How would I approach this if it were an ad campaign? Well, first I'd survey the market. Should I text Amanda? Something like, 'What do you think the sexiest thing about me is?' Immediately, I start stressing about how she'd reply. It would definitely be something non-physical, and that's not going to help in a photo. I'd get something back like 'your laugh', and feel forced to send back the same unattractive topless photo, only with a loop of me giggling over the top of it. God, that is NOT a good idea. I can picture how maniacal it'd sound; like a bunch of demons have intercepted it and made the diabolical equivalent of a reaction video.

I need to think about what women like in *general.* I understand that not all women are the same, but maybe this could work as a springboard… I sit there thinking for a few minutes, increasingly perturbed by how blank my mind is… How can I not have an answer to this? All that's coming to mind are the Athena posters my friend's sister used to have when I was a kid. I literally don't know how I can have to go that far back to think about what women like. I was married to one for over a decade. Might be one of the reasons that didn't work out…

But maybe the Athena posters are a good start. They were everywhere back in the day – that image of the man holding the baby must be locked in everyone's subconscious who was even vaguely alive in the 80s – perhaps that's something I can key into. I look up 'Athena posters' online to see if any of them have poses I can work with. There's the classic 'Guy holding tyres'. Is that doable? Do women still like men who hold tyres? I'm not quite sure what the appeal of holding tyres was in the first place, but it definitely made that photographer a few mill… Annoyingly the man's completely topless, which I definitely couldn't pull off, but maybe if the tyres were distracting enough… Would Mark let me borrow the spare wheel from the back of his jeep? Actually, I'm not sure I could lift it… I think they have the inner bit in too. The idea of getting one of the tyres from the kids' bikes flits across my mind, but I think the scaling might just make me look even fatter in comparison. I click on the 'Man holding baby' poster as an alternative.

This one definitely seems better. The guy's arm, along with the baby, are completely blocking his stomach. That's gold. I should probably cradle something, especially as I have a bit of left tricep. Hey! Maybe that's my good part!?! Those few sessions in the swimming pool before this all kicked off might give the impression that I'm in shape! But what do I cradle? There's no chance of getting a baby, even temporarily. People aren't that willing to loan out their kids at the best of times, and I don't feel a, 'No, you don't understand – I'm trying to use him for a sexy photo,' will justify the lack of social distancing. I suppose I do have Arthur and Carrie, but I don't think asking one of them to nestle (also topless) in my arms will have the desired effect of 'caring father'. More 'perverted kidnapper on a hot day'.

How else could I block my stomach…? Maybe I could be carrying a box or something? Or *flowers*… Yes! That would be good! These are for you! If I had a garden this would be genius. Unfortunately, it'd involve an extra trip to the shop, and it doesn't feel like a good enough reason to catch coronavirus. Especially as they'd probably be out of everything apart from the things old people like and I'd be left with an armful of leathery hydrangea foliage. God! What am I doing? If I'm that ashamed, I should just bloody turn my back to the camera and be done with it!

Actually… that might work.

Slowly, the idea begins to coalesce. I'm pretty sure my back's all right, *and* I could show a little bit of tricep too. Thoughts are flooding into my head – I could even write a little sexy message on my shoulder! 'Can't wait to feel your hands on me!' No, too far. I feel a bit sick just thinking about it. But I try to stay positive. I can even remember Sally telling me once: 'You have such a sexy back!' How could I forget that? Yeah – I'm all about the back. It was staring me in the face. Well, technically in completely the opposite direction – but *figuratively* speaking… *That's* my sexiest feature. As Sir Mix-a-lot once said – baby got back. Actually I'm pretty sure that wasn't about backs at all, but he wasn't a 'sir' either, so you can't take anything he said at face value.

I set up the camera across the room, feeling super positive about this, and change into some jeans for that 'Athena touch'. I put on the tighter ones that I bought for the office, and… oo, they're snug. That tight waistline is doing nothing for the front of my body – my 'abs' bunch up above it like Carrie trying to grab a full water balloon – but when I turn and look at the mirror behind me, it's gone. Back fat: zero. Baby got back! Baby got back!

I put the camera onto timer mode, and press the button, running across the room into position, turning my head toward the camera in a cheeky grin. I dart back to check the photo. Timed it wrong – I'm just looking away. It looks like the kind of thing Carrie would take if I left my phone unlocked. Right, need to try again. This time I get my head round in time, but just look like I've been surprised.

I think I need to go for the ten second setting. I find if I countdown along with it, I can turn my head at the last moment for a more natural look, but every single one of the shots is awful. I am not sexy. I am not sexy at all. But my back doesn't look too bad. That's something isn't it? Maybe she'll be so turned on by my sensual trapezius that she won't even notice how disgusting the rest of me is. After another ten attempts, I manage to create a single one that's vaguely OK and I decide to stick with it, a realisation that the genre of 'Tom's sexy back photos' has already reached it's low-lying zenith growing within me. It's not going to get any better; this'll have to do. Gritting my teeth, I attach it to an email and press 'send'.

Done. It's not good, but at least the ordeal is over.

I change back into comfortable clothes, feeling a shame reminiscent of the sensation I had after my only one-night stand, questioning myself over and over about why I'd done it; what I'd been thinking. This time I wasn't even drunk.

I sit down with my laptop – the kids are on the TV again – thinking I'll watch something to distract myself. And that's when I do something even more stupid. I check my sent mail to see if it's sent all right.

What I am faced with is the email that I just pinged over to Amanda. Only the picture is now taking up a full sized monitor rather than a small phone screen, and something that wasn't previously apparent becomes clear. I have a hairy back.

It's truly disgusting.

I just sent through a picture of myself peeking coquettishly over a shoulder covered in straggly hairs. No one would find that erotic. These days no matter how weird you are, there's a whole community of people online who share your fetish – whether it's feet, cosplay, people with lopsided ears. There is no community for this. Not a single solitary person in the world begging their partner in a desperate whisper: 'Please, no, don't shave your shoulder.'

Hopefully, she'll open it on her phone – it looked OK small, but what if she doesn't? She's just as likely to be on her laptop when it comes through. God! Why did I send an email anyway?!? Why didn't I just message her? Well, because MMS are not included in my data plan and I'm stingy, but that's beside the point.

I run over to my phone and send Amanda a message that simply reads: 'DON'T OPEN THE PHOTO!' Then I send the exact same thing in an email. Hell, if I thought it would help, I'd send a video of me screaming it. What's 55p at a time like this? Thinking about it, that really is a lot…

I get a message back about a minute later.

'Why not? x.'

I start typing. 'Because something went wrong and…' I don't even know what to say. The only thing I can think of is the truth, and that could make things even worse, like one of those monsters that you never quite see, but your imagination makes even scarier. That said, this might be the erotic photo equivalent of that girl in *The Ring*, where the reality far exceeds anything you might imagine, a classic of horror. But before I can compose anything that sounds even partially rational, my phone vibrates.

'I liked it x.'

My heart starts beating again.

She opened it on her phone. Thank God. Well, either that or I'm going out with the equivalent of one of those weird lopsided-ears people. But then she sends something back, and I get distracted again. The same pose I sent her, only a hundred times better. Wow. Maybe I need to start wearing a bra on a day to day basis so that when I take it off for something like this it seems more transgressive.

'I can't wait to see you again x,' I text.

'Me too x,' she replies.

'Oh, and if you care about me even just a little bit, can you promise not to open that on a big screen? Please don't ask why.'

'Ha ha. OK, promise x,' comes back.

Then twenty seconds later: 'Oh my God\. Just opened the one I sent you on my computer. You have to promise me the same, otherwise I'm opening yours NOW.'

I'm tempted to look, I really am – I'm sure she's just saying that to make me feel better – but I don't. I don't even pinch-zoom into it on my phone.

'You have my word x.'

I breathe a sigh of relief. It there's one thing I've learnt, after a failed marriage and four months of vaguely keeping this thing together, it's this: relationships are about adaptation. They're about listening to other people's needs, and accepting them, no questions asked. They're about *trust.*

Oh, and looking at smaller versions of erotic photos.

Tuesday 14th April

My soft porn career behind me, I feel a new sense of freedom. It's like I'm in a new reality. A reality where I can be anyone, any*thing*. I'm no longer just a sub-standard body. I am a *person.* I may be trapped in my home (along with every other person in the country), but the real prison we're all trapped in is in our *minds*.

The feeling lasts all of five minutes. That's when I start work, my kids screaming in the other room, with the knowledge that I can't leave the flat on my own to clear my head for the next two or three months, and realise: the prison is definitely not just in my mind.

What I'm actually doing makes things even worse. I've got to start working on a Father's Day campaign. It's two and a half months away, but that's the timescale we work on. Roll on September when I can get that Christmas-y vibe again. It won't last till Christmas though. Then, I'll just be depressed that I probably won't get any Valentines cards.

I jot down a few 'magical father moments' (none of which I've ever actually experienced), before hopping on a Zoom call with Larousse.

'How's the coffee machine, Big Man?' he asks, as he comes online. He seems to think this is the kind of thing that passes for a greeting these days.

'Good, thanks. Not a thousand pounds-good, but better than what I'd be drinking otherwise.'

'Ha, ha, ha, ha. I'm hearing ya, I'm hearing ya,' he replies, not actually listening. 'Sorry – give me a sec, Amanda's coming in.'

Larousse's eyes scan to the side of his monitor, as he tries to work out how to admit Amanda to the meeting. All credit to him, it's not as easy as just opening your front door. Especially when you pay someone to do that for you.

Seeing my girlfriend's face appear on the screen picks me up a little, even if it is for a work call. She's just got such good energy that I think I'd be stoked if she was just my boss. It reminds me how lucky I am that she's not.

'Morning,' she says to both of us, in a tone that suggests we have no contact outside of work, before turning her back to the camera and winking as Larousse looks away to talk to his nanny. It's pretty cool. Like we're conducting an illicit affair. Not like my ex-wife's one. Like one of the nice ones where you're forbidden from being together because of a family feud, yet your love overcomes societal boundaries and you both end up dead. Maybe not the last bit.

'So, who's got any ideas for this Father's Day thing?' she asks.

'Actually – may have to take a rain check on that one for a little while…' Larousse interrupts. 'We probably need to talk sofas.'

'OK…' Amanda replies. 'I thought that was being signed off?'

'Not quite…'

'OK… So where do we stand?'

'Don't stand on the sofa!' Larousse shouts, in what seems like the greatest over-reaction to a turn of phrase ever, until we realise he's shouting at one of his kids. 'Hualing – you're meant to stop them doing that!'

'Who's Hualing?' Amanda asks, like she hasn't got a pretty damned good idea. Larousse seems to buy it – as if we live in a world where I wouldn't have texted Amanda to tell her he has a live-in nanny the moment I found out.

'Er… my wife. Obviously.'

'I though your wife was called Katherine?' I ask, faux-innocent.

'Yeah – she is, it's a little pet-name.'

'Hualing?' I ask, curious. 'How does it relate to Katherine?'

'Hual*ing*… Kath*erine*,' he says, desperately trying to force them into a rhyme. 'But look,' he continues, clearly glad to have a reason to change the subject, 'we're in a bit of trouble. The sofa peeps have changed their minds. They don't want to do the celebrity thing anymore.'

The Zoom call takes a moment's silence. Eventually, Amanda speaks.

'Erm, you need to convince them that they do.'

'I tried. They've made up their minds already.'

'Fuck,' says Amanda. 'We've spent weeks on it! Look – I should talk to them, see if I can convince them.'

'They're not budging. They don't want to rebrand any of their lines. Apparently, they've got 25,000 copies of their catalogue printed and don't want to chuck them.'

'Surely that costs a lot less than the ad?' I ask. Not to mention the fact there's still a massive shortage of loo roll. Those catalogues could go for a pretty penny.

'I tried everything,' says Larousse. 'But… you know, they're morons.'

'Probably best not to be calling our clients that,' Amanda replies.

'Oh, I haven't finished yet,' Larousse explains. 'Luckily, they've come up with their *own* idea for an ad, which they want us to "finesse" a little – their words. They want to go with a twist on the exact same ad they used ten years ago.'

'All right…' replies Amanda, tentatively. 'And what's that?'

'Strap yourselves in: people sitting down on a sofa and saying "ahhh".'

Silence returns to the call. After everything we've generated for them, this is what they want to go with? Some sub-DFS *nothing*? It's crazy. Eventually Amanda breaks the deadlock.

'OK, they're morons.'

'Have they not thought about how we're going to film it?' I ask. 'Surely we can't even shoot that?'

'Apparently, they have. Their boss knows someone at one of the big supermarkets, and they're filming their Father's Day commercials by delivering the equipment to actors' houses and getting them to film it themselves. They want us to do the same.'

'Is that real?' I ask.

'It is,' says Amanda. 'I've heard about it too.'

'So… what?' I ask, trying to make sense of everything, 'We find some actors – ship over some camera equipment and a sofa, then they film themselves sitting on it on it, and saying "ah".'

'Yeah.'

'How do they expect us to… "finesse" it?'

'Don't shoot the messenger,' Larousse replies. He raises his hands in surrender, before breaking off again to shout something across the kitchen. 'Hualing – do *not* let them break that vase. If they do, it's coming directly out of your wages.' He and his wife have a really strange relationship.

'But what are they thinking *we'll* do?' I ask. 'Change the "ah" to an "oo"?'

Larousse looks as confused as I am, but luckily calm rationality finds its way into the conversation by way of Amanda.

'Look – they just don't know how to make it into an ad. Agreed: they're morons, but I don't think we've got a choice here. We've given them our ideas and they've said no. I guess it's our job to storyboard, get the production company in, and try and come up with a good slogan.'

As much as seeing my work go up in smoke makes me want to disagree, she's right. They're the ones paying us – we can try and guide them, but when it comes down to it, we've got to give them what they want. So… slogans…

Larousse is the first to offer something up. 'How about something to do with lockdown? Like… "Sitting down not locked down", or "Putting the sit into lockdown"?' *Lock* sit *down? Yeah, Larousse, people are always saying that.*

'I'm not sure,' says Amanda, being far more political than I ever could be. 'Good springboard though.'

We all try to think of ways to adapt it, but it appears the springboard has been set up in front of a brick wall. Like a misguided attempt to make the gymnastics event at the Olympics more entertaining.

We sit in front of our screens with our pads of paper, jotting down ideas, not interacting, just being in each other's presence. It reminds me of one of the online play dates Carrie's had recently. Eventually, I have a brainstorm. I actually I might have something.

'What about – "that *ah* moment"? It gives them what they want, plus hopefully the play on "aha moment" will mean it sticks in people's minds.' I pause for a second trying to work out if people think I've just done a Larousse. Their silence makes me stumble onwards, 'The downside is it'll probably spark a thousand internet memes about people taking a poo, but…'

Amanda laughs. 'It probably will – but I think it's good. Larousse?'

I can see the conflict inside him – part of him wanting to agree with the boss, the other half not wanting to support any idea that I came up with, 'Errr… yeah, errr good… they'll probably like it.

Go "Team Us"! Think that springboarding led to something good. Nice one.' *Hmmm… not sure it did. Unless that 'ah' moment, was the sound of someone crashing into vertical concrete.* 'I do have concerns about the loo thing though – maybe bad associations for the brand.'

'We'll just tell them that's good,' Amanda replies. 'It probably is. There's not a single person on the board at that company under 50 anyway – they have about as much in common with the youth as I have with…' She pauses, taking a sip of water while she tries to find a suitable end for her sentence.

'Someone who has a live-in nanny during lockdown?' I suggest.

Larousse stares daggers at me, and Amanda sprays water all over her screen, attempting to cover it up as a coughing fit.

'Anyway – think we're done for today… ahem, ahem…' she splutters. 'Great work everyone. Larousse – can you call them and tell them we think it's great. Tom – call up Sophie from art and try to get a storyboard together. We're going to have to turn this round really quickly.'

'Will do,' says Larousse 'Talk later.'

I wait for him to leave the meeting so I can have a quick chat with Amanda, but he just stays there, waiting, in a moment somewhere between a Wild West gunfight, and two teenagers saying, 'No, you hang up.'

Eventually, Amanda leaves, and it's just me and Larousse.

When I do hang up, it really does feel like an 'ah' moment.

Wednesday 15th April

Finally, a successful trip to the shops. Soap, hand sanitiser, toilet roll, eggs. If I wanted to I could make an omelette with a filling of basic sanitary products. Things are finally getting better. I got pretty much everything I needed. Except peas. You never seem to be able to get peas. Maybe petit pois are the new loo roll…

But things are going well: the storyboard's coming together, the sun is shining, the kids even seem to like me. And I'm sure it has nothing to do with me buying them an extra Easter egg each. Sure, they were reduced, but the chocolate's probably good till Christmas. It's not like the *shape* has a sell-by date. I don't even know why they take the price down… Thinking about it, Easter eggs probably aren't the best use of shelf space. There's a reason they don't package mince in between two consecutive layers of plastic, with a massive hole in the middle. But if anything, I'm helping out by taking the eggs off their hands. Clearing space for essentials in a time of crisis. Now my body's no longer a temple, buying an extra one for myself seems like the moral thing to do.

An aura of positivity seems to surround the whole day. The kids don't argue (even after their mouths no longer contain chocolate), they play together nicely, they do craft, they eat their food without throwing anything, they seem understanding every time I disappear to do some work. And on a more extreme level: they even seem *grateful*. It's like they've been Midwich-Cuckooed. And the small possibility of an upcoming alien takeover is not going to stop me enjoying it. They even try to express their appreciation through the medium of art.

'Daddy, Daddy, we've drawn you a picture together,' shouts Carrie, brandishing a drawing on some A3 paper. *Together? Without arguing?* The act itself is a miracle.

I look down at their collaborative masterpiece.

'Wow, that's fantastic!' I gasp. 'You drew this? You didn't just print it out from the internet?' *Always hit them with affirmations before getting to the real question.* 'What is it?'

'It's *you*, Daddy!' says Carrie.

'That's why we wrote the letters 'Duh Muh' on the body,'

Arthur adds. D.M.? Hmmm… Hope they didn't find evidence of any Dungeon Mastering from my D&D days…

'Me?' I reply. 'Of course it's *me*! I knew that! But what am I *doing*? What does the Duh Muh *stand* for?'

'You're a superhero, silly. It stands for Daddy-Man.'

'Oh cool! And why's there a log hitting me in the neck?'

'That's your cape.'

'Of course it is. I made the same mistake the first time I saw Superman.'

'And we drew you a rainbow behind to say thank you.'

'Like with the NHS,' Arthur explains.

'I think that's just for them, but… Anyway, I *love* it.'

'We thought it was good, because you're like a superhero. You do everything for us, and keep us safe.'

'Thanks Arthur,' I say, feeling genuinely touched by something they've made for me for once, trying to suppress the tears building up in my eyes. Like the massive wuss that I am.

But it makes me feel good for the rest of the day. I *am* like a superhero. Cooking, cleaning, providing. Well, obviously, that wouldn't lead to the greatest Marvel movie ever, but I'm going to take the compliment. It's rare that the kids ever say anything nice to me.

Of course, Mum attempts to undermine it when I show her on Facetime after they've gone to bed.

'You know you did one like that for me?' she says, dismissing it in an instant as just a rite of passage, a 'phase' that kids go through, rather than a genuine show of appreciation. 'Yours was very good. Theirs is good too, but they've gone over the edges with a lot of the colouring.'

I don't know whether to be complimented on the artistic prowess of my youth, or to just interpret it as a diss that if they really cared they would have made a little more effort to stay within the lines.

‘I’ll dig it out for you, if you like,’ she offers.

‘Sure, Mum. That would be good.’

But it doesn’t bother me. I’m bulletproof. Like a superhero. And I go to bed thinking that maybe they’re right, sleeping the sleep of a man who feels like he is fulfilling his role in the world. As protector, provider, and buyer of reduced price chocolate eggs.

Thursday 16th April

The buzz continues into the next day, and by 11:00 am, I’ve got the storyboard completed and signed off on, along with a breakdown for the auditions tomorrow, so I decide to take the kids out for a walk in the park. It’s still sunny, work’s done, what could possibly go wrong?

I could bump into Howard, that’s what.

Howard is one of the dads from Arthur’s school. One of the ones who overbids at every kids’ art auction, just to prove he doesn’t *have* to send his kids to state school, but does so out of principle. He runs a hedge fund, and never seems to work, ever. In many ways he seems quite likeable. But for one thing. He’s Howard. A complete nob. He also goes to the same park as me – out of principle probably. I’m sure he could afford to go to a private park if he wanted to.

‘Tom!’

‘Kids – keep walking,’ I say, trying to usher them forward like blinkered horses. But Howard already has me in his sights.

‘Tom! Over here!’

I have no choice but to go over. It’s annoying – having to avoid people with this whole social-distancing thing has really had its downsides – but now I’m starting to wish they’d up the distance from two metres to ten.

We walk towards Howard, assuming he'll come halfway, but he doesn't. He just stays where he is, bouncing up and down on the spot to keep his heart rate up. Something that I imagine can also be achieved by moving towards the reluctant people you've just called over.

'How you doing?' he starts. 'Isn't this brilliant?' *Talking to someone you don't particularly like? Not the first word I'd have used to describe it.*

'The weather, you mean?' I ask, genuinely confused.

'No – lockdown! Can't quite believe it's happened! So nice to spend all this time with the kids, isn't it?'

I look round his ankles, wondering if his have somehow got particularly good at hiding. Maybe he's been using his new-found free time to help them work on their camouflage skills.

'Oh, *mine*?' he responds, answering the question that my gaze was asking. 'Mine are out with the… wife. Got to take a bit of a break sometimes, haven't you?'

'Well, not if you literally can't.'

'No one literally can't.'

'*I* literally can't.'

'Well, I literally can't either, but you know what I mean.' No, I don't – you're literally taking that break *right now*. And what was with that hesitation before the word 'wife'? I don't want to be overly suspicious, but my spider-sense is tingling. Superhero and all that. 'Plus, of course, there's the online tutoring to be dealing with. Luke's getting ready for the 7+ entrance, so got to be on top of that. Yours doing it? Arthur's year above, isn't he?'

I'm not entirely sure what the 7+ entrance is, but, unless it's going to be a requirement of the kids starting school again when it reopens, I'm pretty sure it's a no. Looks like Howard's days of overbidding in school auctions may be numbered… 'No, they're not.'

'Right, right… Sunshine's great though,' he continues. 'So great to be able to get out and exercise rather than do it in the gym.' Said by someone who clearly hasn't done a work-out in the street with an Ocado driver. 'That – plus time with the kids – it's bloody heaven.'

I look around, hoping for a way out. Where are the police to tell you you-need-to-move-on-as-your-time-out-of-the-house-is-purely-for-exercising when you need them? I really hope that if there is a heaven, they actually make it the same for normals and really rich people. It'd be amazing for most of us, but they'd find it really annoying. And how is he earning anything anyway? I'm pretty sure hedge funds are related to shares which are related to massively crashing markets, but perhaps I've made a mistake. Maybe it's something to do with actual hedges. They seem to be doing OK. If it turns out he's making money from public footpath borders and stopping wandering cattle, suddenly it all makes sense. 'Are you… working?' I ask.

'No – sold the business at the end of last year. Bit of luck really. Put all money into a little company called Zoom, and now… well, let's just say Boom! would be more appropriate.' Agggh. I hate him. I'm going back to Skype. Or sticking exclusively with FaceTime. 'Also, I've got a little invested in Apple and the Skype, in case its retro-charms make a come-back.' Damn it, there's literally no way I can talk to anyone without giving him money. He's like an evil king. I'm not one for conspiracy theories but I'm beginning to worry that he might have created this bloody virus.

'What about you?' he asks. 'You're in advertising aren't you? Must be making you a pretty penny these days, eh?' I literally don't know what the logic to that sentence was. How has this moron somehow made multiple millions? Sally and I were on his team at the school quiz a couple of years ago – he actually didn't know what the capital of Germany was. That's an easy one. Plus he couldn't do basic maths. How can you make a million pounds and not be able to do basic maths?!?

'No. It's literally making me exactly the same as before, but with the added thrill of potentially losing my job.'

'Cool. Of course Sue is setting up her own business now, so that's pretty stressful too.'

'Wow – that's impressive,' I reply, genuinely taken aback. I hadn't realised she did things like that.

'Yeah, they're doing a business hiring out high-end table settings.' He pulls out his phone and shows me a picture of an over-coordinated place setting: a little stack of three plates, a place mat and coaster all in various shades of lavender. As much as these words pain me to even think: my mother would probably cum.

'Um... do people do that? Hire table settings? I suppose for weddings and things?'

'No, not weddings,' he laughs. 'For dinner parties. It's not a caterers! Ha, ha! They're pretty reasonable too. These come out at £60 a head.'

'What? In someone's house?'

'Yeah – you should think about using her next time you have people round.'

OK – first, we need to get through lockdown, then I need to have a dinner party, then I need to find six people who I want to come... but if I arranged all that, why not take out a second mortgage so they have something to eat off?

'I'm sorry – I'm not in the position to buy £60 place settings.'

'Not, buy. *Hire*. And they're not all £60. There's a range – between £50 and a hundred.'

'Are you insane?' I ask, unable to control myself. 'We're about to go into the biggest recession of our lifetimes, and she's set up a business hiring out plates that cost more than the bloody food?' Luckily, he's stopped listening. I can tell because he's started looking over my shoulder, and an expression of panic has come over him. I see his eyes making calculations with the prowess of a solar powered calculator in bad light, before he flicks his eyes back to mine, and attempts to Medusa me with his gaze.

I'm having none of it. It takes more than eye-contact from a man who's missed a haircut for a few weeks to stop me turning around to see what he saw.

'Don't,' he shouts as I start to rotate my head, '…look!'

And I suddenly understand *why* he's been panicking. In the distance is his wife out walking their new dog. Without the children.

As I turn back, my face a question mark, I see him gesturing for her to go away. By the time I look back at her, she's already facing in the other direction, but it's too late. Suddenly, his hesitation before the word 'wife' clicks into place. And I realise what the problem is. He's another bloody nanny-er.

'Where are the kids, Howard?' I ask, not even trying to soften the tone of accusation in my voice.

'I, um, they're, um…'

God, it feels good. Like I've got him on the ropes. 'They're where?'

'At home.'

'They're the same ages as mine though, aren't they?' I say, looking at Carrie and Arthur.

'Tabitha's younger than me!' Carrie spits, mortally offended by the comparison. 'She's a baby. I'm six months older than her.' I suppose when you're under five that *is* a significant proportion of your life.

'A baby, huh? Is she home alone?'

'You know she's not… We've got… a… a, you know, nanny.'

'I knew it!' I shout, almost unable to comprehend that it's happening again. He's another Larousse! Another Covid-skiver!

How many of these people are there?!? 'I can't believe you have a live-in nanny and are pretending you're doing it all by yourself.'

'She's not live-in,' he protests in his defence. But he's just made it worse.

'You're breaking the lockdown?!?' I sputter. At least Larousse has the good manners to lock his house slave in with them in quarantine.

'Shhhh. Keep your voice down,' he says, stepping closer.

'Two metres!' shouts Carrie, and he shoots back to the prescribed distance.

'Please don't tell anyone.' I turn my back on him in absolute disgust, and walk away with the kids.

The revelation colours the rest of our walk. I caught him, but I don't feel good about things. I can't believe that even in this situation people can game the system, buy their way out of hardship as if the rules don't apply to them. I don't know whether I'm one of the good guys, or just a sucker. The fool who waits in the queue for the slip road, while everyone else drives past them on the hard shoulder. Why do we spend our whole lives trying to do the right thing, when all it does is make your life worse?

When we get home, I sit with my phone, my finger hovering over the message box on the parents' WhatsApp group. I should do it, I should name and shame. I go to Howard's and Sue's Instagram – it's filled with pictures of them doing things with the kids, happy family photos with captions like 'homeschooling is hard!' and 'just trying to keep them occupied' while they bake cupcakes. But now I know they're *not* homeschooling – they probably didn't even bake the damn cupcakes. Everybody thinks they're such great parents, but they're rule-breaking liars.

I can feel the resentment building up in me. I want to take them down, to hurt them, to make sure no-one at school ever takes their let-them-eat-cake (on an expensive plate) business even slightly seriously. Maybe I can't make my life better, but I can make theirs worse.

'You look angry, Daddy.'

I look up to see Carrie standing in front of me, framed in the doorway, a look of confusion on her face. I suddenly feel ashamed of myself. Like *I'm* the one that's been caught.

'Daddy's just feeling a bit upset.'

'Why?' she asks.

I hesitate before replying. I know you shouldn't always tell your kids everything, but I want to be emotionally available. I don't want to have the same relationship with them that I had with my father…

'It's just that some people have it so much easier than others and they get away with it. That they don't care about hurting old people, as long as they have it good for themselves.'

'Who has it easier?'

'You know – Howard: having a nanny to help look after Luke and Tabitha.'

Carrie things about it for a second. 'Well, I feel sorry for Luke and Tabitha. I wouldn't want to have to be looked after by a nanny the whole time. It's rubbish that we can't see Mummy for a while, but at least we get to see you.'

And I suddenly realise that I might not be so unlucky after all. That, although my life isn't all Instagrammable moments, and scenes from an ad campaign, I am actually spending time with my children. And it's real. It may have been stressful, it may have been hard, but at least we've been together for all of it – not just posing for a few Instagram photos. Maybe one day that'll mean something. And I can either get resentful and bitter, or just make the best of what I have got, trying to remember, despite it all, how blessed I am.

'Come here, and give me a hug.'

Carrie comes over and wraps her arm around me, giving me a

kiss on the cheek before exiting the living room to go and join Arthur on his iPad.

'I love you, Daddy, try not to be sad.'

'I won't be.'

When she's gone, I close the WhatsApp group, my comment unposted, feeling as if I've been cleansed, purified. There are positives to what I'm going through, even if it is a bit tiring.

I close my eyes for a second and smile, waking up four hours later, when they tell me it's time for dinner. Blessed maybe, but God – this really is tiring.

Friday 17th April

At ten o'clock, the auditions begin.

It's me, Larousse, Sarah (our casting director), and a seemingly endless parade of actors whose job it is to say, 'Ahhhh,' like they've just sat down on something really comfortable.

But I'm starting to get used to all this Zoom stuff. So much so, I don't even bother wearing trousers. If they're only going to see you from the waist up, what's the point? I feel like a newsreader in a comedy sketch from the 80s. It's awesome.

Larousse is setting up the meeting, so he's already on screen when I join.

'Hey, Tommy, ready to judge some people who are more attractive that you? Try not to get a flashback to every nightclub you've ever been to. Ha ha!'

What was that? Was he including himself in that, or just accusing me of being ugly and judgemental…? Not quite sure, but I'm pretty sure both interpretations are pretty offensive.

'Nah, you're not that bad.' Just me. Turns out that interpretation is worse.

'Right – Sarah's coming online. Let me admit her.'

As we wait for Sarah, I start to realise that the sense of ease I had is already evaporating. And I'm feeling a bit threatened by Larousse. That's not normal. There's something different about him. I can't quite work out what it is... He seems a little more sophisticated, intelligent – which makes no sense considering what he's been saying, but there's something... Can't quite put my finger on it.

Sarah appears, a pulsating ball of grins and overemphasised eye brown raises. I've only talked to her once before, but she seems really nice. And intelligent. And sophisticated. In a way that's never struck me before.

What's happening? Have they both got a filter on? I look normal, maybe there's something you can click on? But Larousse's face definitely looks normal. He's just sitting there, normally, in front of his... bookcase.

He's *never* in front of a bookcase. He's always in his Hague Blue kitchen, sitting at the counter, while various members of staff walk past him in the background. I look at Sarah's. She's in front of her bookcase too. Did I not get the memo? Looking down at my shot, I start to realise how awful it is. I'm in my bedroom, a poster of *The National* Blu-Tacked up on the wall behind me in an attempt to create a bit of character after Sally left and took all the pictures. From this angle, it looks like a student bedsit. I look rubbish.

'Hey guys – ready to go?' Sarah asks

'Sure am,' says Larousse, 'Ready and waiting. We've got our first ac*TOR* trying to join the chat right now.'

'Let 'em in,' Sarah pops, like a balloon full of fun.

But I don't feel ready yet. 'Can you just...'

'Hi! I'm Charlie!' Charlie appears on screen, looking incredibly well-groomed and handsome. Maybe Larousse was right; they *are* all going to be more attractive than me. It might just be the camera angle – for all we know he's not wearing any trousers.

‘Hi Charlie! I’m Sarah – this is Larousse, and Tom,’ she replies, her eyebrows bouncing up and down like she’s trying to prove to an interrogator she hasn’t had botox. ‘Can you take a step back so we can get a full length shot?’ He does. Trousers – damn. He’s got *everything*. But it makes me nervous. I’m pretty sure they can’t ask me to do that, can they?

Larousse decides to take over the direction. ‘So, Charlie – assume you got the script?’ *Script? It’s just someone sitting down and saying ‘ah’.*

‘I did. It’s awesome. Very “new normal”.’ *No, it’s not. You’re a suck-up. You’re a complete suck-up*. ‘Before I do one though, what are you thinking with the “ah”? Sort of “ah”, like I’m relieved to be sitting down?’

‘Yeah,’ says Larousse, super-sincere, ‘but also try to bring to it the idea that you’ve had a really hard day.’

‘Good thought, will do, will do…’ Suck-up replies.

Sarah interjects. ‘And you could even add a little bit of “I deserve this”.’

‘Oh, I like that,’ says Charlie. ‘That’s good.’

Am I expected to say something? Don’t want to look like my presence is unnecessary here. That’s probably the kind of thing that loses you your job. Maybe I should say something…

‘And also that it’s really comfortable.’

No reaction.

Am I on mute? What just happened? Where was my sucking up? I’m one of the important people you’re trying to impress.

‘So – shall I do one?’ he asks.

‘Let’s!’ smiles Sarah.

‘Ah!’ says Charlie, a little too much like he’s had a satisfying trip to the toilet.

‘Great stuff,’ says Larousse. ‘A little more comfortable, a little less relieved maybe?’

'Comfortable, good thought,' Charlie replies, enlightened. Didn't I just say that? Didn't I just give him that exact note?

'But good energy,' says Sarah.

'Thank you,' says Charlie, with an air of actorly mock-camp that isn't 100% mock.

'And maybe give it a beat after you sit down before you do the line?' I say.

Nothing. Again. This is really annoying.

'Sorry, Charlie,' I ask, 'can you hear me all right?'

'Yeah,' he says, expressionless. Then with sudden enthusiasm, 'Shall I do another one, Sarah?'

He does another one. It's better. Less toilet-y, but still without the beat I asked for. I don't like him. I don't like him one bit.

'That was great Charlie – thanks! We'll see you next time!' says Sarah.

'Cheers! Bye Sarah… Larousse!' *Ummm… and Tom?* No – he's hung up.

Three more of these go by – with no one seeming to listen to anything I say. It's like they don't respect me. It couldn't be… surely not… it can't be… because I don't have a bookcase? Could it?

I consider going into the living room and sitting in front of my shelves, but what if they read the titles of the books? I've already made the observation that Larousse likes Gabriel Garcia Marquez and Murakami (I bet he doesn't – he probably paid some staff to put fake covers on his Andy McNab), and Sarah's more of an Austen fan. And I've completely judged them on it. There's no way they're not going to draw some conclusions when they see a row-full of spines with Elven warrior-mages all over them.

As the next actor, Samira, comes on the call, I have an idea. I open up a new window and start doing an image search for 'bookcase backgrounds zoom'. Ten seconds later, I've got one downloading. I can use that 'change your background' thing, and suddenly my opinion is going to be something worth listening to.

Samira does a few 'Ah's, ignoring every note I give her (although she is actually reasonably good), and I realise I've got to do it. I've got to 'relocate to my library'.

I open up 'photos', the library picture's right there. I'm ready.

'Guys,' I interject, ''scuse me, for a second – I've got to change rooms – I keep losing reception.'

No one reacts once again. Well, on the upside, it should mean I might get away with this.

I close my laptop (keeping my hand between the screen and trackpad, so I can do a little virtual magic) and shuffle around a bit, before clicking and opening the screen back up.

I can see it in their eyes. They're paying attention to me. Realising, for the first time, that I'm actually there.

But not in a good way.

It seems that with the screen closed, I've managed to click on the wrong picture. And the background I've chosen is not a library. It's a picture of me, looking flirtatiously over the shoulder of my naked back.

Oh my fucking God.

'What is THAT?!?' Larousse asks.

'I... I... I don't know how that got there!'

'That is really not appropriate,' says Sarah.

Samira just delivers her line again, but with completely the wrong motivation behind it. 'Ahhhhhh!'

'I'm sorry – I don't what's happening, my computer's spasming.'

'Is that meant to be sexy?' asks Larousse.

I'm desperately clicking trying to get rid of it, but I can't make it go.

'No... no... I'm... checking a mole. The doctor asked me to take a photograph of it. No one should have seen that.'

'Why are you smiling then?'

''Cos I've found it. And it looks fine. Wouldn't you be happy if your mole looked fine?'

'I'm not comfortable with this, Tom,' Sarah protests. With my mole looking fine? With me having a clean bill of health? Why do I feel she doesn't believe me?

'Back in a sec,' I blurt, shutting the computer in horror. What the hell? I'm never going to live this down. I can't risk opening it again. Even for a second. What if Larousse decides to shame me and takes a screenshot…?

I go into the other room, grabbing some trousers as I walk – I don't want to tempt fate – especially as Fate currently seems to see me as her prison wife.

'Kids, get into your bedroom!' I shout as I move. 'I need the lounge!'

The kids seem to grasp the desperation in my voice, and scatter out of my path like bowling pins as I run into the living room.

I pull out my phone and open up the Zoom app, taking my place in front of my bookcase as it boots up.

For a moment before they admit me, I get a sneak preview of what they're going to see. A fully grown man, a mild look of panic on his face, sitting in front of what looks like the 'literature' section of Forbidden Planet.

But I no longer feel bad about it. After you've shown some people you barely know your attempt at an erotic photo, sitting in front of a few shelves of fantasy novels really doesn't seem like an issue. Hell, I could probably be next to a life-size cutout of Galadriel and it'd be an improvement…

I take a deep breath and press 'Join'.

***

When I tell Amanda what happened later she doesn't laugh for once. She seems genuinely terrified for me. Apparently, the company's doing its second round of furloughing after the shoot, and exposing myself to colleagues isn't going to help put me on the 'must keep' list. Making sure this sofa ad turns out all right is my best chance of keeping my job. Knowing that isn't doing anything for my stress levels.

'I suppose one of the positives is it actually could have been you checking a mole,' she says, offering up a sliver of hope.

'The photo I sent was that sexy, huh?'

'Didn't I tell you about my clinical examinations fetish?'

I laugh. The embarrassment still burns, and I can feel the stress bubbling up underneath, but there's something about being with someone you care about that seems to make everything better, even if they are mocking you. I guess that's why lockdown's been so hard for everyone, we're missing the healing power of presence.

We don't even talk much as the evening goes on; instead just sitting there watching a movie, at either end of the virtual phone line. Amanda's wanted to show me Baz Luhrmann's *Romeo and Juliet*, and tonight's the night. I've never seen it, but, luckily, she's made it very clear she loves it, so I'm able to keep all my sarcastic comments about people speaking strangely and Juliet ending up as a bipolar CIA analyst to myself.

It's strange. All we do is watch TV, but I end up feeling like I've had a great night, my embarrassment fading into the background like a feud between two houses both alike in dignity, in the presence of love.

The thought makes me feel a bit nauseous. If I get any soppier I'm going to end up at the bottom of a balcony before next weekend. But most of all, as I lie in bed a few hours later, I just feel happy.

Saturday 18th April

Ain't no party like a lockdown party.

It's our first day of big social events since the virus hit, and we're doing it with a bang. There's not one, not two, but *three* lockdown parties today. I guess lockdown parties are like buses, you wait ages for one, and then they're a bit shit.

I check the schedule to make sure I've got the timings right. We've got two Zoom parties for the kids (first at one, second at three), and then Mark has his at eight. Amelie's is the one o'clock. It's been the bane of Mark's existence that his only child was born on the same day as him. It was the only time I'd ever seen him lose it with Karen before this whole trapped-in-a-house-with-the-person-you're-meant-to-love thing happened. 'She could have done me a favour and held it in for another bloody day,' I think were his exact words. 'She only did it to spite me.' He has since expressed his regret. With the fervency of a Hollywood star who said something homophobic in the 90s.

The three o'clock is Jacob's. Jacob is a boy Arthur was at nursery with. Arthur doesn't remember him, and this time every year we have the same conversation.

'You were at Montessori with him.'

Blank expression.

'He's the boy whose party you went to last year and you didn't remember.'

'Oh, yeah.'

It's become this very weird cycle with Jacob's only memorable feature being Arthur's not remembering him. Still, Sally's good friends with the mum, so Arthur's stuck with him.

It's 12:55, when I get the text from Sally.

'Is Arthur ready for the party?' *No, of course he's not ready for the party, it's not for two hours.* Except I don't text that back.

Because, scanning back through the texts that Sally's sent me i.e. looking at the one above it on the page (they're kind of infrequent), I can see, it's not at 3:00. It's at 13:00. Meaning I've fucked up.

'Yes of course!' I text back, deleting the smiley face at the last minute. I never thought I'd be someone who overcompensated in emoji.

'Right kids,' I say, rounding them up and dragging them to the computer. 'Great news!'

'What? Is the virus over?' asks Arthur.

'Have you bought me a bike?' asks Carrie.

'No, not quite that great. But pretty darn great. You're about to go to a double party!'

'What's a double party?'

'Two parties at *once*. Doesn't that sound cool?! Only it'll be like a game, because you can't let the people whose party it is know you're at the other party.'

'Like Fatty undercover?'

'What are you talking about?'

'In the *Find-Outers*,' Arthur explains. Phew! Enid Blyton reference. I thought they'd found a DVD of that Hollywood star's hilarious fatsuit comedy from the early noughties.

'Yes! Like Fatty undercover!'

The whole thing's worked out in my mind – I'll have one party going on the laptop and one on the iPad next to it. They'll be sitting there looking in vaguely the same direction, all I have to do is flip the mutes from one to the other and everything should be plain sailing. I feel like some kind of genius. A genius who's so absorbed with profound and creative thoughts that sometimes he misreads the time.

The parties start well. And by that I mean terribly. Kids and Zoom parties don't really seem to mix, which for my purposes is ideal. Turns out if you confront two kids with the faces of another twenty kids on screen, they just sit there in silence looking a bit confused. Annoyingly, the parents at both parties seem committed to keeping the whole charade going, and everything gets jollied along by a directed question every few seconds or so. As Sally's on Jacob's party Zoom, she seems keen on getting Arthur involved.

'You like that as well, don't you Arthur? Do you remember Jacob, Arthur? From nursery?'

I hold up my finger for a second, plugging some headphones in the side of the iPad so I can keep track on Amelie's party, before unmuting the mic on the laptop.

'You can speak now, Arthur.'

'I don't remember Jacob from nursery, but I remember him from not remembering him last year.'

'Ha, ha!' says Sally, trying not to acknowledge the fact that he really shouldn't be here. 'I suppose nursery's quite a long time ago. It's difficult to remember people!'

'No, I remember Mrs Goldman, and Harold, and Louisa, and Edward. I just don't remember Jacob…'

Sally's awkwardness is interrupted from some mumbling on my headphones. Shit, incoming. It's Mark. It takes me a second to tune into the question.

'What was your tooth fairy called again?'

I raise a finger. Hopefully, Sally will interpret that as me wanting to have a chat with Arthur off camera to tell him off for being rude to Jacob. Mute, headphone swap, turn to Arthur and relay the question while trying to look like I'm a bit angry from the laptop angle.

'Goldmember!' says Arthur.

'Ember!' I correct.

The flow is a bit better on the other call (probably due to Arthur actually knowing who he's talking to), which means I have to look like I'm listening really actively to Arthur and he's just not quite looking at me. I'm sure Sally's getting suspicious, but thanks to the presence of twenty other parents at the 'party', she's unwilling to take a risk and call me on it, and thirty-five minutes in, I'm starting to think I've got away with it. A quick search on my phone tells me that the maximum free length of a Zoom call is forty minutes, explaining why both the parties officially end at 1:40, and I feel like I'm on a countdown to success. As the fortieth minute hits, Amelie's party ends with no ceremony and I realise I've done it! I've pulled off the double party manoeuvre! It reminds me of the time I was dating two women in my early 20s. It seemed like I'd pulled off something remarkable. Except it wasn't. As the second girl said she'd go out with me, I was so overcome with guilt that I went straight to a payphone and left a message for the other one that I had to cancel our date. My whole career as a dating-bigamist lasted less than four minutes. I'm probably not exactly playah material. But it did provide a similar thrill for those with a rigid sexual morality.

But forty-one minutes in, I start to worry. The Jacob party's still going on. They must have paid for a subscription... That means this party could potentially go on for*ever*.

'We've got to go in a sec!' I say, smiling. 'Really lovely to see you Jacob!'

'Why?' asks Sally.

'Because we've got another party to go to.'

'I thought we weren't mentioning that?' Carrie asks.

'Why wouldn't we mention that?' I ask, laughing. *Mute*. 'Shut up.' *Unmute*.

'Who is that again?' Jacob asks, talking to his Mum who has briefly walked away from the camera, clearly not remembering Arthur that well either. Unfortunately, Arthur doesn't interpret what's happening completely correctly.

'Is Jacob at another party at the same time as well?' he asks.

'What's he talking about?' asks Sally.

'Because Jacob's talking to his mum off camera.'

'He said "as well".'

'Of *course* he did. If you think someone's at a second party, of course they're at a second party as well.'

'What are you doing, Tom?' Sally asks, seeming to have forgotten that there are twenty other sets of parents who we no longer know staring at us.

'I…'

It's a terrible thing to see your own look of panic relayed back to you on a computer screen. If anything it only makes me feel more panicked, which makes me look more panicked, which makes me feel more panicked, onwards and onwards in an endless feedback loop that might actually end in my face splitting down the middle like an overcut hasselback potato. But nothing can calm me down. Not even my upcoming prize for most middle-class comparison ever.

'I… I…'

In a moment of sheer madness. I reach forward and click the 'Leave now' button.

And then they're gone.

It's over. I didn't get away with it, but I managed to… get away. With no consequences. I suddenly realise that maybe Zoom parties are exactly what I've been looking for all my life. How many awkward exchanges could I have avoided if I could have just left conversations halfway through and claimed it was because of my broadband? My mind starts turning over, searching for a physical equivalent I could start using… Hearing aids! Of course! A couple of fake oversized hearing aids, and I could just claim they've broken as soon as a conversation starts to get uncomfortable. Maybe I should order some for after lockdown ends?

That said, I don't want to offend anyone who's actually got a problem with their hearing, but if something medical's got an unintended secondary application shouldn't we use it? It's like when people discovered that prostate drug also helped with male pattern baldness. This is a bit like that for the deaf. If indeed there are any…

My phone pings. Hm – second text from of the day from Sally! Maybe she's starting to miss me. 'What the hell was that?' Guess not.

'Sorry, internet went down.' (Nearly wrote hearing aid). 'All good x.'

She messages a few things back using vocabulary that is outside the remit of predictive text. But I suddenly realise I can ignore it. It's not right, but my phone could have died. *Plausible deniability.*

Ah lockdown! Finally you and I are learning to work together…

***

The evening party doesn't go quite as smoothly. I join about half an hour late because the kids won't go to sleep.

'Tommmmmmmmm!' shouts Mark as I join the call.

'Sorry: kids wouldn't go to sleep, so I…'

I suddenly realise everyone's stopped what they were doing and started looking at me. If this was a real life party, I might be getting paranoid. Then they all look disappointed and take a swig from their beers.

'Well, no worries!' Mark continues. 'I've upgraded to a paid subscription. We're going to go on all night!!!!!'

Fuck.

'Hey Tom! How's it hanging?' In the centre of the screen is Mark's work friend, Ranj. I can't quite believe he remembers my name. That said, he did just hear it. And it's written at the bottom of my little window. 'You got here just in time. We're doing a drinking game!'

Fuck.

I don't like drinking games at the best of times. I can't drink very much and I'm really bad at games, but playing one sitting at a computer monitor seems like a new low. It's basically getting drunk on your own in your house. I'm pretty sure that's the first stage of alcoholism…

'Get your beers lined up, Tommy Boy!'

'I've actually only got two in the house.'

'No other booze?!?' he scoffs, like I'm a member of the temperance movement.

'No. Well, except for a bottle of Baileys that my Mum bought me at Christmas.'

'Get that! Get that! Get that!' he starts to chant. Everybody else joins in. What the fuck is going on? My hearing aid/hanging up technique seems like the best way out, but for some reason I can't bring myself to do it. The peer pressure is too strong.

Head bowed, I go off and get the Baileys.

I get back and everyone downs their beer. Then Ranj explains the rules to me. 'Right – every time someone joins the Zoom, or goes off camera and comes back, you have to drink.' OK, well, at least that explains the awkwardness when I joined the call. Hopefully.

'For example if I were to go…' Ranj ducks out of the shot and reappears, 'you all have to drink. That was not a drill, people. Get it fucking down ya!'

Wow. I hate this party. I thought Zoom parties were great, but it turns out I'd underestimated the power of the real life phrase 'sorry, got to mingle!'.

'Come on, Tom, that means you as well.'

I drink, feeling utterly bullied. In the top right corner of the screen, I spot Karen in a window of her own. They've decided to do this in different rooms. Maybe I *should* start worrying about their relationship. She's looking like I feel: like she'd rather be anywhere else in the world, but stuck here because of an obligation to her nearest and dearest.

I type her a message in the chat. 'Whose idea was this?'

She messages me back immediately. 'Mark's originally. Ranj seems to be taking it a little too seriously though.' A few seconds later: 'BTW – is this our affair starting?'

I spit out my beer in laughter, and Mark's on me immediately. 'What was that? What's funny?'

'Nothing's funny… I reply. Everything's just *fun*…!'

I jump out of shot and jump back in.

Ranj cheers and everyone downs their drink, while I turn back to the chat.

'He didn't say that to you as well, did he?'

Karen laughs. 'Oh SO much more,' she types back. 'By the way, please don't jump out of shot again. Ranj is desperate for everyone to get wasted, so he can get off with Lou.'

'And how exactly is he going to do that?' I type.

'Don't think he's thought it through…'

Lou (who I don't know) is in a box at the bottom left. A few shots later, and Ranj starts throwing our a few compliments. But not at her.

'But I just think: hey, so what if I get drunk?' he slurs. 'After all, I wouldn't mind seeing *you* double… Jenny. Rest of them I could do without, eh? Ha ha ha!'

Jenny? I thought it was Lou? 'Jenny?' I type to Karen.

'He's doing his "negging",' she replies. I suddenly remember his pick-up techniques from when I've hung out with him before. I think he read *The Game* as a teenager and never really grew out of it. He always compliments the 'second hottest woman' to make his real target insecure. I have to admit it's effective. I feel a little 'negged' myself. Why doesn't he want to see *me* double? I made an effort for tonight and everything.

What worries me more is where he thinks this is leading. Come 10:00 pm, is he going to be changing his background to 'boudoir', and slipping into something more comfortable? Well, joke's on him. Even though I'm in a nice shirt, I'm also wearing jogging pants. So who's comfortable now?

What follows are a few more attempts to have 'fun' (*'Let's change our backgrounds.' Cue someone bringing up a picture of fish, and pretending to swim.*) and lots of drinking. No one's even close to having a proper conversation because everyone else is listening, so I spend most of the time making sarcastic remarks to Karen in the chat, with a brief interlude to 'go to the toilet' (empty out the bottle of Baileys and replace it with milk). (Although it turns out shots of milk don't go down particularly well after two cans of lager either.)

By 11:00 pm, everyone is a complete mess apart from me and Karen (who followed my milk lead and replaced her Chardonnay with apple juice), and someone even suggests doing a 'line'. I'm not a druggy at all, so at first I think they're intending to create some kind of virtual conga, but no, and, seconds later, let's call him 'Lemmy' has disappeared below the camera and comes back into frame with his face covered in more white than a witness at a bakery explosion. Ranj doesn't miss a beat.

'I think that's a cue to drink!' he wa-heys, and I've got to admit I'm a little impressed. People have started doing Class As, and Ranj is still playing drinking games. But then he ups the ante.

'Do you know what we should do?' he suddenly announces. 'A quiz!' *Read the room, Ranj, read the virtual room.*

'Yeah, I fucking love quizzes,' says Lets-Call-Him-Lemmy, before disappearing again in an attempt to deviate his septum.

'Quiz! Quiz! Quiz! Quiz! Quiz!' everyone chants. Turns out Ranj has read the room better than I thought.

'Except not a normal quiz. A strip-quiz!'

Oh God no.

'I'm not comfortable with…' I start to protest.

'You fucking pussy, Tom,' Ranj laughs.

'Yeah, you're a fucking pussy whatever-your-name-is,' echoes Lets-Call-Him-Lemmy. *Make an effort – it's literally written at the bottom of my window.*

'No, I reply. 'I've got kids in the next room.' And I now know what I look like with my top off.

'Lock your door, Tom! Or are you worried we'll *see* your pussy!'

Strangely, the comment doesn't seem to turn the whole party against him. That really seems like a cancellable offence. I can feel myself dying inside, but salvation comes in the form of a message from Karen.

'Think we've seen the next stage of Ranj's plan,' she types. 'Want to bail and have a private chat instead? Promise I'll let you keep your clothes on.'

I make my excuses and leave, feeling slightly guilty that we're abandoning Mark, but really pleased to finally have my other friend back.

We chat for a few hours on FaceTime. She's more interested in what's going on with Amanda than Mark ever is, and it feels really nice to be listened to for once by someone who isn't my girlfriend. I even go as far as telling her about my back-hair photo. Judging on how badly they seem to be getting on at the moment, I'm counting on her not telling Mark…

After a while, I try turning the conversation to what's going on with the two of them. She doesn't bite, and I don't feel I can push it to get an answer. I really hope that Mark's wrong about their relationship, as they're so great together. I'm worried he's getting so paranoid that he's going to screw everything up.

Unfortunately, I get a bit more insight into what's going on between them than I bargained for, when Mark storms in just after midnight.

'What are you doing?' he cries, pouncing towards the laptop. 'I knew it! It's an affair, you're having a virtual affair! ... With Tom?!? You're having an affair with Tom?'

'For God's sake, Mark,' Karen shouts. 'I'm chatting to my friend.'

'Chatting? *Sexy* chatting more like... talking about... sexy things!' He's so drunk he can barely get his words out.

'We were talking about normal things, Mark. If I was going to talk about sexy things to someone, it wouldn't be Tom.' *Um, that's fine, but... feeling a little singled out.*

'Who would it be then?'

'No one... You.'

'*Me*? When was the last time you talked to me about... sexy things? You never talk to me about sexy things anymore.'

I feel I should hang up. 'Um... Mark?'

'What, *backstabber*?' he spits.

'Maybe I should go...'

'Oh, you'd love that, wouldn't you?!? You'd love that!' he slurs, and I get the impression that even *he* doesn't know what he means.

'For God's sake, Mark. Leave Tom alone – he's the last person I'd ever have an affair with!' *Last? Really?* Maybe not first, but surely top three? Should never have told her about the back hair... 'I don't know why you'd even care, anyway. All you've seemed to want for the last month is to get rid of me.'

'Get rid of you? Potty... kettle,' he says, pausing unsure whether to correct himself, then carrying on regardless. 'You've wanted to get rid me of *me*!'

'No, I haven't.'

'Then why do you always find me so annoying?'

'Because we're stuck in a house together and you *are* annoying. It doesn't mean I don't love you. You're not going to pretend you don't find me annoying?'

'I find you *really* annoying,' he slurs. 'But I love you… And you still love me?'

'Yes.'

'And you find me attractive?'

'Yes.'

'More attractive than Tom?'

'Mark – I don't find Tom attractive at all.' *Oh, come on. That's just not necessary.*

'I don't find Tom attractive either,' he slurs. *For God's sake – no one was even asking you.*

'Erm… Mark?' I ask, trying to get a bit of context on the full situation.

'What?' he replies, his words containing slightly less vitriol than the last time he addressed me.

'Why are you naked?'

Mark looks down, as if he hasn't realised until I mentioned it. Unfortunately he angles the laptop slightly as he does it, and I get a brief glimpse of penis.

'I'm not very good at quizzes all right!?!' he shouts, before he calms down again. 'I think I might be a bit drunk…'

'I think you might be.'

'Let's get you in some pants and I'll tuck you up in bed, all right?' says Karen from off camera.

'OK…' Mark replies, taking on the demeanour of a child who's been allowed to stay up too late.

'Night, Tom,' Karen says.

'Night, Karen. Oh, and Happy Birthday, mate,' I reply.

‘Thanks, Tom. Sorry, I said you were a backstabber. I’ll make it up to you.’

‘Just make sure I never see your penis again; that’ll be more than enough.’

As they hang up, I hear Mark mumbling to Karen about how much he loves her. Maybe they will be all right after all. Perhaps all it took was the context of his other annoying friends to realise what a good one he’s landed. And, despite the fact that I’ve spent the last few minutes being told how unattractive I am, it makes me smile.

Because it seems that maybe there’s hope for us all.

Sunday 19th April

Turns out an alcohol/milk hangover is just as bad as non-dairy ones, so I stumble through the first few hours of the day, unable to even face hair-of-the-dog-ing it with some cereal and a latte.

But, as I sit on the sofa with the kids watching cartoons, my hangover gradually fades, and I feel happy to be back in my life again, away from the virtual debauchery of last night’s party. Well, for a while. Rather than concentrating on the escapades of an animated Mr Bean, I stupidly start checking Facebook. I manage to ignore a few postings from Mark’s party (Ranj is now ‘in a relationship’? How did that happen?), then come across a letter that all the parents from the school seem to be sharing and find myself sucked in. It reads:

Dear parents,

Don’t stress about schoolwork. In September, I will get your children back on track. I am a teacher and that’s my superpower.

Signed,

All the teachers on planet Earth.

There are a few other things too, but that's the gist. Let's just say, my back is officially 'got up'. *All the teachers on planet Earth*? What kind of a ridiculous statement is that? Sure, some of them are brilliant and can probably drag my now-backwards children out of the mire, but *all*? That's the biggest case of mass delusion since the medieval dancing plagues.

Case in point: next year Arthur's got Ms Newman. She does *not* have a superpower; or if she does it's one of the ones no one wants. She's Color Kid. The DC character who has the ability to change the colour of an object at will. *You're about to shoot me with that red gun? Not any more! Ow. You shot me with that blue gun!*

As far as I can see the closest she's got to any kind of extraordinary ability is being able to bamboozle people at parents' evening. At the last one, I asked her how Arthur could get better marks in Geography, and by the end of the first sentence she was talking about her problems with the shared coffee kitty in the staff room. I literally have no idea how she got there. Her brain is like an internet rabbit hole. She free-associates thoughts like a series of drunken clicks, logic-be-damned, till she arrives at some random place. On the upside, although Arthur won't have a basic grasp of English by summer 2021, he may have got to see a rare interview with Orson Welles on *The Dick Cavett Show* from fifty years earlier.

Well, as it's looking like Arthur's got the only muggle who's teaching at Hogwarts, I realise I have to get my act together and *not* rely on the teachers to get the kids back on track. No more will their school work consist of making rainbows out of household objects that embarrass their father when uploaded online! I'm going to take my kids to the top – school or no school! The other thing this smug shit of an educator-letter decided to tell me is 'No kids are ahead. No kids are behind'. Well – I've got news for you: mine are about to get *way* ahead.

Tomorrow: I'm taking homeschooling to the next level.

***

I'm talking about this with Amanda in the evening, when she decides to drop another bombshell.

'I'm coming back to London.'

The news knocks me for six. Amanda – the woman I love – is coming back. She's coming home.

'That's… that's amazing.' I can feel the warmth growing within me, like kindling on a bonfire about to catch.

'Yeah, I've been well for a while now, so I guess I'm clear to travel. My parents haven't got it either, so I reckon there's more chance of me killing them if I stay – you know, through murder – so I thought: why not head back?'

But then suddenly the reality of the situation hits me. She's coming back to London. Not to me. The warmth I was feeling fizzles into nothingness like a spark on wet tinder. All this means is that instead of her being trapped thirty miles away, we'll be separated by five – holed up in different parts of London, an untraversable distance still between us.

I mean, I'm pleased for her. Well, relieved. Relieved that she can finally get away from her parents (I can't imagine being holed up with mine for all of this), but having her so near, yet so far away is almost more painful.

'When are you coming?' I ask.

'Probably next weekend. I maybe should have done it today, but I guess… I guess I was scared. Of travelling. Of going out into the world… Does that sound ridiculous?'

I think about it for a second, and I realise it doesn't. It suddenly strikes me that maybe I'm a bit scared too. As desperate as I am for everything to get started again, the idea of it is paralysing. It's amazing how quickly you get used to this whole situation. Everybody's calling it the 'new normal', but I've never thought before about how normal it's actually become. At how quickly the four walls around us have become our only places of safety in the world – the only place where the big bad virus can't come and get us. When there's a threat that you can't see, it's everywhere, omnipresent, like God. Well if the presence of God had symptoms clearly defined by the NHS. Even then people would probably be claiming it was just 5G…

But it makes me wonder. How the hell are we ever going to come out of this? As a nation? As a world? If going for a walk seems like a big deal, how are things ever going to be normal again?

'No,' I reply, 'it doesn't seem ridiculous at all. I think maybe everyone's a bit scared.'

She pauses for a second before continuing. 'Anyway, I reckon I'll wait till after the shoot – you know how full on the prep always is – so I guess I'll head back next Sunday or something. If I leave first thing I can miss the traffic, so it should be pretty quick back to… my flat.'

The pauses between the words hang around longer than the words themselves. Hovering there like open doors waiting to be walked through. But neither of us knows where they lead, what the other one's thinking. I want to be with her, I want it more than anything. But what are my options? Asking her to move in? It's too fast – too full on. I don't want her thinking I'm a psycho. But what if she's thinking the exact same thing? No – it's too risky. Maybe they're not doors after all, but traps; great big spike-filled holes just waiting for some fool to walk over them and have the ground fall away beneath them…

'That sounds like a good plan,' I reply.

'Yeah,' she echoes.

We chat for a few more minutes, but after that everything seems more strained, as if not mentioning it was just as bad as blurting it out, and pretty soon we're saying our goodbyes.

'I miss you,' she tells me before hanging up.

'I miss you too,' I reply.

But then I'm alone on my bed once more. My head perched up against the headboard in an uncomfortable position, the pillow between doing little to negate the obtuse angle of my neck. I shift my body down the bed, and rest my head in the pillow properly, a valley of goose down forming around my ears.

I don't know why I feel any different. She wasn't going to be here either way, yet somehow it *feels* different. It suddenly hits me how much of our world is imagination, at how the thought of her being one place or another seems so significant, and yet the reality is – either way, I'd be here alone. Staring at the same white ceiling, the same imperfections in the paint work looking back at me. For this whole time, that's all I've been: alone.

Conned by a few pixels dancing on the screen of my computer.

Monday 20th April

Next level homeschooling begins at 8:00 am with me downloading Arthur's work from his *actual* school. As predicted it's almost nothing. Well, strap in Arthur, Daddy's about to Google some 7+ papers.

Howard's comments about the 7+ have been rebounding around my brain for the last few days. I had no idea what it was a week ago (having not gone to anything like the type of school that might need it and there being no chance of Arthur ever taking it), but I'll be damned if Howard's dumbass kids can pass it and Arthur can't.

So, after Arthur's 'Welcome Back' assembly on Microsoft Teams, I give him his first 7+ maths paper to do. And it turns out I'll be damned.

After about twice as long as the time you're allowed in the exam, Arthur's finished. He's left about half of the questions blank, but, on the upside, he has drawn a really nice picture of Captain America and made an origami frog. Pretty sure neither of those were on the test.

I sit down and start to mark it, finding myself penning cross after cross after cross. Arthur looks over my shoulder, and I can see he's starting to get a bit upset, so I decide to just tick the correct ones. Let's just say I won't be rushing to buy a new marking pen.

'Well, Arthur – well done for giving that a go!' I say, radiating enthusiasm like a Soviet power plant on the brink of meltdown.

'Did I do well?' he replies, buying it hook, line, and bribed communist official.

'You did OK...'

'What did I get?'

'Three!' I say, trying to maintain my hyperactive zeal.

'Out of what?'

'Erm... eighty.'

'Is that good?' Christ! Why am I surprised he found the fractions section difficult?

'It's not... great. But it's a good *start*. It tells me what we need to work on.'

'And what do we need to work on?'

'Everything.'

For the rest of the morning, I teach him basic maths, while at the same time trying to organise a Covid-friendly ad shoot. I can't believe how little he's learnt at school. His teacher this year has been lovely – all smiles, warmth and 'if you were an animal what would you be?' – but it turns out she's not exactly hot shit in the academia department.

It's soul destroying. He can't even do basic subtraction, so when the paper gets to the 'applied' stuff ('If John has 12 apples, and he gives away 5 apples, how many does he have left?'), it feels like I'm asking him to explain Heisenberg's uncertainty principle.

My frustration starts to spill over into the phone calls I'm making in parallel, and I find myself talking to one of the production company runners, Barto, as if he's a confused seven-year-old. 'OK, Barto. If training the actor to use the camera themselves takes *one* day, and we have to film on Friday, when does the actor need to receive the camera by?'

'First thing Friday morning, like we arranged.'

No, you bloody moron. The day before. Cross. Zero out of one. He probably doesn't even know how many apples John has.

Of course that's not what I say.

'Well, why don't we get it there first thing *Thurs*day, just to be on the safe side?'

'Sure thing. You never know if the actor will need an extra day to learn it! They're not always the brightest!'

'Yeah, not always the brightest…'

As a pleasant interlude from all the stress, I also have the privilege of a Zoom with Larousse to discuss the casting decisions.

'What a fucking bitch,' is today's opener. It's like I'm breathing in a rainbow.

'Look – I know your daughter's a bit annoying, but that seems a little harsh.'

'HA HA HA HA HA Tom,' he spits sarcastically. 'You're hilarious. I'm talking about my nanny.' Wow. That almost seems more offensive than if he'd been talking about his kid. You might almost think he wasn't a very nice person.

'Look – if she's quit on you, that's her right,' I try to explain *(please let her have quit, please let her have quit)*. 'Technically, she shouldn't have been there in the first place—'

'She hasn't bloody quit, you idiot. The cow's gone and got bloody coronavirus.' I'm amazed that the selfishness of spoilt rich people still has the power to surprise me, but this is really something else.

'Um… poor her?' I reply, attempting to tap at the casing of his moral compass.

'No. *Not* poor her,' he explodes at me, like I'm a moron. 'She's *fine*. Poor *ME*. She's sitting in bed with a bit of a temperature, but the chances of her going down with it are sub-zero. She's got the constitution of an ox – and her lungs… they're inhuman. At Lizzy's last birthday party, she was inflating balloons with a single breath. There was a candle that Lizzy hadn't managed to blow out, and this bloody woman extinguished it with an exhalation from across the room. She's superpowered. We've got a hundred and twenty foot garden, and this morning she called me when I was at the bottom of it. Her window was closed.'

'Well, she's probably suffering and feeling vulnerable.'

'Suffering? She's sat up in bed watching TV on her phone and getting *paid*. *I'm* the one that's bloody suffering. Thanks to that selfish bloody woman, I'm no longer allowed to leave the house. She rang the NHS – without my permission I should add – so now it's on record that we have a carrier in our 'bubble' so we have to self-isolate. The whole family. Not only that – I've got to cook *her* dinner *and* bring her drinks, *and* watch the bloody kids. When did I sign up for this? When did I become a bloody carer? And I can't even fire her! She says she'll get a bloody tribunal! THIS is why you hire illegal immigrants – they can't take you to court if things go wrong.'

I literally can't believe what I'm hearing. Part of me wants to slam him down, but there's another part of me that's sort of rejoicing. As long as this poor indentured servant isn't actually seriously ill, I can't help but feel like Fate has finally intervened and dispensed her divine justice. At long last, there's something Larousse can't buy his way out of!

'Luckily I've managed to hire a new nanny who can look after her as well, but she doesn't start till tomorrow. No wonder they're calling this whole thing a crisis.'

And my heart sinks a little more. The trajectory continues when we get to our actual business. It turns out the client wants to hire Samira i.e. the only actor who has seen me grinning sensually with my top off. Apparently, it was neck and neck between her and someone who hadn't felt the erotic charge of Tom Cooper's hairy back, but the director liked the décor in her flat so much (thanks to Covid we're going to be filming there), that the scales tipped in her favour. Next time, I'll try to reveal myself to someone who hasn't got such a good sense of interior design…

My attempt at multi-tasking continues into the afternoon: Carrie sits next to us doing colouring, while I teach Arthur more basic arithmetic over the course of a few hours than he's learnt over the past year. I want to scream at him while he's doing it, to unleash a barrage of, '*Do you not realise your father used to be an accountant?!?!*', a phrase I never thought I would utter without obscene levels of embarrassment, but the fact that not even a sliver of my ability made it into the spermatozoa that formed him makes me feel slightly ashamed.

Work continues to be just as frustrating. Barto – who I'm pretty sure is actually called Bartholemew – is one of the most incompetent men I have ever met. I have no idea how he's got a job. The only thing I can put it down to is that he's part of a positive discrimination outreach programme for ex-Harrow students. I guess the production company were lacking diversity in the public schools their employees once attended.

Needless to say, by the time I've got the kids to bed, my tolerance is spent. So, when my mother calls and starts having a go at me, I'm not in the most tolerant of moods.

'You didn't call us earlier.'

'No, but I didn't say I was going to.'

'Erm, yes you did – at the weekend, you emailed to say we'd FaceTime in the afternoon.'

'Fuck.'

'Please don't use that language with me, Tom.'

'Sorry. I've been pretty busy with work and school stuff.'

'Well, a little more consideration for other people wouldn't do any harm.'

'Are you joking?'

'No, I'm not. We'd been looking forward to speaking to the children. I'm assuming they've gone to bed now.'

'Yeah, but… Do you realise what I'm having to do?'

'I'm sure it's very difficult, but you've got to understand *we're* having a really hard time too.'

The words prompt a thousand silent expletives in my head, but this time it's too much, and the floodgates of my frustration finally give way, sending a torrent of grievances tumbling in her direction.

'Why? Because you can't have your hair appointments? Because you can't swan off to the thousand and one clubs you seem to belong to? To tai chi? To basket weaving?' I try to stop myself but I can't. There's an ocean of annoyance within me, and it just comes pouring out. 'I bet Dad's having the time of his life! Not having to leave the house – not having to help me. I wouldn't be surprised if he turned out to be the one who introduced the bloody virus into the world in the first place. A cabal of pensioners who smuggled infected bats into China so they didn't have to look after their grandkids for six months.'

'Tom, let's talk about it this another time. I can see you're in a bad mood. And we'd be very willing to help with the children if it wasn't for the virus.'

'Oh, give me a break. I didn't see you for three months before this started. You were good when Sally first left, I'll give you that, but after Christmas, you just disappeared, swanning off on your various trips!'

'We'd booked a *cruise*,' she explains as if it'll soon be introduced as a new type of plea in the English legal system. 'A *year* earlier. That was before anything went wrong with you and Sally. How were we to know?!?'

'But it's always the bloody same, isn't it? Travelling here, car shows there, trips to the NEC, trips to see friends. You never bloody prioritise *me*. Mark and Karen have their parents helping *every* weekend, *and* they've got each other. I've been doing it on my own for nearly five bloody months now. Without a single day off. When did you ever fucking have to do that?'

'I can see you need someone to take this out on Tom, but it's not our fault we can't help. I get that things are really difficult for you, I was just saying they're hard for us too.'

'How? *How*?' I spit, sarcasm dripping off my words like an over-toasted marshmallow. 'What exactly is making it so bloody hard?'

'Because…' She pauses for a moment. Because she can't think of a reason. Because there *is* no bloody reason. But then I see her stolidity start to crack, revealing fault lines, like a mask of dried clay. '…Because…' I watch as her eyes moisten, the tears forming barely visible through the lo-res camera of her ageing iPad. 'Because we don't know how long we have left.'

The words come like a punch in the gut.

'We're old, Tom. We might not have many more springs, many more summers. I know we're not having to deal with what you're having to deal with, but it doesn't mean it's not difficult, all right? I'm going to go now.'

'Oh Mum, sorry, I didn't mean—'

But she's already left the call. I put down the receiver. I can feel the space where my frustration had been filling up with guilt, like a hole in the sand dug too close to the sea.

And I feel like such a dick.

I try to call her back a few times to apologise, but after a few answerphone-less tries, it begins to look like Dad has unplugged the phone, an honour they normally reserve for people outside the family.

After half-concentrating on an episode of *The Stranger*, I realise that this is not something I'm going to be able to fix tonight, so I head off to my bed, to a night of dreams of angry queens and incompetent servants called Barto, and, trapped in the middle of it all, is me: a mouthy court fool. Who just happens to be a bit of a dick.

Tuesday 21st April

I wake at 7:00 am, my mind still in a haze of guilt. I slept terribly, but I suppose that's to be expected, what with the ad, my underperforming kids, the weirdness between me and Amanda, and the discovery that, as well as being a mediocre father, I'm also a terrible son.

I reach for my phone to turn off the alarm, and before my eyes are properly open I'm performing the ritual of my morning email check.

Surprisingly, there's nothing new. Not that I normally receive a flurry of late night communications, but today: nada, not even a daily deal from Bulk Powders. I feel a bit offended. Since I bought an industrial amount of vitamin C from them a few weeks ago, they've been really good at keeping in touch. But this morning, there's not even a discount on protein shakes. It's almost as if my lack of response to every other thing they've sent has made them doubt my future as an international bodybuilder.

But it's when I don't receive my regular message from my close friend 'iPhone-storage-almost-full', that I really get suspicious and realise I'd better check the router. I wander to the living room in my charming get-up of dressing gown and pants (briefly catching my reflection, and considering whether Bulk Powders might have been hoping to recruit me as a 'before' model), only to find a steady orange light glowing back at me. It's happening. The Internet's out.

A few restarts later, the orange light is still there, like a traffic light on pause, and I can feel my to-do list starting to get restless, screaming at me from behind like a crush of angry motorists.

A raised voice outside draws me to the window. Kerry, my neighbour, is ranting down her phone line. The rattle of my pane draws her eyes up in my direction.

'Sorry,' she apologises, 'my internet's out.'

'Mine too.'

'I'm on the phone to them now. Said it probably won't be working till ten tonight. Fucking idiots.'

I go back inside so I can start panicking about work, heading to the bathroom's reception hotspot to text Amanda about what's happening. After a while it sends, and she texts back, telling me not to worry, that she'll keep on top of Barto and just to call her when it's back on.

'We're not going to do anymore of those 70+ papers are we?' Arthur asks as he walks in for a wee. *Missed it by a factor of ten, but the answer is still no.*

'No, today it's just the normal stuff.' No more taking his maths up to the standard where he can get into a posh school. Or nursing home.

He considers my response as he hikes his trousers back up.

'Were they to teach me something about being bored? Now I know about being bored, do I not need to do them?'

'No, they… Look, the Internet's down. And, anyway, they're not boring if you know how to do them…' I begin, stopping myself just in time. In his eyes, I'm doubling down on the boredom right *now*.

'How will we get the other work?' Carrie asks, joining us. 'Isn't that on the Internet?'

Shit. She's right. Literally *everything's* on the Internet. 'Um… yeah, so… I guess you're not doing any work today either. Which means… we're going out for a walk!'

So, after an express breakfast, we head towards the park, and, strangely, the kids actually seem to be *enjoying* it. It's like Arthur's first experience of actual work yesterday has given him a new appreciation of the natural world. I find him talking about the flowers in people's front gardens, and pointing at pigeons as if seeing them from the first time. Carrie's the same, developing an enthusiasm for the native fauna that might suggest a future career as a botanist. When we get to the park, they play around at the stream. It's lovely; like something from an Enid Blyton novel. Without the sizism.

I try to call my mum a few times while they're playing to apologise, but there's still no response. It might be that Dad's forgotten to plug the landline back in. Old people may be some of the top door-lockers in the country, but when it comes to technology, there're less good at remembering the basics. I'm hoping. It's probably just that they still don't want to talk to me.

I stay out with the kids for as long as possible to extend our one permissible daily walk, then we return to the flat, all feeling a bit confused, as if we've forgotten what there is to do in life, but after a while we find a flow: spending the day playing games, reading books, talking, hell, we even watch *terrestrial*. I'd kind of forgotten that existed.

It's amazing how quickly the boredom transforms into a kind of calm. Like the whole thing is a window onto a past age. Is this what life used to be like? I can't even remember. I suppose if there'd been a lockdown in the 80s it would have been *exactly* like this. Well, we might have been in a slightly bigger flat (probably with a garden and everything), but the world… it would have stopped. The economy would be tanking even faster, we'd all be feeling more isolated, maybe they wouldn't even have *done* a lockdown. Instead, we'd all just be going about our business, getting sick, while half a million people died…

But the headspace is nice. Perhaps this is what all the people who are 'enjoying' this are feeling? The ones without the hassles of jobs and solo childcare. The feeling is so good that it almost makes me forget my resentment, and I get a sensation that anything is possible. That I can grow as a person.

After the kids have gone to bed, I try to call Amanda from the bathroom, but can't get enough reception, so I head to the living room and uncharacteristically pick up the copy of *Great Expectations* that Sally left. I start to read. It's great. And it makes me *feel* great. I'm reading a classic novel and *liking* it. This must be how sophisticated people feel. No wonder they act a bit smug. Perhaps I *am* clever enough to enjoy the finer things in life. I even notice that 'Magwitch' (the convict) is like 'magician' and 'witch' combined. I'm not just reading the story, I'm *getting* stuff. Maybe I could enjoy Proust, Dostoyevsky. I could read philosophy, bits of the newspaper that didn't have titillating headlines about celebrities. Imagine how impressed Amanda's going to be when she catches me reading *Romeo and Juliet* in one of those big collections of Shakespeare. Maybe I'll send that through as my next erotic photo.

I'm four chapters in, when my phone beeps. It's Amanda saying goodnight, that she's sorry we couldn't talk, and it's got the familiar blue background of an iPhone message that's been *delivered over Wi-Fi*. I look at the router, and the teenage boy inside of me jumps for joy. The Internet's back on! It's back on!

I send Amanda a 'goodnight' back (not wanting to call in case it's from a while ago), and then check the news to make sure I haven't missed anything important. Hm! Harry's been texting Meghan's dad! I read about that for a while then check my Facebook and Twitter, Reddit and email, and order a landline phone from Amazon, just in case this ever happens again. Before long, I'm watching random YouTube videos, scanning the comments while the video plays in the background, as if experiencing one thing at a time couldn't possibly be enough.

And that's when I notice my book, still open, spreadeagled on the floor next to the sofa, a vague memory of another world I was in a few minutes earlier calling to me to return. I'm halfway through a chapter, I should probably finish that at least. But then I remember I'm also halfway through an episode of *The Stranger*...

I turn on Netflix and start to watch. *The Stranger*'s rubbish, but I can't help myself. Just sitting there – it's so *easy*. Who was I to think I could read a difficult book anyway? I read two and a half chapters – that's probably more than most people manage. I stand up and put it back on the shelf, my eyes fixed on some low quality British drama, chucking a few strange figures the kids and I drew in a game of consequences away as I move, a strange kind of sadness coming over me that I try to ignore.

The feeling continues as I lie in bed reading through Amanda's old messages. Not speaking to her today has made me miss her more than ever. I don't want it to be like this between us, it doesn't feel right. What my mum said about 'not knowing how long we have left' is hovering round my mind... who in life ever *does*? It feels ridiculous wasting my time pining for this woman when we could be together, like staring at a phone screen while life in all it's richness goes on around you.

The prospect of me asking her to move in begins to raise its problematic head again, and I start to consider it as a possibility. Watching Karen and Mark arguing had helped to put that idea to bed, but seeing them reunited, tender and loving, has started to make me think that relationships can work out. That what I've got with Amanda is the real thing.

So I'm going to ask her. I'm going to ask her.

Wednesday 22nd April

I wake up with the question still going round my head. Do I ask Amanda to move in? In the naked light of day, the answer isn't quite so obvious. I don't want to rush it. To pop the question and be met with a blank face, a pasted on smile. It's only been a few months, and I haven't even seen her for a third of that time, just an image on a screen that looks similar. I can't even remember what she smells like. Hmm… that sounds suspiciously close to one of the Covid symptoms…

But we've talked and talked and isn't that what attraction's really about? I don't know – I get on amazingly well with Mark, but I'm not asking him to move in with me. And would we even be allowed to move in during the lockdown anyway? Me and Amanda, not me and Mark. What are the rules? I don't even know. Not being allowed doesn't make sense (considering if we'd done it for a single day before she'd got trapped at her parents no one would raise an eyebrow), but maybe it's not worth the risk. The social stigma.

And what about Arthur and Carrie? They're lovely, but kids are difficult. Four of us trapped in this flat would be a nightmare. It's a ridiculous thought and I've got to forget it. There's plenty of time to move our relationship forward when this is over. Besides, there's far more chance of her saying yes if it's face-to-face and she's enraptured by my enticing scent. Given my current level of conversation and appearance, that's the only thing I can put us still being together down to.

The decision made, I FaceTime her at lunch with a renewed sense of confidence. Even though nothing's been said, it feels like things are instantly better between us. Maybe it's just her relief at not having to stay with her parents for much longer.

'It's like a reprieve from a death sentence. Four more days, then I'm free.'

'Well, unless your Dad locks you in your bedroom again.'

'I told him he had to take the lock off the door.'

'Really? I can't believe he did it!'

'Well… he didn't. But I stuffed Blu Tack in the hole, so now he can't get the key in.'

We chat for about an hour, and everything seems right again. I feel like I made the right decision, that the strangeness between us is a thing of the past. Well, until the conversation turns to something real.

'Can I tell you something weird?'

'Yeah, of course.'

'I'm a bit worried.'

It doesn't faze me too much. I get it; it's normal to be scared at the moment. 'I know – you said. About going back into the world. It makes sense.'

'No, not about that. Well, yeah, about that, but also, I'm a bit worried about… being home.'

'What are you talking about? You've hated being at your parents. It'll be amazing.'

'I know, but then it'll… just be me. In an empty flat.'

'I'm happy to spend a few hours a day talking to you if you're lonely. I could even send you a few more sexy photos.' She laughs, but I regret saying it even as a joke. It's like offering to re-enact a traumatic experience from your childhood.

'Thanks. But not seeing anyone, not being with anyone… I'm worried it's just going to drive me mad.'

There's an awkward pause, while some calculations go on in my head that I'm not even party to, and before I've even realised it, the words slip out of my mouth. 'Well, why don't you move in here?'

What comes next sends shivers down my spine. A blank face, what looks like a pasted on smile. And then the screen goes blank.

I try to call back but my phone's not working, and a trip to the router reveals the Internet's down again. I can't believe it. I've fucked it. And I can't even call back to say it was just a joke, to bat it away. And then I remember my newly purchased landline. I was right to order it. I'm a genius; I'm a bloody genius.

As I walk towards the phone, it starts to ring. I left the number on my voicemail message – Amanda must have got it there. It's going to be all right. It's going to be all right!

'Hey!' I say, picking up. 'Look, about that…'

But it's not Amanda. It's Dad.

'Hello, Tom.'

'Oh, Dad, Sorry – I can't talk right now.' It's the first time I've heard his voice since the start of lockdown, but compared to having probably fucked up my relationship, currently being in the doghouse with him and Mum doesn't seem like a big deal.

'It's important.'

'I know. I really want to talk to Mum and smooth things over. I was an idiot the other day, but I think I might have just messed things up with me and Amanda…'

'Mum's in the hospital.'

The words bring me to a halt like a cyclist who has put his brakes on too fast. 'I…'

'She had a temperature, but she didn't want to burden you with it. She knows you've got a lot on your plate.'

'I don't understand. She was fine the other day.'

'We thought we'd better go in and get her a test. And well, it was positive.'

'Oh my God.' I feel myself flying forward into the unknown, with no idea whether I'm ever going to land.

'They were just keeping her in for observation. But… but overnight her breathing got worse, so they put her in intensive care.'

'I… Why didn't you call me?'

'I was going to leave a message, but… she didn't want to worry you. We thought she'd be coming out this morning… we… we…'

And then he starts to cry. I've never heard my dad cry before. Not when I went off to university, not when he gave up his business, not when his parents died – I once saw his eyes vaguely moisten when he saw a Volvo P1800 – but it was nothing like this. Nothing real.

'I don't know what I'm going to do, Tom… if she… if she… She's all I've got, Tom.'

I can feel the tears infecting me down the phone line, but I realise that I've got to pretend to be the strong one here. For him.

'She'll be fine, Dad, she'll be fine.'

'It's a third that die, Tom. And that's including the young ones. I looked it up.'

'Mum's tough. She's a fighter – she'll be fine.'

'You're right, Tom, you're right.' Those are his words, but his tone says anything but. And beneath them all I can hear is, 'She's gone, Tom. She's gone.'

Dad coughs. I have a slight moment of worry that he's got it too, before I realise he's just clearing his throat, trying to brush away his emotions. He's not comfortable with feelings. The idea of what he's just shared with me is probably as petrifying as what's happening to Mum, but I'm glad he did. He's shut up in their empty house all by himself, not sure if the woman he's given the whole of his adult life to is going to live or die. Just because he's cooped up, it doesn't mean his feelings have to be.

'Anyway, we'll see. I'll keep you informed. I've got to go now.'

'OK, Dad. But if you need to call me, just call me, OK? Anytime.'

'I'm fine.'

'Alright.'

'Oh, Mum dug out an old picture you made for her – she wanted to show it to you on FaceTime. I'll take a photo of it, and email it.'

'Sure. That'd be nice. Thanks.'

We end the call, and as I hang up I feel my world shattering around me. The walls of my flat no longer seem to offer protection, not when there are people out there in the world that I love; that are vulnerable. I look up the stats online – they vary, but Dad's pretty much right: 33% of intensive care patients end up dead.

I sit on the edge of my bed, my head in my hands, and tears run down the insides of my wrists like rain on a window pane. I can't believe that was the last conversation I might ever have with her. How many years did she put in to raise me? How much love did she send in my direction? I know what it's like to be a parent now – how hard it is, how all-encompassing – and although she's maybe slacked off a bit in recent years, she was a really good mum. As fucked up as my life is, none of that was down to her. She always made me happy, she always made me feel loved.

And to think that's how I sent her off, the bottle broken to launch her into the afterlife, a rant of accusations and incriminations. All I can feel is shame. That that was my thank you, my goodbye, my au revoir.

I walk back to my bedroom, curling up in a foetal position on the bed.

'Are you all right, Daddy?'

Looking up, I see Carrie standing in the doorway.

'Yeah, I'm fine. Daddy's just a bit sad, that's all. Can I have a hug?'

Carrie comes over, and puts her little arms round me, her hands unable to meet behind my hunched up form.

'I really love you Carrie, you know that, don't you?'

'Of course,' she replies, like it's a stupid question. 'Why are you sad?'

I start to fob her off with a 'nothing', but stop myself. I don't want to be my dad, unable to tell his kid what he's feeling. I've got to protect her, but it's got to be for her sake. Not mine.

'Granny's ill. She's in the hospital.'

'Granny Jan?'

'Yeah.'

'That's worse.'

'I know.'

'Did she fall over?'

'No.'

'Does she have koroner… korowner…'

'Coronavirus. Yeah.'

'Is she going to die?'

'Hopefully not.'

My phone beeps behind me, and I reach over the bed. There's a message from Amanda up on the screen 'Lost reception – can you talk?', but there's also something from my dad. Carrie joins me for a cuddle as I lean back against the headboard, nuzzling into my armpit as I open my father's email.

'I don't want Granny to die,' Carrie whispers as I do so.

'I don't either.'

I click on the attachment Dad has sent through, and a dog-eared piece of A4 from the 80s appears, all faded felt-tip and edge-transgressing colouring, Mum clearly having mis-remembered how good I was at staying within the lines back then. In the centre of it is a picture of my mum – badly drawn by me at the age of six or seven – a superhero costume on, the words 'I love you Mum' scrawled around it.

'Look at that,' I say to Carrie. 'It's like the one you and Arthur drew.'

'The one we drew was better.'

'It was. I was never much of an artist.'

And suddenly I can see my whole life ahead of me. The picture they drew of me disappearing into an attic (if I can ever afford one), only to be dug out in old age, a memory of what once was, nostalgia in marker pen and crayon. A kid at the other end of a phone line, whose memory of loving me that intensely has all but faded, their affections transferred to children of their own, who will one day forget theirs in turn.

But then Carrie rests her head on my chest, and I remember what I have now. That, though what she feels for me will disappear off into the ether, it's there in this moment, and at least my mum had that. The joy of getting that card from me that said she was the best thing since sliced bread – or Spider-Man, who at that point I massively preferred to sandwiches – the feeling of my arms wrapped around her knowing that she was the most important thing to me in the world. I take refuge in that thought, as I take refuge in Carrie's warmth, and for a moment I see things as they are. That there are no parents, no children – just caretakers for a love that will be felt through a thousand generations.

But I can't stop hoping that I can at least get to say goodbye.

Thursday 23rd/Friday 24th April

The next few days go by in a blur. The whole Amanda thing is there somewhere in the mire, but it's dwarfed by what's happened to Mum. I feel like I've lost her already. I've never had anyone close to me die, which I guess makes me unusually lucky, but it's such a weird feeling, so alien, sort of like being in purgatory. The only reference I can find is the feeling when Sally left. That same sense that nothing was ever going to be the same again. It never has been, but I don't think losing Mum is going to have the same upside. At least, what happened with Sally meant I got to meet Amanda. And she's amazing. *Was* amazing, before I fucked it up. But I'm not going to be meeting a new mum. It's one and done.

I try to concentrate on work and the schooling, and I'm surprised how quickly Arthur improves on the tests. It's good to have something to take my mind off things, but it makes me really resentful towards his teacher. She's definitely one of these 'I don't really focus on the academic side of things – I just want to make sure that they're having a nice time' people, but how's that meant to help when they still can't read properly at ten? The fact that I have doubled Arthur's maths ability in three days (his ability, not his score. I'm not boasting about him landing a '6' in his latest paper), makes me think a little less 'nice' might be good. 'Cos I'm definitely not as nice as she is. Well, unless Mrs Raleigh at some point has shouted at her kids, '*It's just basic adding! If you can't work out how many bloody sweets he has, then you may as well go and sleep in a box, because that's how you're going to end up!* Yeah, no one's going to accuse me of 'nice'. Potentially child abuse, but not that.

I call Amanda to tell her what's happened, and she's all sympathy, but it doesn't feel like things are going back to normal with us. Everything's shot through with this weird tension, that reminds me of this girl I was going out with during my finals: I kept asking her what was wrong, and she'd reply 'nothing, nothing' and then, the day of my last exam, she broke up with me within an hour of finishing the paper. Said she hadn't wanted to be responsible for me messing up my degree. It feels like Amanda's doing the same thing – playing the part of the attentive girlfriend, ignoring the massive foot-in-the-mouth comment I made until my mother's prognosis comes back, and then our relationship will be no more.

But I can't think about that. I've got the final prep to do for Saturday's shoot, so I grind away sending emails and making phone calls, trying to forget that every moment that passes is just one less moment in my mother's life. And that I'm probably never going to see her again.

Saturday 25th April – Day of the Shoot

The Zoom call starts at 8:00 am. With all the social distancing going on, this will be where the magic happens today, with us, the client and production company all on a single video call, a live feed connecting us to the shoot. Even with everything that's happening in my life, I'm feeling an overwhelming sense of pressure to make sure that today goes well. If it doesn't, I'm probably going to be furloughed (at best), which means I'm not going to be able to pay my rent, which means I'm going to be absolutely fucked. So, fair to say, I'm not feeling that relaxed.

I join the Zoom early, with Larousse the only other person on the call so far. He's being his normal pleasant self, complaining about how his new nanny has failed to turn up, and how his old (currently-sick) nanny is being far too fussy about which herbal teas she's drinking. Despite the awkwardness between us, it's a welcome relief when Amanda joins us a few minutes later.

'Morning!' she beams, a picture of professionalism. 'How you doing, Larousse?'

'Good. Everything's fine,' he sulks.

The director and the producer soon join next, followed by more and more people until all our faces have shrunk to the size of postage stamps. It looks like one of those montages they do at the end of films that screams, 'LOOK HOW MANY PEOPLE THERE ARE IN THE WORLD!' The head of the sofa company, Mr Parkinson (not sure if he has a first name), seems just as harsh and old-school as I've been led to believe, but he's the guy we've got to impress, so everyone's happy to use his requested honorific. Finally, we patch into the feed from the actor's house where the shoot's taking place. Samira appears on the monitor.

'Morning Samira!' says Jo, the director. Jo's great – really nice, and actually competent. It's funny how those things don't seem to be mutually exclusive in directors.

'Morning, Jo!' Samira replies. 'Larousse! Amanda!' *Tom?… Nope.*

'Are you feeling ready?' Jo asks, a bit of small talk to ease everyone in.

'Always ready!' Samira responds, which prompts more laughter than it could possibly deserve.

'Right, down to business,' Jo continues. 'Can you point the camera at the sofa and we'll try to work out the lighting set up?'

Samira looks confused, turning around to look behind her. 'This is it!' she says, displaying as wide a smile as a face can feasibly cope with.

'No...' replies Jo, her voice marinated in scepticism. 'That's *not* it. The walls were green, these are white.'

'Oh did you want to do it in *that* room? Sorry, but I don't think we can move the sofa through there!'

There's a pause for a second, while I see Jo type something into the chat, the producer replying a few beats later.

Jo looks back up to the monitor. 'It's OK, we're going to send some people round to your house – they'll lift it for you.'

'Oh. I don't know if I'm comfortable having people inside my house.'

'It'll be the same people who were there the other day. They'll be in masks and gloves, and you can leave the room while they're there.'

'Still, I'm not sure it's going to work...'

'Samira, you agreed to this when you signed up for the ad.'

'I know, it's just...' She's wrestling with herself with a subtlety that puts her acting showreel to shame. 'Um, it's just... the pictures I sent of my flat... weren't *actually* of my flat.' Cue twenty people's mouths dropping open. LOOK HOW MANY OPEN MOUTHS THERE ARE IN THE WORLD! 'Sorry – I got them online. I know it was a bit naughty, but I just really needed the job!' Samira shrugs her shoulders with a little half-smile as if to say – *I'm cheeky, but it's no big deal.*

Jo flashes a pretend smile back that's a darn sight less convincing. 'We're just going cut off your feed for a second, Samira, OK? Back in a tick.' A few clicks from the technician later, and Samira is ejected from the call like a drunk from a nightclub. The expression on Jo's face changes like a jump cut in a horror film. 'I want to fire her. NOW.'

'Sorry Big J, no can do,' Larousse interjects. 'We're on a schedule here.' And also because actors aren't just illegal nannies – they've got contracts and everything.

'She's got white walls. I'm not working with white walls.'

'Too patriarchal?' asks Larousse, nodding thoughtfully.

'No, Larousse. They *look* shit.'

'Because they're patriarchal?' Jo's expression suggests she may try to fire him as well.

'Sorry, Jo,' Amanda interrupts, 'I just don't see what we can do. This is what we've got.'

'Then I'm sorry – I'm out.'

'You're what?'

'I can't put my name on it – it'll look rubbish. It's my reputation, Amanda – I'm sorry, but I can't do it.'

'But…'

'Sorry, Amanda,' interjects Sherry, the head of the production company. 'We can't have one of our directors putting in substandard work because of the actor you hired.'

'But… you approved her… we couldn't know she was going to do this.'

'Like Jo said, it's our reputation. We've got to protect ourselves. Love working with you guys though. Hopefully, we can find another project to do together in the future.'

And suddenly they're gone. And we have no director. There's *zero* chance we're doing a project with them in the future. They've screwed us. They've completely screwed us.

'Um… is this normal?' asks Mr Parkinson, his face turtling forward towards his webcam, as suspicious as he indeed should be.

'Yeah, totally!' says Amanda. 'It always happens! To be honest, we usually just have the director on the call as a back up – they're not really necessary. By the way, your connection's really bad. Do you mind hanging up, and rejoining again?'

'Um… no, that's not a problem. As long as everything's all right.'

'Everything's fine!'

Mr Parkinson hangs up and we patch Samira back in.

'Well, Samira,' Amanda begins. 'Thanks to you, we now have no director or producer, so you're going to be taking notes from us, and acting like it's completely normal, all right? Luckily, our DP seems to be sticking around…' She hesitates for a moment. 'You are, aren't you?'

Drake, the director of photography, nods despondently from his one inch box. 'Yeah. I wouldn't normally, but I need to get paid.'

'Good enough for me!' says Amanda, doing little to hide the relief in her voice. 'Looks like we're still shooting! Let's set up a camera in front of some white walls!'

Mr Parkinson rejoins the call a few minutes later, and we spend the next hour watching Samira attempt to compose the shot with her boyfriend, Ross, assisting her. Ross seems to fancy himself as something of an auteur, and starts suggesting alternative lighting set-ups, talking about 'fills' and 'mise-en-scene' in a way that makes you think perhaps he's missed his true calling. Of working in a video shop.

But Samira's screw-up puts me a bit more at ease. If this goes completely wrong, it won't just be my fault. And, as we approach the first take, I actually start to feel that it's going to go well. Amanda seems to be doing a really good job of directing. She's amazing with visuals. Maybe she'll end up moving into directing properly after this. My mind starts wandering into fantasy, forgetting the fact that our relationship is probably about to end, and I get flashes of her walking up the red carpet at a Hollywood premiere with me on her arm, her token bimbo ex-accountant who happened to get in there before she was famous…

'Give me a sec – I just need to get my charger,' Amanda announces, before muting her feed and wandering off. So director-y. I bet Werner Herzog always gets his charger before the first take. Even if he's got 90% battery.

However, thirty seconds later Amanda still hasn't reappeared, and when she does she's wearing a mask of calm, a maniacal panic leaking from beneath. 'Bad news, I'm afraid – I'm going to have to leave the call for a bit, as we've got an emergency with another shoot. Larousse and Tom will take the reins while I'm gone though. They're both very experienced with directing. You're in *very* capable hands!'

What?!?

Amanda hangs up, and Larousse and I look at each other while everyone else watches, desperately trying to understand what the hell's going on. Another shoot? There's no other shoot. What the hell is she talking about?

My questions are answered a second later when my phone pings with a message from Amanda. 'Parents locked me in again.'

Fuck. I message her back. 'Are they in the house?'

'No. Might be few hours. Stuck in living room. Charger in kitchen. No way of getting it. Do NOT mention. Can't look any more amateur in front of client.'

I look back up at the screen, and smile.

'Well,' I say, ('I HATE them' pinging up on my phone screen as I talk) 'as Amanda said, Larousse and I are in charge, so… let's… make a… do a… take! Make/do… whatever. Ha ha ha ha!' *Make do?* Shit. That sums up what's happening far more than I hope anyone realises.

We shoot a few takes, each one of them worse than the last. Annoyingly, Samira seems to ignore every bit of feedback I give her again, which basically means Larousse is co-directing with Ross. Unfortunately, Larousse is busy half the time making a cup of tea for his nanny, and Ross clearly has aspirations to use this as a showreel for his move into features. It's not a winning combination.

'Sammy – you need to ask yourself *why* you're so relieved to sit on the sofa,' he muses. 'What has been *happening*? Has your lover left you? Did you shout at him one too many times about the washing up? Perhaps you've realised that you'll never achieve the dreams of your youth... That you're stuck in adverts in your early 30s and will never be a star.' Wow, that sounded far more specific than was necessary. 'Just trying to help her connect with something,' he tells us. 'Trust me – I've read Meisner.'

Meanwhile, Mr Parkinson is beginning to look extremely dubious about the whole thing, scanning our faces for signs as to whether this is going as badly as he thinks it is. Samira looks like she's on the verge of a nervous breakdown, Larousse is trying to read the small print on an individually wrapped teabag, and I've got a smile so fixed it looks like I'm wearing the mouthpiece from *Speak Out*.

'Guys, I've had an idea!' Ross suddenly exclaims. 'I'm just going to turn down the fill light and make it a bit more moody!'

'Do NOT do that,' Drake shouts.

'I think it'll work,' Ross insists.

'If you touch my lights without my permission,' Drake explains, 'I will come round to your house and cut off your balls.'

Ross seems to take it on board. Note to self: maybe start making more threats to balls. They really seem to create a sense of authority. What's wrong with me? That's no way to think. How long till I'm looking to Vlad the Impaler as a role model? How long till I start ending my feedback with 'or you'll get a stake in the butthole'?

Unfortunately, it might be necessary. Samira's ignoring every note I give her. Annoyingly, she *is* actually listening to Ross and on the next take comes in like she's suffered an existential crisis. When she sits down on the sofa and says 'ah', it's like she's asking how a slightly comfortable seat can take away the emptiness of existence.

'That was great!' Ross announces after prematurely shouting 'Cut!'. 'Really felt it meant something. I'm not bothered about the white walls at all now. That was like Beckett or something.'

'Ross,' I reply, trying to be diplomatic as I can. 'It's not really what we want. It's a sofa ad – it's got to be light and happy. So maybe you could… stop contributing? Samira – can you make it more like you're having a good day and the sofa is making it even better?'

No response. For fuck's sake. Am I muted or something?

'Make it more happy, Sammy – can you do that?' asks Larousse, still focused on the ingredients list of 'Moment of Calm'.

'Sure thing!' she replies. I check my screen and no, I'm not muted. I don't understand what's happening. He doesn't even have a bookcase today. 'So like the world is falling apart, but the sofa takes it all away?'

'*We do not have lemon and ginger!*' Larousse screams in response to something off screen, before reengaging with the task at hand. 'Yeah, whatever. Sounds great.'

I hold my head in my hands as they get set up for another shot, only for a message from Amanda to ping up on my screen 'Going OK?'

I start to type 'If we were trying to sell sofas to people during communism,' but I stop myself. She needs this to work – I've got to project confidence.

'Really good!' I message back.

'Mr P?'

I look over at Mr Parkinson's window. His facial expression suggests he's about to have an aneurysm.

'Really happy!'

'Phew!' she replies. 'Down to 5% battery. Also need wee :('

'Is there a window?'

'Parents have urn. Can use that.'

'Where will you put the ashes?' I type back, trying to hide my shock. That is Vlad the Impaler level disrespectful.

'*Punchbowl* urn, idiot.'

'Right.'

'All right – let's do another take,' Ross announces.

The action on the screen begins, and this time Samira's depression on approaching the cushion becomes a joy so intense that it looks like she's taking the piss. Either that, or she's sat on something that isn't a cushion.

'Cut!' I shout, really starting to panic. 'Samira – just be *normal*, OK?' No response *again*. Why couldn't Ross have been the one I need to correct? No one's taught me how to have authority over someone without balls.

'One more, a bit happier before you sit down,' asks Larousse. 'By the way, which do you reckon is closer to lemon and ginger – spearmint or camomile?'

The next take is even worse. It looks like we're doing a spoof of a sofa commercial. I look over at Mr Parkinson; his teeth are bared like he's about to lunge in and bite his monitor. I can feel the rage building inside me, a deep rumble struggling to find a fault line in my Englishness. These fuckers are going to lose me my fucking job.

'It's not really working,' I explain.

'I loved it!' says Ross.

'It felt good actually,' Samira agrees. 'Unless of course you have any thoughts, Larousse?'

And suddenly I lose it. Everything within me explodes to the surface like a geyser that has been blocked with a glut of herbal teabags.

'For God's sake – LISTEN to me!'

A silence spreads over the Zoom call, as if everyone *else* has suddenly muted. Actually, everyone is on mute apart from Samira, Larousse and me, but now it really *feels* like it.

'Ross,' I spit. 'You're not to say another word. If you do, Drake will do something to your balls. Samira – you need to listen to me and do EXACTLY what I say. If you do not, again, Drake will come to your house do something to Ross's balls.' At least I managed to hold back on the butt-staking. 'Now pay attention: You're going to walk into shot, *slightly* happy, then you lay back on the sofa, and it makes you slightly happi*er*. That's when you say 'ah'. Not as if you're unsure whether life is worth living, not as if you're having an orgasm, but like you've just had quite a nice cup of tea. The proper stuff, not a bloody peppermint.'

'I actually quite like peppermint.'

'DON'T. TALK. This is a sofa advert, it's *not* a piece of art. It's the same sofa advert we've seen a million times before. Nothing is different and nothing *should* be different. Do you understand, Samira?'

Samira stares at the camera like she's a hostage who has been forced to make a statement, while someone's standing with a gun/butt-stake outside the frame. 'Yes.'

'Good. Now, let's do a take.'

We do a take, and I begin to realise how uncomfortable I am with how I've just acted. I look over at Mr Parkinson, unable to read his expression, then type him a message in the chat: 'BTW – NOT the same sofa ad we've seen a million times before – just trying to get through to the actor. Smiley face.'

No response. Shit.

But the take is perfect; and a few seconds later, a message appears from Mr Parkinson. 'Dear Tom, Please do not worry. The take was excellent. Very happy with that one. Yours sincerely, Mr Parkinson.'

Boom! Turns out *that's* the way to get some respect and some results: shout at people and threaten to hurt their boyfriends. No wonder Vlad was so successful. Also kind of explains all these toxic work environments. Maybe there're just lots of desperate men who are panicking because their far more competent girlfriends were locked in a room attempting to do a wee in an urn.

I think it's best that I never direct again.

***

The adrenalin buzz of the shoot lasts for all of two minutes after the call ends and my thoughts turn back to Mum. I've never really bought the whole compartmentalisation thing before, but maybe it's true. I didn't even think about her during that whole fiasco; now it's over I can't think of anything else.

I go into the living room and tell the kids that they have to turn the TV off. They seem to find it difficult to compute after their four movie marathon, looking at me with an expression that asks, 'What do you mean "off"?' But as I give them a big hug on the sofa and tell them about my first foray into the cinematic arts (the threats to people's balls finding their way onto the cutting room floor), I realise they're the ones who are going to get me through this. That one day – maybe today, maybe tomorrow – I'm going to lose Mum. That's a definite. But unless I'm really unlucky – they're still going to be here, Amanda or no Amanda, and together we can get through anything.

Together we will be all right.

Sunday 26th April

The landline rings at 8:00 am.

I'm half-asleep, having been awake on and off for most of the night. The kids are watching TV again. I didn't want to let them, but I've got to think of my upcoming entry for *Parent of the Year*.

I know it's my Dad. My mobile's back on, and no one else would willingly choose the landline with other options. I rub the sleep from my eyes, grabbing my dressing gown from the end of the bed as I bound through to the living room. The kids are watching *Teen Titans*, which I've told Arthur Carrie is too young for repeatedly, but all I'm thinking about is the black handset upright in its base on the window sill.

I stand over it, not wanting to pick it up. Maybe this is it. The end. Of possibility. Of hope. The moment where multiple realities collapse into one. Where the box is opened. And the cat is dead.

'Hello?'

'Hello, Tom.' It's my father's voice. He sounds weak, humbled.

'Dad – what's happening? Kids – turn the TV off. Press pause, I can't hear.'

The kids freeze the screen, leaving teenage Robin suspended in the air over a pool of molten lava, his future undetermined. Suddenly, the room seems empty, as if I've lost my connection with the rest of the world.

'Dad – is she all right?'

There's silence on the other end of the phone.

It can only mean one thing.

From down the phone line, I hear a faint sobbing. He's crying. My father's crying again.

'She's out.'

'I… she's what?'

'She's out, Tom. Of intensive care I mean. She's getting better.'

It takes me a moment to realise what's happening. That the tears he was shedding were tears of joy, of relief. Because she's alive. Because my mother's going to make it.

'Oh, Dad. That's amazing.'

'I know. I was so worried, Tom. I was so worried.'

'Me too, Dad, me too,' I reply, through tears of my own. 'But like I said, she's a fighter.'

'She's not a fighter. I only agreed with that to make you feel better.'

I find myself laughing, as much through relief as anything. 'You wouldn't say that if you'd tried to stop her booking hair appointments before the lockdown kicked in.'

'No, I suppose I wouldn't.'

'Tell her I love her, will you?'

I suddenly feel embarrassed for having said it. As if the amnesty from the awkwardness that surrounds any expression of emotion in our relationship has already ended.

But Dad replies. 'She knows, Tom, she knows.'

And then we say our goodbyes, and I hang up the phone.

Arthur and Carrie are staring up at me, their attention for once completely off the TV.

'Is Granny all right?' Carrie asks.

'She is,' I reply.

Carrie smiles. 'I knew she would be.' And a second later the TV is on again, Robin having saved himself from death by performing an elongated splits manoeuvre over the mouth of a home-made volcano. And the world is right once more.

It's a matter of moments till my mind turns back to Amanda, my relief as transient as life itself. I can't help but feel the countdown to the end of our relationship has just been started. She's coming back to London today. I think. She may still be trapped in her parents' living room… She messaged me late last night to say how impressed the client was with my directing and that she was leaving early, but not much else. I thought that was because I was in a funk over Mum, but maybe she was just trying to minimise contact.

I message her to let her know what's happened and she gets

back to me a few minutes later with a 'So pleased Tom x', but that's it. It's probably because she's driving. Probably.

The hours pass, and I become more and more convinced it's the post-finals break-up all over again. I take the kids out for a family walk and then attempt to bake a chocolate cake without any actual chocolate, but as far as distractions go they don't really cut it. I can't shake the feeling that this is the end.

At lunchtime, I finally cave and call. There's no point in postponing the inevitable. Now Mum's out of the woods, there's no reason for her to pretend any more, and it's not like she can be waiting to tell me in person. But part of me doesn't want to give up. Part of me feels if I can just say the right words, I can pull things back from the brink. The call goes straight to voicemail, so I leave a message.

'Hey Amanda. It's me. Look – um, hope you're having a good journey, and that the traffic's not too bad. At least it's sunny eh?' I realise I'm waffling, that I have to get to the point. 'About what I said the other day, about moving in with me. It was stupid – I realise that now. You don't want to be living with a couple of kids, and it would be weird for them too, so… ignore it, all right? It's a weird time – I think lockdown was just getting to me, and I was trying to be nice, but I overstepped the mark, and, you know. Blah, blah, blah. Anyway, I take it back. Sorry. So, um, bye.'

I hang up. Reasonably confident those *weren't* the right words.

As more hours pass, I can feel the resentment building up within me. I don't know why she's doing this. She could at least text and put me out of my misery.

It's only after the kids have gone to bed that I start to worry something's happened to *her*. I've been so self-obsessed that, for all I know, she's been in a car crash or something, and I haven't even considered it. Images of her concertinaed up behind a steering wheel on the side of the M3 fill my brain. I don't know if it's because I'd been expecting a death, but suddenly it all seems so vivid. I suddenly realise that I care about her even more than I care about *us*. What if she's hurt? What if she's gone?

I get up from the sofa and start to pace around, realising I have to check on her, that she's safe, that she's alive. I start to type.

'I know that you probably don't want to talk to me, but I just want to check you're OK? Can you text me please?'

But before I can press send, a message appears on my screen. From Amanda.

'Thomas, Thomas, wherefore art thou Thomas?'

I stand there, staring at the screen trying to work out what the hell it's meant to mean. Why my moment of panic is being responded to with a mangled *Romeo and Juliet* quote?

A few seconds later, another text appears.

'Look out of the window, stupid.'

I throw my phone onto the sofa, and run to the window. And there, outside, sitting on top of her car, is Amanda. I smile creeps across my face, and I throw the sash upwards.

'So, I hear you don't want to live with me anymore?'

'I...'

'You know, before you start saying that, it's usually polite to have asked someone to move in in the first place.'

'What are you talking about? I asked you and then you hung up on me.'

'Um... no.' Suddenly it all makes sense. The connection must have dropped just as I asked her – my garbled bloody phone message was the first she'd heard of it. Relief washes over me, and I find myself laughing despite myself.

'What are you doing here?' I ask.

'I wanted to surprise you. I thought it would be romantic.'

'It would've been. It *is*. I just... I've been trying to call you all day.'

'My car broke down. I've been sitting on a motorway verge in a reception dead zone. I had to walk twenty minutes to call the RAC.'

'I'm so glad you're all right.' Across the street, I see Mr Perry peeking out from between his curtains, but it doesn't even bother me. I just feel so *happy*. 'God, it's so nice to see you.'

'It's nice to see you too,' she replies, her smile as big as mine. 'Nice banner by the way.'

'Yeah – there's been a bit of a competition going on; you probably heard.'

Amanda pauses, then smiles. 'So, are you going to come down and chat to me, or are you expecting me to climb up to your balcony?'

'I'll come down.'

I go and check the kids are asleep, then head downstairs. The window's open so I should be able to hear them if they start crying. Hopefully.

We chat for about an hour, me standing in our front garden, her on the pavement, the other side of a low wall. Even though we're two metres away, I can smell her perfume on the spring breeze, feel her presence in a way that technology will never be able to recapture. Every so often I feel the curtains opposite twitch, Mr Perry probably considering whether to shop us, unsure whether our observation of the social distancing rules is sufficient, but I don't care anymore. She's here. And I love her. And I get the feeling that she loves me too.

'I'm so happy to see you.'

'Me too. But then again, the only people I've seen for the last six weeks are my parents, so I might not be in the best place to judge.'

She smiles, and I smile back. I want so much to kiss her, to just lean across the wall and feel our lips meet, but I can feel all the eyes looking down on us in the semi-darkness. It's not just Mr Perry now, the houses either side of him have had a look to see what's going on. I can feel the TV from the downstairs flat behind me, its volume pointedly turned up. I think if there was any physical contact, someone might send in a strike team. Well, *kissing* – I think I read that sex was OK as long as you wear masks, but I don't want to try that in our front garden. Besides, what if I really liked it? I don't want that to be my thing. It'd be such a hassle having to keep the bedside drawer stocked even after this whole thing passes.

'So, you said you didn't want to live with me anymore?' Amanda asks, hesitantly.

'Um, no, I didn't say that. Well, I did, but I didn't mean it. I just… my kids, they're a nightmare, and… wait a minute, do you *want* to?'

'I suppose I do,' she says, but then she stops and hesitates. 'I don't want to mess things up though. To go too fast and wreck what we've got. We shouldn't jump into things just 'cos everything's weird, because we feel lonely, isolated. If we did it and it screwed everything up, I'd never forgive myself.'

I nod, disappointed but happy.

'This really means a lot to me,' she continues. 'Us. I really care about you.'

I nod. 'I really care about you too.' I pause, unsure whether to continue, but something about it feels right. Even with the darting eyes that pepper the gaps between the first floor curtains above, even with the theme music to a nature programme playing through the glass behind me. 'I think… I think I love you.'

It's the first time I've ever said the words out loud, and they feel strange on my lips; but she doesn't leave me hanging, doesn't let me stew.

'I think I love you too.'

Amanda holds out her hand across the wall, and I reach mine towards it, not quite touching, as if there is an invisible barrier between us like Spock and Kirk in *The Wrath of Khan*. It strikes me I might be one of the great romantics. She's got *Romeo and Juliet*, but I've got *Star Trek 2*.

'It's OK,' Amanda tells me. 'I've got anti-bac.'

The barrier disappears, and our palms meet, our fingers interlinking, desperately searching for some kind of profound connection. And somehow finding it. I close my eyes for a moment, and the sensation of touch becomes everything, a time out from the madness, the stress, the frustration. For the first time since lockdown began, I feel free, as if the intertwining of two lives can offer something other than just obligation, a passing relief from mutual need and loneliness – but a genuine escape. To a world where everything is better.

I open my eyes, and we let go of each other's hands, our eyes still locked.

'Oh, anti-bac,' Amanda suddenly realises, pulling out a travel sized hand sanitizer from her pocket. She doles out a couple of splodges into our palms, and we both rub it in, amused for a change at the ridiculousness of it all. 'I'd better go,' she says. 'Still got to drive across London.'

'I should probably go and make sure that the kids haven't woken up. They'll go into a panic if they think I've gone. Carrie's very concerned about having access to breakfast products.'

'OK,' she says, beaming from somewhere deep within. 'See ya.'

'See ya… Why don't we check in when things get back to normal and sort out the whole living arrangements thing?'

'Sounds good to me.'

'I'll probably call you before that though.'

'Probably.' I'm pretty sure she knows I'll be calling her the moment she gets home.

I watch on as Amanda goes round to the passenger door of her Mini. We're both grinning like teenagers. I stand outside my building until she's gone, watching as her car disappears round the end of the street, hovering there long after she's out of sight, not wanting the moment to end. So what if the kids have woken up? Maybe it'll make them appreciate me a bit more if they think they've been abandoned. Although I'm definitely only thinking that because I'm pretty sure they're still asleep. I reckon if I heard so much as a whimper from the upstairs window I'd be sprinting up there at 30 miles per hour.

It's a few minutes later when I go back inside, a warm feeling within me. It's over. Not lockdown – who knows how long that's going to last – but the worry, the anxiety. She loves me, and I love her too, and if that's the case I can bear anything that life throws at me. Even if we're apart, it doesn't matter. I now know we're truly together.

As I shut the door of the flat behind me, I can feel her touch still lingering on my skin. The kids are in their beds fast asleep, so I head to the living room, collapsing on the sofa and linking my hands behind my head as I look upwards at nothing in particular.

A smile on my face that feels as if it will last forever.

Also by the author:

THE REBUILDING OF TOM COOPER

By Spencer Brown

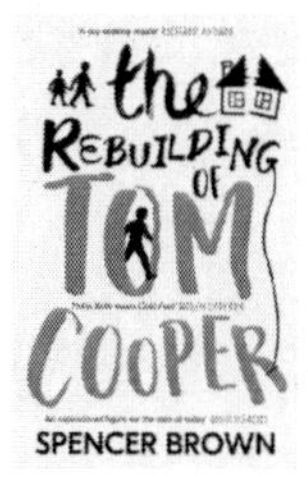

Tom Cooper's life has fallen apart.

His wife has left, dropping him into a world of solo childcare, he's stuck in an accountancy job he hates and he can't even call on the grandparents for support – they're too busy – after all, a Scrabble trophy won't engrave itself.

But when a creative position opens up at the advertising agency he works for, he sees the opportunity to turn things around. All he has to do is pitch a product to a new market, convince Maestro J he is sufficiently finger-clickingly 'creative', beat his weaselly co-worker/nemesis John to the job, and try not to fall for his new mentor, Amanda. Oh, and try to blend in with people 10 years younger than him, survive the office obstacle course using his imaginary agility and stop accidentally turning up to work in the exact same outfit as Doug.

Find out how the journey began in the first book in the Tom Cooper series, *The Rebuilding of Tom Cooper*, a laugh-out-loud comedy about life, love and 21st century manhood.

'A gloriously self-aware satirical romp through the terrors of relationships, family life and survival. Philip Roth meets Cold Feet'
Helen Lederer

'Hilarious and heart-warming' **Andi Osho**

'A joy-seeking missile' **Richard Ayoade**

'Very funny. Peep Show combined with Outnumbered. But you know. In a book' **Josh Howie**

'An aspirational figure for the men of today' **Omid Djalili**

If you enjoyed reading this and want to hear about future books by Spencer Brown, sign up for the mailing list at:
www.spencerbrown.net

Serious about Funny

Acknowledgments

Once again, the largest thank you of all goes to my amazing wife. Without you, God knows if this book would even exist – thanks for being truly great. Thanks to my agent, Richard, my editor, Sarah, Katherine Stephen for proofreading and Liam Relph for another fantastic cover! Thanks also to all the people who read the work-in-progress extracts from this as it was being written during lockdown itself – your support really meant a lot, and let me know that the book was actually worth writing! Thanks to my kids for not being too noisy during these difficult months (and being generally wonderful), and to my parents.

About the Author

Spencer Brown began performing comedy with the Cambridge Footlights alongside John Oliver and Matthew Holness, before becoming an internationally acclaimed stand up. He has performed everywhere from London's *The Comedy Store* to Mumbai and the USA and his TV credits include *Nathan Barley*, *Edinburgh Comedy*, *Last Comic Standing*, and his own special on Swedish television, as well as the lead role in the 2019 horror comedy movie *Shed of the Dead*. As a TV presenter, he fronted *ITV*'s *Lip Service* alongside Holly Willoughby, and *Five*'s *The Sexy Ads Show*. He is also the writer-director of the multi-award-winning short film *The Boy with a Camera for a Face*. *The Lockdown Diary of Tom Cooper* is the follow up to his hilarious debut novel *The Rebuilding of Tom Cooper*.